# A
# Christmas
# Romance
## in the
# Scottish
# Highlands

# BOOKS BY DONNA ASHCROFT

Donna Ashcroft

# A Christmas Romance in the Scottish Highlands

bookouture

Published by Bookouture in 2024

An imprint of Storyfire Ltd.
Carmelite House
50 Victoria Embankment
London EC4Y 0DZ

Storyfire Ltd's authorised representative in the EEA is Hachette Ireland
8 Castlecourt Centre
Castleknock Road
Castleknock
Dublin 15, D15 YF6A
Ireland

www.bookouture.com

ISBN: 978-1-83618-167-5
eBook ISBN: 978-1-83618-166-8

*Jules Wake/Julie Caplin*
*Thank you for talking me down and helping me believe xx*

# 1

## ELLA

Ella McNally took in a deep breath of cold air. Fighting a wave of tiredness, she perused the pretty row of thatched cottages framed by the Mistletoe mountain range, which was glittering after hours of non-stop snowfall.

She pulled on her dog's leash as her tenacious bloodhound, Wyatt, ground to a halt and dropped to his haunches. The dog usually enjoyed their twice-daily walks, but the wind was glacial, and he was irritated that Ella hadn't let him run free. Mostly because the last few times she had, he'd vanished until she'd been forced to tempt him back with handfuls of treats.

'Come on,' she pleaded as Wyatt refused to budge and she tugged at the lead again. A car revved somewhere in the distance and her pet growled, seemingly echoing its refrain, before sinking lower onto the snowy pavement.

'Please, Wyatt. It's cold. I'll feed you when we get to my stepmother's house,' Ella promised and sighed in relief when his dark eyes twitched with interest. 'Good boy,' she soothed as he suddenly shot to his feet, his long limbs ramrod straight and his droopy ears fluttering like festive bunting in a breeze.

He woofed hungrily, glaring to his left, and Ella glanced

across the road and immediately spotted a cat on the pavement. 'No!' she yelled just as Wyatt barked again and bolted forward, making her drop her handbag and dragging her along with him. Ella tugged at the lead so fiercely that it slipped through her gloved hands and the forward momentum made her trip and face-plant in the snow. '*Orff!*' she exclaimed as frigid ice stabbed her cheeks.

Wyatt must have heard her yell, because he forgot the cat and spun around just as Ella looked up, swiping snowflakes from her eyes as a silver Volvo did a fast wheel-spin onto the top of the road.

'Wyatt, run!' Ella screamed, her heart thumping wildly as the car appeared to speed up. Her whole body stiffened, and she watched dumbstruck as it headed straight for her pet. The bloodhound barked, his eyes widening as he spotted the car – Ella assumed he'd move, but he stood mesmerised as if frozen in place by the glare of its headlights.

The driver must have realised her dog wasn't going to shift because they simultaneously pressed the horn and slammed on the brakes. But it was too late, because instead of coming to a stop, the Volvo began to skid.

'*Eejit.* Don't you know how to drive in the snow!' Ella shrieked, and pushed herself onto all fours, desperately hurling her body forward as she attempted to reach Wyatt's lead.

The breath left her throat as she caught it and heaved her dog out of the way, mere seconds before the gliding Volvo hit him. She hugged Wyatt tightly to her chest and momentarily shut her eyes as the vehicle skated past, spraying pellets of ice all over them both before it finally came to a stop at a right angle across the road.

Ella let go of Wyatt and sprang to her feet so she could stomp towards it, attempting to hold onto her temper. She rarely lost her cool, but the bampot driver had almost squashed her dog – what sort of person would drive that fast

in a snowstorm, especially if they didn't know the correct way
to brake?

Ella heard the car's engine fire up as she approached. *Was
the jackass leaving?* 'Wait!' she yelled as irritation ignited and
flared. She broke into a trot and bent on impulse so she could
grab a handful of snow. Then she hurled it at the side of the car
– intending to capture the driver's attention before they drove
away. Only the icy globe hit just as the window slid halfway
down.

As Ella drew to a jerky stop beside the driver's door, she saw
a man sitting behind the wheel wincing as he swiped clumps of
snow from his jaw.

'Um,' Ella began as she watched pieces of ice slide down his
cheeks and onto his chin, before dropping like watery tears into
his lap. She gritted her teeth to stop herself from laughing – or
worse, apologising.

'Do you realise you could be charged with assault?' the man
said slowly.

'For throwing a snowball?' Ella snorted as he turned to glare
at her, and she took a moment to catch her breath.

He was handsome, with a chiselled jawline that he was
flexing in displeasure. His hair was the colour of jet, and his
chin was peppered with matching snow-speckled stubble that
made him oddly endearing. Ella had spent many happy hours of
her life sketching – she was usually drawn to things like
colourful birds playing in the trees and fluffy cats intent on
mischief. But in this instant, she found herself itching for her
pad and pencil so she could recreate this man's gorgeous face.
Her reaction to him was ridiculous and no doubt due to the fact
that she hadn't dated at all during the last year.

'Do *you* realise you nearly killed Wyatt?' she ground out,
ignoring the way her pulse skipped up as his dark eyes glittered.

'Then perhaps you should teach him that roads are for cars,
and not dogs,' he shot back, his eyes scouring her face angrily.

He heaved out an irritated breath and then switched off the
engine and opened the door before climbing out. He was taller
than Ella had expected – definitely over six foot because he
towered over her.

He wore a navy jumper and dark trousers that were splattered with ice blobs and watery stains which she refused to feel
guilty about. His shoes were no more suitable for the weather
than his driving, and Ella saw the man's eyes flicker with annoyance when they sank and were swallowed by a drift. 'What
were you thinking, letting him sit in the road?' he asked, shaking
his head.

Ella blinked, surprised. 'He wasn't sitting, he was stalking a
cat,' she explained, instantly regretting sharing that particular
piece of information, cursing her openness.

The man's eyebrow arched as he made a point of looking at
the empty pavements. 'Aye. Well – I suggest you keep a better
eye on him. A tip?' The eyebrow arched higher. 'Dog restraints
work better if you hold onto them; perhaps you should try that
next time he spots the Cheshire cat?'

Ella opened her mouth to give the man a piece of her mind,
but the accusing look on his face had her stumbling over the
words.

Was this really all her fault? Her stomach squeezed with
the familiar ache of guilt which she quickly squashed as she
narrowed her eyes at his car. 'Perhaps you should try driving a
little slower too?' she suggested, wondering what had got into
her. She normally went with the flow – this was so out of
character.

'Thankfully, he got out of the way just in time – so at least I
won't have to bill you for any damage to my car,' he continued.

'Damage?' Ella echoed.

Wyatt – who'd obviously followed her – let out a low snarl.
Ella grabbed his lead and tugged him closer so he couldn't
lunge.

'I'm in a hurry,' the man snapped, eyeing her dog warily and then glancing through his open car door at the clock on the dashboard. 'I've got places to be – important places and I don't want to be late.' His eyes swept Ella's face as if he were taking her in for the first time. For an instant, he looked surprised, then he seemed to gather himself and nod. 'I assume neither of you is hurt?' he asked brusquely.

'Thanks for asking finally,' Ella muttered. 'We're not hurt, more upset.' She glanced down at her soggy clothes and shoved her hands into her pockets because they were shaking and she didn't want him to see.

'Then I'll be on my way,' he said abruptly, ignoring Wyatt as he let out a warning bark.

'You're leaving?' Ella gasped as he folded his long legs back into the car.

'I think we're done,' he said as he closed the door with a snap and started the engine.

Her mouth gaped as she watched him drive off, feeling helpless and weary.

Their encounter was such a mirror of her life. Her left picking up the pieces and sorting out the mess – and no matter what she tried nothing ever worked or changed.

'What a horrible man. I hope I never see him again,' she grumbled as the Volvo accelerated, took a right and disappeared. Although as Ella turned and tugged Wyatt back onto the pavement, the man's face flashed back into her mind, and she realised she might not be being entirely truthful with herself.

# 2

## ELLA

Ella stopped on the pavement, wriggling as a tiny pebble of ice stuck inside her jumper melted on her back. Shivering, she grimaced and tugged Wyatt's lead, wearily pulling him along.

'That's enough moping. I'm not going to let the idiot ruin my first day off in three weeks,' she promised, swiping the ice from her hat as a bird began to sing. Ella twisted around, and spotted a small robin perched on the birdbath and waved, feeling a little better.

A few houses away she paused at the front gate that led to her family home and took a moment to admire the pretty double-fronted thatched cottage. Despite it only being the first of December, the Christmas decorations were already up, courtesy of the four lunch breaks she'd skipped the week before. Ella lived in a small fixer-upper a couple of streets away and hadn't had a chance to decorate it yet, but she planned to do it later this afternoon. If she found the time. There always seemed to be so much to do.

She trod carefully along the snowy pathway, heading for the front door. 'Is anyone home?' she called out as she unlocked it, just in case one of her stepbrothers had decided to pop in. They only seemed to do so when they ran out of food.

She unclipped Wyatt's lead and the dog immediately scrambled towards the kitchen in search of food. Ella frowned at the soggy footprints he'd made on the tiled floor which merged with the ones that had been left by a pair of man-sized boots. She sighed wearily, knowing she'd have to mop them up before leaving or she'd receive a barrage of calls from her stepmother complaining about the mess.

Her shoulders sagged as she entered the kitchen and spotted the sink, which was piled high with washing-up. The kitchen counters were also littered with breadcrumbs, plates and empty cups. Ella shook her head as she went into the larder and quickly fed Wyatt, then she scoured the surfaces, looking for the letter her stepmother had promised would be here. It was propped against the kettle beside a note.

*Dear Ella,*

*As I mentioned in my text this morning, this letter arrived from the bank yesterday. Can you sort out whatever they want? I assume it's about the loan your father took out. I don't have time to deal with any Magic Mops paperwork. I have my part in the pantomime and your stepbrothers to think about – and you know your father expected you to take care of all that for us.*

Ella's eyes filled with tears at the mention of her da and a hundred different memories flooded through her. He'd died a year ago after a short illness, and she still hadn't come to terms with the loss. It felt odd when she walked into the house now and found it empty. She still expected to find him cooking pancakes for her in the kitchen or tinkering out in his shed. Ella could remember the sound of his voice and how he'd always had a new joke to tell her, hoping to make her groan. She'd returned to Mistletoe to care for him eighteen months before, intending to go back to her life when he got better. But instead, he'd begged her to take care of the family and business just before he'd passed – and she hadn't been able to bring herself to leave.

> *While you're here could you do a quick tidy round? After all, this will always be your home too and you know how much your da hated mess. Also, I've written a list of things I'd like you to pick up from the shop. I know it's your day off, but it won't take long.*

'I've got an art lesson later,' Ella muttered as Wyatt finished his food and wandered across the kitchen to join her. 'But it's fine,' she said, glancing around. If she got started on the cleaning now, she'd have time to do the shopping and still arrive at her lesson promptly for a change.

> *I'll be in touch later. There's a lot to do in the run-up to Christmas, and I thought we could share the chores.*
>
> *Lucinda McNally*

Ella put the note from her stepmother back on the counter and stared at the unopened letter from the bank, feeling sick. Then she heaved in a breath, picked it up and ripped it open.

Tears pricked her eyes as she scanned the contents. The bank was giving them until the end of February to pay the outstanding payments of her father's loan. He'd taken it out the year before he'd died to buy essential equipment, but now, if they didn't pay, the bank would seize all the company assets. It would spell the end of the family business.

Ella sighed as her stomach roiled. Her parents had established and grown Magic Mops into a thriving company when they'd both been alive – and she'd done everything she could since she'd been old enough to hold a broom to help it to flourish. She had no intention of letting it go.

She twisted around and wandered to the sideboard by the back door. On it, Lucinda had arranged a series of picture frames containing multiple photos of Ella's stepbrothers playing sport; one of her da and Lucinda on their wedding day, along with a small one tucked at the back of him hugging Ella when she'd been around eight.

'I dinnae know what I'm going to do,' she whispered to him as she folded the letter into a tiny square and put it in her pocket. 'The business account's been in trouble for a long time, and it doesn't improve no matter how hard I work.' She sighed. 'Things have just been getting more and more expensive: equipment, advertising, even the cleaning gear. We need more clients, but that means more employees and we're paying out more in wages than we're bringing in, which means we've defaulted on a couple of loan payments. The shortfall's been building up for a while...'

She rubbed her eyes feeling weary. 'Oh, don't listen to me, Da. I made you a promise and I'm not going to let you down. I'll work this out.'

Ella's mobile began to ring, and she pulled it from her pocket. Then she winced when she saw the name Clyde McNally on the screen. Her stepbrother was supposed to be doing a deep-clean in one of their client's properties ready for a party tomorrow.

'Clyde,' she said as she picked up, holding her breath because she suspected he was about to deliver bad news.

'Hi, sis,' her brother wheezed. 'I'm sorry this is short notice, Ella. But I need to finish work now. I've done some of the cleaning, but I've just got an appointment with the doctor for this cough. I think I might have bacterial bronchitis, or maybe something worse. I've googled my symptoms, and it could be really, really bad.' He paused long enough for a coughing fit, and Ella had to admit he didn't sound well. 'I've been feeling pretty rough.' He cleared his throat. 'I wasn't going to come to work today, but I didn't want to let you down again.' He gasped.

'Oh Clyde,' Ella said worriedly. She knew Clyde had been fighting a nasty case of the flu for the last two weeks. 'What can I do?'

'I'll only get to the doctor's surgery on time if I leave now,' he shot back. 'But the stairs and both of the top floors in this building haven't been finished. Plus, I'm only halfway through the kitchen.' Ella heard the sound of a hoover in the background – was Clyde trying to work while he talked? 'I called Dane, but he said he's at the dentist for another root canal and Mam's gone shopping and you know she hates being disturbed.' Clyde paused. 'That only leaves you.'

'That's true.' Ella sighed. She looked after the staff rotas, so she knew exactly where everyone was supposed to be. Which was how she already knew there was no one else to fill in.

'Sorry, sis,' Clyde said, stopping as his cough kicked off again, quickly escalating until he sounded like he was fighting for air.

'Are you all right?' Ella asked as her heartbeat skipped up. He sounded terrible.

'Yes, but is it okay if I go?' her brother finally choked. 'You know I'd finish the cleaning if I could.'

'Of course it's fine,' Ella soothed, pulling up her sleeves and perusing the mess she had to clear up. 'I've got spare keys to the client's house, so take yours with you. If you leave all the equipment exactly where it is, I'll finish everything.'

'Thank you. I owe you, sis,' Clyde said before he hung up, leaving Ella staring at the phone.

If she got started now, she could clean, do Lucinda's shopping, walk Wyatt, finish Clyde's work and if she were lucky, she might even make it to her lesson on time. Ella sighed wearily as she turned on the taps thinking about the man in the Volvo again – wondering how some people got to waltz through life doing exactly what they wanted, while others seemed to be here to simply mop up after everyone else. It would be nice to swap places, even if it were just for a while.

# 3

## ALEX

Alexander Forbes-Charming drew his silver Volvo to a stop in front of Pinecone Manor. It had been a challenging drive from Edinburgh this morning. Made worse by the snowstorm and the woman who'd accused him of almost running down her dog.

Had he been driving too fast? Alex shook his head chalking the faint stirrings of guilt up to hunger pangs. Instead, he checked his Rolex and calculated that he'd shaved four minutes off Google Maps' predicted arrival time, despite the unexpected pitstop. There were a couple of colleagues at work who'd be impressed when he messaged an update and if he was lucky, his father – a man who'd dedicated his life to being first in every way – might give him a rare thumbs up.

Alex kept the car engine humming as he took a moment to peruse the striking building he was facing. He hadn't known what to expect when his father had informed him that he was going to spend the next month on sabbatical with Henry Lock-hart – one of Scotland's foremost watercolour artists – but it hadn't been this.

The double-fronted grey-stone building was vast and sprawling, with a large oak front door and imposing porch positioned in the centre. Numerous sections and extensions had been added to either side – some that even included turrets – all obviously designed to harmonise with the original structure.

Logic said it shouldn't have worked, but somehow the expansive building was stunning. The Scottish mountains in the distance offered the perfect backdrop, and Alex wondered if Henry had moved here because of how lovely the scenery was. The artist was famous for his watercolours and Alex guessed he probably loved the beauty and isolation of the place.

Lockhart clearly had a keen interest in gardening as well as art. There were pots of winter pansies and multiple rows of trees on either side of the building – all already decorated with festive lights that looked like tiny fireworks exploding from each of their branches.

The driveway circled the manor, but Alex couldn't see any other cars. He switched his off and got out before grabbing his suitcase, laptop bag and portfolio from the back and trudging his way up to the front door.

As Alex approached the porch, he heard 'Paint It, Black' by The Rolling Stones blaring loudly inside. He rang the bell and texted his father to tell him he'd arrived, informing him of the exact time it had taken. Then he waited, putting the luggage on the ground and shoving his hands into his pockets when a sudden gust of wind almost knocked him off his feet.

Alex shivered and stamped his feet on the mat which lined the porch. It had a picture of a Christmas tree on it, but the word 'welcome' was nowhere in sight. Was that an omen? He rang the bell again and waited, checking his watch. Three minutes later, he rang it again.

Stamping his feet once more, Alex's attention caught on a garish Santa Claus ornament in the corner of the porch which seemed out of keeping with the style of the house. On impulse he knelt and lifted it, immediately spotting a brass key, which he picked up. 'Father's rule of success number one: *use your initiative, you'll never go wrong*,' he said quietly.

Michael Charming had a verbal rulebook which he added to from time to time. He'd shared his wise words with Alex over the years and considered them a vital part of his parenting, believing they'd mould his son into a man he could admire. At least that was the hope.

Alex used the key to open the door as another gust of wind propelled him through it. 'Hello!' he shouted as he closed the door and then he stared. The hallway was beautiful with a shiny black and white stone floor and swirling staircase which had been layered with lush, thick red carpet. A curved banister had been decorated with wreathes of fresh holly which he could smell as he drew closer.

Alex was used to beautiful spaces – his family owned eleven houses which were scattered across the world, and he'd been raised to appreciate all kinds of architecture, interior design and decor. But this went far beyond that. Perhaps because it was so inviting?

He put his luggage on the ground and shoved his hands into his pockets as The Rolling Stones stopped singing, but Alex barely noticed; he was so absorbed. He looked up at the huge glittering chandelier before his gaze swung to the walls. They were peppered with an abundance of Henry's watercolours, some of which had tinsel wound around their frames. There were a couple of interesting line drawings dotted in between the others – one of a bloodhound with soulful eyes and Alex found himself drawing closer so he could study it. Why did it look familiar?

His stomach clenched into an uncomfortable knot. He knew he was a talented artist, but this work was exquisite – the details so perfect that he wouldn't have been surprised if the dog had suddenly come to life and licked his cheek. There was something whimsical about the image, completely out of keeping with Henry's usual style. But Alex found himself unusually drawn in.

'You found your way inside then?' A loud voice rasped, and Alex only just stopped himself from bellowing in surprise before he spun round. 'I'm Henry. Sorry no one was here to greet you. My housekeeper walked out again last week – I can be *difficult* apparently.' The man checked his watch. 'By my calculations she's due to put in an appearance sometime today – she always forgives me in the end.' He lifted an eyebrow as he grinned. 'So, you're Michael Charming's lad, are you?'

'Aye,' Alex said as his heart rate began to return to normal. 'Alex Forbes-Charming. Forbes was my mother's surname,' he explained. 'Nice to meet you, Mr Lockhart,' he said formally.

'We'll see,' Henry said.

The artist was a surprisingly imposing man up close. Alex had read as many articles and profiles on him as he could before leaving Edinburgh, because forewarned was forearmed – and he always did his homework.

He knew the man was sixty-eight and almost six foot four, which meant he was a full inch taller than Alex. He'd been expecting that but still found himself feeling at a disadvantage. The older man's hair was snow white, but long enough to brush his shoulder and there was plenty of it. It matched his tidily clipped beard and the overall effect was elegant and distinguished, despite the well-worn jeans and Rolling Stones T-shirt he wore. There were a couple of paint splodges on his hands and arms, suggesting Alex had interrupted his painting.

'I appreciate you having me,' Alex said stiffly, offering his hand.

The older man gazed at it before taking it and meeting Alex's eyes, his expression assessing. 'You can thank your da,' he said gruffly. 'Charming Capital Management has made me a lot of money over the years, and I owed him a favour. *That's* what got you through the door. I'm sure Michael told you I only open my house and studio to one artist a year?'

He paused for effect, perhaps to underscore exactly how much of a privilege it was for Alex to be standing here. 'The lad who was supposed to come broke his arm last week and you're only here because he's not.' He shrugged. 'Well, that and because I was on the phone with your da when I found out he couldn't make it.'

Henry blinked, his eyes emotionless. 'The pictures your da sent me of your work proved you have raw talent, but raw is as far as it goes.' He heaved out a breath. 'I'm sure you're used to people being impressed by you, but before we go any further, I need you to understand something.'

He wagged a finger looking serious. 'From this point on, I don't care if your da is Michael Charming – or how many degrees you have, your job title, stock portfolio or—' His eyes narrowed as they skidded across Alex's face. 'That you have a very fine bone structure.' He shrugged. 'From this point on, I *only* care about the art.'

'I understand that,' Alex murmured. He didn't bother adding that he was used to it. His father had made him earn every accolade, compliment and promotion since birth. There was no room for sentiment in his world. Everything had to be earned.

'You need to be focused for every second that you're staying with me,' Henry continued. 'If you're not sufficiently talented or don't put in enough effort, I will ask you to leave.' The threat hung between them like a dark cloud.

'I *will* be good enough,' Alex promised. He knew that sounded arrogant, but he also knew people responded to confidence. 'Hard work doesn't scare me.'

The artist nodded as if he'd expected nothing less. 'I'll also want you to rip open your chest and show me the essence of your soul if I ask you to.' Henry paused and narrowed his eyes. 'And if you think I'm joking about that, lad, you're wrong.'

'Right.' Alex drew out the word. None of this fazed him, but just for a moment, he felt weary. He was used to proving himself – but for the first time in a long time, he wondered if he'd ever reach a point in his life when he wouldn't have to. Whether he'd ever be enough just as he was? He shook himself, disgusted. Feeling sorry for oneself was an indulgence.

'That's what my artists have to do when they're with me,' Henry continued. 'You have to learn how to tell the truth with your work – and that means I expect you to show me exactly who you are.' He waited as if expecting Alex to argue with him.

'Aye,' Alex said. 'That's fine.' He'd been raised to win and to accept nothing less; it's what his father demanded. Michael had told him if he was going to waste his time on a hobby like painting, then he might as well excel and earn money from it, which is why he'd insisted he come here. Now it was up to Alex to prove to Henry and his father that he had the talent and dedication to succeed.

The older man nodded, and then frowned. 'Aye, well, words are easy, lad. We'll see what you're made of when you bleed. I'll expect you've brought more work to show me—' He opened his palm, indicating to Alex's portfolio which was resting on the ground beside his suitcase.

Alex was about to pick it up when he heard a loud yapping from somewhere in the bowels of the house. Seconds later, a brown Yorkshire terrier wearing a set of antlers charged into the hallway and stopped before dropping onto its haunches and barking wildly at Alex's legs. Alex stared at the fluffy bundle as it continued to yap, unsure of how to react. He'd never had a pet. The dog suddenly whined and launched itself closer to Alex, perhaps attempting to knock him over in the hope of gaining access to food?

'I have nothing,' Alex said, showing the dog his empty palms.

'This is Sprout,' Henry explained. 'Named for that.' He wagged a finger at the tuft of blonde-coloured hair that sprouted from the top of the dog's head. 'It has *nowt* to do with vegetables.' His deep frown indicated this was an important distinction. 'He seems to have taken a liking to you.' He sounded amused, and he watched the dog nuzzle closer to Alex's leg. 'Don't let it go to your head.'

'What did I do, and how can I stop it?' Alex asked gruffly. He decided against shaking the animal off because he didn't want to upset the older man. But what was it that the dog liked so much?

'A smart lad like you will figure that out. Although why you'd want to try, I've no idea,' Henry said airily. 'Grab your things and follow me.' He spun on his heels and marched down the hallway at speed.

Alex quickly grabbed his luggage and followed, ignoring the dog as it whined, and only realised the shiny floor was slippery when he almost went flying.

They charged through a large door into a lounge where a fire burned in a stunning brick fireplace. Four dark green, high-back chairs faced the flames, and an enormous Christmas tree twinkled beside it.

Alex didn't get a chance to see more because Henry disappeared through another doorway and suddenly, he was following the artist up a set of stairs. The older man was surprisingly fast for someone in his late sixties, and Alex was out of breath when they reached the top. He carefully put everything on the ground when he realised they were now in Henry's studio.

It was a huge room and must have covered at least a third of the house. The ceiling was vaulted and there were dozens of Velux windows at all sorts of angles scattered across it. Someone had hung fairy lights in between them – and Santa and reindeer swirls dangled down.

'I wanted natural light in my studio whatever time of the day it was,' Henry explained before Alex could ask him about the windows. 'There are more over on the right side of the room, because I like to be able to see the gardens when I work.'

Alex nodded and walked up to them, perturbed because Sprout shadowed him mere inches from his heels. He ignored the dog and took in the view – from here, he could see they were on the opposite side of the building to where he'd parked.

Snow was still falling outside, and the trees glittered with fresh flakes. Beyond the house were fields separated by hedgerows and in the distance, he could just make out a sheep. The view was beautiful, and he stared at it mesmerised until Henry cleared his throat.

Alex swung around, taking care not to tread on the terrier, and took a moment to peruse the rest of the room. There were numerous easels positioned around the space. On one he could see a line drawing of a cat drawn in the same style as the bloodhound in the hallway. It was almost finished and just as perfect, and he felt that same pinch of longing that he'd had downstairs.

There were multiple canvases piled up in the far corner of the room facing the wall and he itched to flick through them. Instead, he peeled off his coat because the studio was warm. His mouth felt dry, and he wished he'd thought to bring his water bottle in from the car.

'I have underfloor heating,' Henry explained, reading Alex's mind again – although he didn't offer refreshments. 'Put your work on that table over there, lad.' He went to pluck a pair of gold-framed spectacles from beside an easel and put them on.

Alex picked up his portfolio feeling anxious. He didn't usually question himself. But there was something about this man that made him nervous. Perhaps because suddenly he really wanted to impress him and stay?

He unzipped the case and spread it wide, tugging out one of his favourite pieces. It was a landscape he'd painted earlier this year whilst in the garden of his father's home on the Isle of Skye. He knew he'd caught the exact angles of the cliffs and the wildness of the sea which had been boisterous, sweeping onto the beach in foamy arcs. When Alex looked at it now, he could almost feel the wind on his face and the wet flecks of spray. He was proud of the painting and knew it was the best thing he'd done, but sharing it now made him feel exposed.

'The perspective's slightly off. How did you feel when you were looking at that view?' Henry asked, plucking the picture from Alex's hands and frowning as he looked closely at the detail.

*Angry*, Alex thought. Michael had just berated him, because... He scratched a hand through his hair. He couldn't remember the reason now. 'Happy,' he shot back, his response automatic, feeding the artist the words he guessed he'd want to hear.

'That's not the truth,' Henry said, his words puncturing something deep in Alex's chest and he couldn't help gasping.

'Don't worry, lad, I'll give you a reprieve because we've only just met,' the older man said, looking at him closely. 'You can have a couple of days to get to know me, then I'll expect you to unravel.'

Henry chuckled and moved closer to the table so he could flick through the rest of the work. He didn't say a word, but Alex could tell by the set of his shoulders that he wasn't impressed. A part of him deflated, but he was determined not to show it.

It's why he was here, to learn from the best. His father had told him that he planned to hang the painting Alex created in the reception area of the Charming Capital Management offices – so he wasn't going to mess that up. He liked the idea – it was his one chance to impress his father, so he had to paint something incredible, however much time and effort it took to get it right.

'I thought you might have arrived,' a voice suddenly admonished from the top of the stairs. When Alex turned, he saw an older woman with bright red hair wearing a black and white apron edged with silver tinsel. She was carrying a tray and Alex almost wept when he saw the pot of tea and plate of mince pies. There was a young boy wearing a royal blue school uniform beside her, and he was staring at Alex.

'Hi, lad,' Henry said before turning to the older woman. 'Aggie McBride, I *knew* you'd be back.' He walked up and took the tray from her hands, taking a moment to ruffle the boy's hair.

The woman shook her head as she came further into the room and the dog immediately hopped up and began to growl.

'Oh, don't be dafty.' She scrubbed a hand over Sprout's head, then pulled a carrot baton from her pocket and fed it to him.

'I'm not here for you,' she said to Henry. 'I'm here because of the lad.' She gave Alex a wide smile which lit her face. She was round and attractive with blue eyes and wrinkles that had obviously been there long enough to make themselves at home. Her red hair was long and she'd tied it into a bun, and then decorated it with tiny multicoloured baubles. Alex tried to guess her age, but it was impossible.

'Alex Forbes-Charming.' He nodded.

'It's good to meet you, lad. This is my grandson, Hunter McBride.' Aggie pointed to the young boy beside her. He was skinny, with short red hair and freckles that ran across the tops of his cheeks and nose.

'My name is Hunter Rufus McBride, actually,' the young boy corrected. 'My da's name is Rufus, but he lives near London, so I don't see him very much. He's got a very important job.' The boy offered Alex a proud smile, his small chest inflating his sweatshirt to almost twice the size. 'You've got a good job too. I know that because my nana told me.'

'Aye,' Alex said, taken aback by the boy's bluntness.

'I'm an artist,' the young boy continued, his eyes shining. 'I'm going to draw you a picture to keep. I'm in the village pantomime and we're doing *Cinderella* – it's on Christmas Eve. I'm playing Patch, the mouse.' His voice raced, and Alex wondered how he found time to breathe. 'Will you come?'

Alex gaped. He had no experience with children. They were as alien to him as pets. 'Um, I'm not sure.' He took a step back.

'Shush, lad.' Aggie gave the boy a gentle smile. 'Let's give the man a chance to settle in before we mob him. I made up your room,' she said kindly, looking pointedly at Alex's suitcase, which was still on the ground. 'I assumed Henry wouldn't have thought about it – or that you might be hungry after your journey.'

The older man grunted but didn't comment. Instead, he poured two mugs of tea and put a mince pie on a plate, then handed them to Alex.

'When you've finished torturing him, take him to the west wing. I've put him in Andy Warhol – because that room's warmest and has the prettiest views,' she said. 'Also, Ella hung some Christmas decorations there last week.'

'Where is the lass?' Henry asked grumpily, glancing pointedly at his watch. 'She was supposed to be here thirty minutes ago. We have a lesson booked, and I wanted her to meet Alex.' He turned and his attention rested on the line drawing of the cat. Was this Ella responsible for drawing it? Alex frowned.

'She's running late. She messaged me because she knew you wouldn't hear your phone over your music. I told her I might be seeing you today.' Aggie beamed at Alex again. 'If you need anything while you're here, just ask me.' Her tone was warm. 'I try to come once a day and I'll be making all your meals, so you don't have to worry about food poisoning or the old man forgetting that humans actually need to eat.' She shot Henry another exasperated look, but this time, it contained a flicker of affection. 'Don't keep the lad up here for long – I'm sure he's tired and would like to settle in. Lunch is at twelve o'clock sharp in the main dining room.'

'I'm coming too!' Hunter beamed.

'You'd better not be serving soup.' Henry shoved out his lower lip.

'Aye, parsnip,' she said gleefully before turning and disappearing down the stairs.

'I don't like parsnips,' Henry shouted before shaking his head and turning back to Alex. 'Aggie's been working at the manor for over forty years,' he explained, turning again to look at the portfolio before shaking his head and closing the lid on the rest of the work, leaving Alex feeling disheartened.

'I inherited her from the last owner, and it was just easier to let her stay. She's an excellent cook, aside from her obsession with *soup*.' He sighed as his attention fixed on Alex's suitcase. 'I suppose you'd better unpack, lad. We'll meet here for your first lesson after lunch – hopefully, Ella will have arrived by then. She's another protégé of mine. Gifted, but lacking in focus. You're going to be seeing a lot of her, and I'm sure you'll get along.'

He grinned before he turned on his heels and headed for the stairs. Alex quickly zipped up the portfolio, then grabbed the rest of his luggage and followed. Wondering who this mystery Ella was, and why someone as famous as Henry Lockhart would give up his time for somebody who so clearly didn't deserve it.

He definitely wasn't looking forward to meeting her. No matter how long he stayed, there was no chance he was going to like her at all.

# 4

ELLA

Ella slid the Magic Mops company van to a stop at the front of Pinecone Manor and gulped when the vehicle shuddered and whined. It had been playing up all morning and was due an MOT in the next few days, which she suspected it wouldn't pass. She eased the tension from her shoulders as she checked her watch and grimaced. 'Crappity drat,' she said wearily, because she was over an hour and a half late for her lesson with Henry.

'Come on, Wyatt!' she called into the back seat as she opened the van door and jumped onto the icy snow, barely registering the slivers of ice as they seeped into the not-very-sensible slippers she wore while she was cleaning. She'd forgotten to change them after mopping the hallway tiles in the house Clyde had left her to clean, because she'd been in such a hurry to leave. It meant she'd also left her boots sitting in the client's hallway, she realised with a groan. So she'd have to figure out when to get them back.

There had been a lot more to do at the house than her step-brother had led Ella to believe – and it had taken her three very long hours to finish. Clyde had barely touched the kitchen and hadn't ventured onto the second or third floors at all. The four sitting rooms hadn't been polished or hoovered, and all five bathrooms had been filthy. In a moment of rare irritation, Ella had wondered if he'd done anything other than raid the biscuit tin and toss crumbs all over the floors. But she'd quickly shaken off the feeling – he'd been ill, after all.

Wyatt climbed slowly from the van onto the ground. Then he stopped, his black nose twitching. Ella was so absorbed in grabbing her art supplies and locking up that she missed him approaching the silver Volvo that was parked a few metres to their right. He growled suddenly, the sound low in his throat, and Ella spun around and then went to join him so she could see what the problem was. She reached Wyatt just as he cocked his leg.

'No!' Ella wailed as Wyatt peed all over one of the car's shiny wheels. 'What are you doing?' she admonished, as she picked up the dog's leash and tugged him away. Then she stopped as she studied the vehicle, and her mind began to whir.

'Is that...?' she gasped, quickly skirting around the car with the dog lead loose in her hand. The bloodhound went to sniff at the handle on the driver's side, before dropping his nose to the snow. 'It is!' Ella gasped, watching Wyatt sniff again before following the scent.

'It's the car that almost squashed you. The one the eejit was driving,' Ella told her pet as Wyatt – who'd obviously already worked that out – continued to smell the ground, leading her towards the front of Pinecone Manor. 'What's it doing parked here?' The dog didn't respond, and suddenly tugged the leash forcefully, almost pulling Ella over. She righted herself just in time.

'Hang on!' Ella said as she skidded behind Wyatt, almost tripping again – clutching even more tightly to her bag of art supplies.

As they reached the porch, Ella heard 'Honky Tonk

Woman' playing inside the manor and guessed Henry must be painting in his studio, which meant she'd probably missed most of her lesson.

Wincing with guilt, Ella rang the doorbell and immediately dropped down to lift up the Santa Claus ornament where the older man usually left a key, but it wasn't there.

Wyatt whined as a gust of wind barrelled into them and Ella rang the doorbell again, pressing her ear to the wood panelling, hoping to hear footsteps. She knew Henry wouldn't hear his mobile if she called and had no other way of getting in. Although she could try Aggie? Ella was searching in her bag for her mobile when the door swung open.

'Ach, lass, what are you doing standing out here?' the house-keeper asked, dragging her and Wyatt into the hallway before frowning at Ella's outfit. 'Did you come straight from work?' she gasped. 'Are those *slippers*?'

Ella pulled a face. 'I was late for my lesson, and I forgot to change into my shoes.' Aggie tutted. 'Is Henry in his studio?'

The housekeeper didn't have a chance to respond because Wyatt suddenly pressed his nose to the tiles and then growled before leaping forward. As Ella was still clutching his lead, she found herself being dragged towards the sitting room door.

'Aye, lass,' Aggie shouted as the dog pulled Ella through it. 'Henry's in the studio with his latest protégé. I'll meet you there in a minute – I just want to fix you some lunch. I'm guessing you didn't find time to eat again.' She had to shout the last few words because Wyatt had already hauled Ella to the opposite side of the sitting room and was now racing up the stairs.

By the time they reached Henry's studio, Ella was out of breath, and she'd lost one of her slippers somewhere on the journey.

She stood at the top, her chest heaving, and let go of the lead, watching as Wyatt charged up to the man standing in front of one of Henry's easels. Then the bloodhound began to growl.

Henry switched off the music and grabbed Wyatt's lead. 'Calm down, lad,' he soothed as Sprout leaped in front of the bloodhound and began to yap too. 'What's going on?' the older man asked Ella, raising his voice above the din.

'This gentleman.' It took all of Ella's willpower to call him that. 'Was driving his car too fast and almost knocked Wyatt down this morning.' She took a step forward, and the man lifted his dark eyes to meet hers.

'We've been through this,' he said testily, and his shoulders tensed as if he were gearing up to argue with her. 'I think you'll find the fault lies with your dog.'

Wyatt barked again, then glanced at Ella as if asking for permission to yell more – but she reluctantly shook her head.

'Could be you were both at fault,' Henry suggested, glancing between them, picking up on the obvious tension.

'I'm a very careful driver,' the man insisted, but when Henry frowned, he dipped his chin. 'But you're right of course. If it was my fault that I almost hit you, then I apologise.'

He addressed the words to Wyatt who glanced at Ella again. This time when she nodded, the dog took a step away. Ella didn't want to make up with the man, but it was clear he was Henry's latest protégé. If he was going to be working here, there was no point in prolonging their fight.

'You're late, lass,' Henry said gently as the tension finally eased. He swept an arm towards the easel where Ella usually worked. 'And that's been gathering dust.'

'I'm really sorry,' she said quietly, wiping her hands on her jeans. 'Something important came up,' she admitted.

There was no point in elaborating. Late was late and Henry didn't need to know about Clyde's doctor's appointment. Besides, he might not be very sympathetic. She'd missed an art lesson the week before because Dane had booked to see the dentist, and she'd had to clean four rental cottages for him which had taken a whole afternoon.

She heard the man at the easel make a *tsk-tsk* sound under his breath, but when she glanced his way, he was staring at his blank canvas. She wandered up to her easel and put her bag on the ground.

'I'll start with introductions,' Henry said. 'This is Alexander Forbes-Charming, he's going to be studying with me until Christmas.'

'You can call me Alex I suppose,' the man said reluctantly.

Henry smiled. 'This is Ella McNally. She runs Magic Mops. The team help Aggie to keep the manor in order. Ella could be a very successful artist.' His tone grew dark. 'If she committed herself.'

She sighed. Henry knew about her promise to her da and obligations to the family, but to him, the world revolved around art and nothing else. 'I'll be teaching you together as often as I can.'

Neither Ella nor Alex spoke, but the heavy silence communicated their disappointment at the news.

'It's fortunate you're getting the chance to meet now, because Alex will be at the pantomime rehearsals tomorrow evening. I'm sure you'll make him feel welcome.' There was a hint of mischief in Henry's voice. Ella saw a flash of surprise flicker across the younger man's face before he hid it.

'I will?' Alex asked roughly.

'Aye, why do you think my protégés always come here in the run-up to Christmas?' The older man chuckled. 'I take care of all the scenery for the annual village pantomime – and I like to hand-pick my assistants. You'll be helping me while you're staying for at least two nights a week, starting tomorrow.'

Henry winked as Alex's mouth bunched. 'Perhaps your da forgot to mention it. Then again, I may not have remembered to tell him.' He gave the younger man an amused look, and Ella had to give Alex points for staying silent because it was obvious he was horrified by the idea.

From the look of his designer haircut, fancy clothes and shiny car, Alexander Forbes-Charming wasn't the type of person who'd usually be seen dead at a village pantomime, let alone helping out with the scenery. He was probably too busy mowing down pets.

'Ella is in the pantomime,' Henry said proudly, but Alex's expression didn't change. 'The cast is in the fourth week of rehearsals which is around the time I like to visit to consider scenery options. We'll leave here after dinner tomorrow and you can drive.' Henry shot Alex a long look. 'Assuming you haven't got any other plans?'

'Nope,' Alex murmured, his expression dark.

The older man tutted when Aggie suddenly appeared at the top of the stairs carrying a tray.

'More soup?' Henry asked sharply as she sidestepped him.

'Not for you. But I noticed that you managed to force all yours down at lunch,' she shot back, looking smug.

'Only because I was starving.' Henry looked embarrassed.

Aggie ignored him as she fussed around Ella, supplying her with a bowl of steaming soup and a crust of bread before putting down bowls of water for Sprout and Wyatt. Both dogs immediately buried their noses in them, and Alex looked more relaxed.

Henry left Ella to eat and turned towards Alex before pointing to the blank canvas. 'What are you going to paint first, lad?' he asked as Ella dipped a spoon into her bowl.

'I like that view.' Alex pointed past Ella to the row of windows.

'Why?' Henry asked, his gaze fixed on the younger man's face. Ella sipped the soup, watching him too. He really was quite beautiful – with an angular jaw, dark eyes and a full mouth which didn't look like it had ever smiled. Did he have a reason to be sad? Perhaps she'd been too hard on him...

Alex looked pained. 'It's... pretty,' he offered, obviously caught off guard.

Henry shook his head before he turned to Ella. 'And what do you want to draw next? That cat is almost finished so I'd like you to start thinking about your next project.' Ella quickly swallowed another mouthful of soup, considering her walk earlier.

'A robin,' she said simply.

'Because?' Henry asked.

Ella considered. She knew what Henry wanted so took her time. 'There's one that visits a garden I walk past. He's friendly and sometimes when it's quiet and Wyatt isn't around, he sings. Those moments make me feel –' She pressed a hand to her chest as she tried to find the right words. '– Like I've got a candle burning inside of me. That robin doesn't want anything but my company, and I'd somehow like to capture the joy of that.'

She could have sworn Alex snorted, but when she checked, he was staring out of the window again.

'Aye.' Henry nodded before he turned back to the younger man. 'That beats "pretty", doesn't it, lad?'

Alex's cheeks reddened, and Ella felt a twinge of guilt. She hadn't meant to make the man look bad.

'Before you put a pencil to that paper.' The artist pointed at the easel. 'I want you to think about how your picture is going to make you feel. Because that will show in every stroke of your brush.' His tone was intense. 'You want to make whoever sees it feel exactly like you. If you want them to love, hate, cry, laugh – you have the power to do it. But you're not going to achieve anything if you're aiming for something as mundane as pretty.' With that, Henry turned away.

As he did, Ella caught Alex's eye – he looked lost. For a nanosecond, she wanted to reassure him, but then his face changed as if a shield had slid down, blocking any emotions he might be feeling.

'I'm sure I'll work it out,' he said, his voice flat. He gave Ella a brief glance, which was anything but friendly – then he turned to face his easel again. Leaving her wondering if Alex Forbes-Charming had any feelings, or if he was just as cold as he seemed.

# 5

## ELLA

The Art House on Mistletoe's high street was quiet when Ella entered, and she dragged Wyatt across the threshold before he got distracted by another cat. She was bone-tired and couldn't wait to get home, but her godmother had asked her to pop in on the way and she could never refuse her Aunt Mae.

'Hello!' she called out, as she wearily made her way across the stunning gallery. It was light and airy due to the huge windows in the roof. Columns set into the wooden floor exhibited striking pottery and sculptures – and a multitude of thick white panels showcased pieces of eclectic art, hand-picked by Mae. Ella paused at a landscape she recognised as one of Henry's and winced at the price tag. Her problems would be solved overnight if her art could earn even a fraction of that. She'd pay off the company debts and find a new staff member to help out. Then she'd have time to paint.

'Is anyone there?' Ella called again as she passed a Christmas tree decorated in red and green baubles.

'Ella,' her godmother said brightly as she emerged from her office at the back, looking cool and collected in a pristine crimson suit. Mae Douglas had been Ella's mother's best friend from school up until her mother had died when Ella was almost five. Mae was a beautiful woman – she'd been a model before opening her art gallery. Despite being in her early sixties, Mae's shiny blonde hair was styled into a modern, chin-length bob which complimented her pretty heart-shaped face and made her look younger than she was. She always looked immaculate – but was very sensitive about her age.

'Wait a second, I've got a couple of things I want to give you,' Mae said in a deep Scottish drawl, and Wyatt barked with excitement as she disappeared into her office, emerging seconds later holding bags. 'Aye, lad. I've got something for you,' she cooed offering Wyatt a bone-shaped biscuit, which he quickly gobbled down. 'Did you have a good day off?' Ella grimaced. 'Let's sit over there, you look tired.' Mae pointed to two red leather sofas by the Christmas tree.

When they were seated, Mae put the bags on the table and crossed her long legs.

'Clyde was sick,' Ella said, rubbing her eyes.

'Let me guess.' Mae sighed. 'You had to do his work again?'

'You know both of my stepbrothers have health issues,' Ella quickly shot back as she took in her godmother's expression.

'They seem like a couple of very healthy twenty-two-year-olds to me. What they're both suffering from is a bad case of lazyitis,' Mae said dryly. 'They've only been working with you for six months. But they've been incapacitated for more days than they've worked, and you look more tired than I've ever seen you.'

'I'm fine.' Ella shoved her hands into the pockets of her coat. 'It's winter and there are lots of bugs around.'

'You know, it could be time to finally make a change, leave the business and concentrate on your art,' Mae said softly.

Ella shook her head. 'You know Da made me promise to

take care of the family and Magic Mops when he died. I'll go back to art college when the business is on track.'

Mae pulled a face. 'That's not going to happen, lass, until someone other than you steps up.' She trailed off when she caught Ella's expression. It was a conversation they'd had a thousand times. But Ella had made a promise to her father and that was that.

'Aye, well...' Mae sighed and, after a long pause, she nodded. 'Perhaps these will cheer you up.' She handed one of the bags to Ella. 'I made my reindeer cupcakes.'

Mae had been making her Christmas cupcakes for Ella since her mam had passed a few weeks before her fifth birthday, almost eighteen years before. Now Christmas wouldn't be Christmas without at least a dozen crooked reindeer cakes.

Ella pulled a tin from the bag and opened the lid. Inside was a plate of the skew-whiff cupcakes decorated with pretzels, candy eyes and sweets which were supposed to resemble reindeer – but looked more like four-legged monsters.

'Thank you.' Ella's eyes pricked with tears, and she popped the lid back on. 'I'll take them home.'

'Don't share them,' Mae said sternly, and Ella nodded. Last year, she'd taken the cakes to Lucinda's and her stepbrothers had gobbled the lot.

'There's something else wrong.' Mae looked at Ella carefully and leaned forward studying her face. 'Did you see the eejit artist today? Did he upset you?'

'Henry was fine – I was late to his lesson again, that's all,' Ella said as Alex Forbes-Charming's face flashed into her head.

'Ach, it'll do the bampot good to wait for somebody for a change. Perhaps his head might finally shrink to the size of his brain,' Mae said darkly.

'He's not that bad.' Ella shook her head at her godmother's comments, wondering again where the anger came from.

The couple had begun a love affair at the start of the year

and from what Mae had told her, it had been both tumultuous and passionate. By the summer, things had started to get serious, and they'd even discussed Mae moving into Pinecone Manor. Then something had changed in the autumn and since then, her godmother had refused to speak to Henry. Whenever Ella had tried to grill the older woman about what had happened, Mae had declined to share. But something had hurt her; it was written all over her face. Henry randomly asked questions about her godmother, looking more and more dejected when Ella had little to offer him.

'Maybe you should talk to him?' she suggested.

Mae's expression was grim. 'We're past talking, lass. The less said about Henry Lockhart, the better as far as I'm concerned.' She let out a long breath, visibly relaxing. 'You should get yourself home. I just wanted to see you to give you the cakes.'

Ella stood and gave her a quick hug. 'Will I see you at the pantomime rehearsals?'

'Aye, wouldn't miss it.' Mae nodded as she stood. 'I am the director, after all. Oh, that reminds me.' Mae picked up the final bag and pulled out a pair of pretty, transparent high heels. 'Blair McBride found you some glass slippers and asked if I'd give them to you.' She offered them to Ella. 'If you're going to be playing Cinderella, you're going to have to look the part.'

They were delicate, covered in sparkly jewels and looked about the right size. 'I'll try them on when I get home,' Ella promised, taking the bag.

'Don't forget to bring them to rehearsals tomorrow.' Mae leaned in to kiss Ella's cheek. 'And try to take a little time for yourself and your art, lass. I know for a fact that your mam – and da – wouldn't have wanted you to waste all that talent running about after—' She frowned. 'Well, you know what I mean.'

Ella nodded and squeezed her godmother's shoulder before

heading for the door. She hadn't shown an interest in art before her mam had passed and her da definitely wouldn't want her to abandon the family or Magic Mops.

Which meant Ella would do whatever was necessary to make sure both thrived. She'd just work even harder so she could do it all.

# 6

## ALEX

'We're here!' Henry said from the front seat of Alex's car as he drew his Volvo to a stop outside of the Mistletoe Village Hall. It was snowing again, and he'd taken extra-care on the drive here, in case Ella's huge, gangly dog decided to sit in the middle of road again.

He gazed at the building as he put on the brake. It was bigger than he'd expected, with multiple windows and a tall triangular roof. Colourful drawings, paper chains and Christmas decorations had been hung across the windows. The effect was charming and unexpectedly quaint.

Alex's mobile began to ring, distracting him from the view, and he switched off the engine and reached for the door handle so he could get out.

'Take the call, lad,' Henry insisted as he opened the passenger door, letting Sprout leap from where he'd been travelling on his lap. The dog landed in the snow and immediately turned to gaze at Alex, his nose twitching in raw delight.

Alex tried to ignore him, feeling uncomfortable. He wasn't used to being adored. It's not like he deserved it. He'd barely looked at the animal since he'd arrived at Pinecone Manor yesterday morning and deliberately hadn't touched it. So, why was he the object of so much affection?

The terrier had even tried to sneak into his bedroom last night, and when Alex had shut the door, it had whimpered outside. He'd almost relented, but then Henry had called Sprout away. Alex had checked his pockets this morning to ensure he wasn't harbouring carrots or something equally tempting, but he'd found nothing to explain all the continued doggy love. He was obviously missing something.

He let out a sigh of relief when Henry got out and shut the door before walking towards the village hall with the terrier. The dog looked back towards the car a couple of times, his face a picture of confusion, but he didn't try to return. When they both disappeared, Alex answered his mobile which was still ringing.

'Iceman,' the caller said, using the nickname Alex's colleagues used at work.

Alex rested his head on the steering wheel, letting the familiar voice wash over him. 'Stan.' He could hear relief in his voice and wished it wasn't so obvious or sincere.

Stanley Bailey had been his best friend since they'd met in boarding school when they were six. They'd been like pieces of the same puzzle – utterly inseparable – from that moment onwards.

They'd both played rugby for the county, attended St Andrews University together, after which they'd risen through the ranks of Alex's father's firm, Charming Capital Management. They'd competed for every promotion, bonus, award and client – each of them striving to outperform the other. His friend had been the closest he'd ever come to trusting someone – to letting them into his head or heart. But Stan had suffered a health scare six months ago and since then his whole personality had changed.

'How are you doing?' Alex asked, sitting up. 'Which

country are you in now? I hope you're close to a decent hospital in case your heart decides to stop pumping again.' Despite the joke, he regularly relived the awful moment his friend had grabbed his chest and slumped to the floor in the company boardroom. Every second had felt like a nightmare and Alex still hadn't come to terms with his sense of helplessness, the utter terror he'd felt.

'I'm in New Zealand. All of my organs are working fine and I'm feeling better than ever. Thanks for asking,' Stanley said, sounding relaxed. 'How are things going with you?'

'Great.' Alex kept his tone light. In truth, he wasn't sure how things were. He wasn't used to wasting his time looking inwards. Henry kept asking how he felt about what he was going to work on, and he had no answers for him.

*Why did it matter?* Surely the only thing that did was how the artwork looked? People didn't buy feelings, they wanted beauty – more than that, they wanted something to covet and own. Desire and money made the world go round. Nothing else counted. Which meant he was out of his comfort zone with no idea of what he had to do to succeed – and he hated it.

'What are you up to at the moment, are you bored? When are you coming home?' he asked, desperate to change the subject.

'I'm not up to much.' Stanley sighed. 'I met a couple of people on the beach picking up shells this morning. Have you ever wondered why people do that?'

'Because they've got nothing better to do,' Alex suggested, hoping his friend would get the hint.

'I think it's because of the colours,' Stanley continued, his tone wistful. 'I've never thought of looking at them before today, but they're incredible when you get close up. A kind of mini miracle.' He sighed.

'You need a holiday from your holiday, you're not making sense,' Alex said brusquely.

Since his friend had left for his trip, his existence had become aimless and unfocused, and Alex was worried about him. If Stanley told him he was going to take up yoga or meditation, he knew he'd have to fly to New Zealand to stage an intervention.

'Are you planning on returning to work soon? Your office is gathering dust, and I've heard tales of people eyeing it up for their own,' he lied. No one would be allowed to so much as look at Stan's desk so long as Alex was around.

'I've no plans to return to the office.' Stan chuckled, but Alex didn't see what was funny about that. 'Remember, there's an open invitation if you ever fancy joining me. You haven't taken a proper break since we left university. You might be surprised at how much you enjoy being aimless if you do.'

'I'll pass.' Alex choked imagining what his father would say. Michael Charming's second rule of success was, *'holidays are for those who lack ambition'*.

Alex understood why Stanley had wanted to take a step away from his life for a few weeks, but his continued desire to separate himself from the bright future he'd been heading towards was baffling. And Alex missed him. Stan was the only person he'd ever met who he really understood – or who got him, in return. But he barely recognised his friend now.

'Why are you calling?'

'I just wanted to catch up. How are things in Mistletoe Village with the artist?' Stan asked.

Alex took another look at the red brick building that was Mistletoe Village Hall. It was a large structure for such a small village – perhaps because there was so little else in the area to do? He wondered if the woman he'd met yesterday – Ella – and her bloodhound were already inside, although it seemed unlikely. She hadn't turned up to her lesson this afternoon. According to Aggie she'd been detained at work, although Alex wasn't sure he believed the excuse. But her absence had irritated him more than it should have, considering they'd only just met.

Then again, people with talent like Ella's should want to develop it. The fact that she couldn't be bothered to take advantage of her opportunity with Henry Lockhart was a pitiable waste. Although Alex guessed if he worked hard, it would be easy for him to outshine her, so she was doing him a favour really. 'Things are odd. He's making me help him with pantomime scenery,' he answered, fairly sure his friend would laugh.

'Really. Which panto?' Stanley asked eagerly.

'*Cinderella.*' Alex's tone was dark.

'I'd love to see that.' Stan chuckled. 'What does your dad think about it?'

'He doesn't know,' Alex admitted. He wouldn't be telling him either. Michael Charming would be horrified at the idea. He'd expect his only son to focus on creating the perfect canvas, not painting cardboard boxes in village halls. 'I'm not sure why Henry wants me here,' he mused. 'I'm supposed to be learning from him, but so far all he's done is make me take walks around the grounds of his house. I'm supposed to *feel* something apparently.'

'You sound frustrated,' Stan observed.

'I think he's just trying to see how far he can push me before I lose my cool,' Alex admitted. 'He's trying to get inside my head; asking questions, wanting me to talk about my feelings...' He stopped suddenly. 'I'm sorry.' He straightened his spine, embarrassed. 'I'm complaining, aren't I?' Which was one of the deadly sins as far as his father was concerned.

'You're venting and you need to stop feeling guilty for expressing your feelings. It's a wonder you allow yourself to have them at all.' His friend sighed. 'Take a deep breath and give it time,' he said. 'I'm sure your artist knows what he's doing. You need to chill out.'

Alex had a sudden memory of Stanley standing in his office wound up like a coil and ranting because one of their clients had asked if he could have a croissant with his morning cup of coffee before their meeting began. It had taken the client only four minutes to eat it, but Stanley had charged him an additional two hours for wasting his time.

Even Alex had thought that was excessive. But he missed that side of his friend, he realised. At least that was a person he could make sense of. For years, it had been the two of them against the world, even as they were competing side by side. Now he felt alone.

'I need to go,' he muttered as he watched three people wrapped in enormous coats tramp across the car park and enter the building. 'I think I'm going to be needed inside soon. Call me when you've finished collecting those shells...' The words sounded more sour than he'd intended, but his friend just laughed.

'Maybe. Let me know when you're ready to join me. I'll guarantee it's a lot more fun than you think. I'll call again in a couple of days.' With that, Stan hung up, ensuring he got the final word.

Alex flashed the mobile a wide smile – at least that hadn't changed.

# 7

## ALEX

The village hall was huge inside. The ceiling was vaulted and there were multiple windows across two of the main walls – all covered in the decorations Alex had seen from outside. He guessed they let in plenty of daylight, but since it was dark now an abundance of LED panels kept the room warm and bright. Someone had hung fairy lights along the edges of the walls, which made the place look festive, and Alex couldn't stop himself wondering if Ella had been responsible. From what Aggie had told him, she'd decorated most of Pinecone Manor, which explained why he had a Christmas tree in his bedroom.

A large stage framed by thick red curtains took up almost the entire end of the main room. It was an impressive set-up, and Alex guessed the panto might be more professional than he'd first imagined. It probably explained why a man of Henry's stature had agreed to help out.

Alex walked further into the room searching for Henry. There were clusters of people sat on chairs, some holding mugs of tea and a few tucking into mince pies. Some milled around the empty space chatting, many of them slathered in sparkly pantomime makeup. A few glanced curiously in Alex's direction as he passed.

'Are you okay, lad?' a woman with high cheekbones and a tidy blonde bob swerved from where she'd been heading to cut him off, her expression friendly. She held a large clipboard in one hand and wore a billowy green velvet dress which accentuated her generous curves. She looked him up and down, her mouth bowing up at the edges. 'I'm Mae Douglas, pantomime director. I'm also playing the fairy godmother – so if you have any particular wishes you want granted, don't hesitate to ask.'

Alex decided not to ask if she could arrange for him to be anywhere but here.

The woman flashed him a grin as if she'd read his mind exposing deep dimples in both cheeks. 'If I had to guess, I'd say you must be the artist who's staying at Pinecone Manor.' Alex gaped and she giggled. 'Getting that right isn't a demonstration of my magical powers, lad; some of the villagers have been talking about you, and you're the only handsome stranger here tonight.'

He frowned.

'Don't worry, you'll get used to being the centre of attention. That gorgeous face will guarantee at least a few extra looks. Besides, new blood gets the gossip mill churning at twice its normal speed. Everyone will get over it as soon as there's something else to blather about. It's good to meet you.' She offered a hand.

'Alex Forbes-Charming.' He took her hand and shook it. 'Everyone's talking about me?' He looked around the room. A few people were glancing their way, but most had gone back to their conversations. In the distance, Alex spotted Aggie with Hunter by her side talking to a woman who looked identical to her.

Mae nodded still grinning.

'What are they saying?' Alex asked, wondering why he cared.

'That you're very attractive.' She raised an eyebrow. 'And an artist. I've also heard you drive too fast.'

Alex sighed as understanding dawned. 'You've been speaking to Ella McNally.' He shouldn't be happy that the younger woman had been talking about him, but a flicker of pleasure still danced in his chest.

Mae glanced over her shoulder, and Alex immediately spotted Ella with a couple of young men. They were both tall, with brown hair, and even from here, Alex could see they were handsome. He worked hard to keep his expression blank even as his insides lurched as he fought a rush of jealousy.

His attraction to Ella was baffling and unwelcome, but he'd rarely experienced anything quite so fierce. He wasn't sure what it was about her that drew him to her. Certainly not her height – she was around five foot six, which was average in most circles, but he usually preferred dating women who were loftier so he didn't feel freakishly tall.

Her hair was odd – most of it was an unremarkable chestnut brown, but she'd childishly streaked multiple strands in different shades of red and green. Alex supposed it was a nod to Christmas, but its frivolousness still confused him. Her glossy mane stopped just below her shoulders – it wasn't extraordinary in itself, nor were her large blue eyes. But there was something about the overall combination and the way her cheeks blazed when she glowered at him that made his blood pump faster.

He'd known from the moment they'd laid eyes on each other that Ella didn't like him very much. Normally, that wouldn't have bothered him, but for some unknown reason it did this time – and it didn't seem to matter that he didn't particularly like her either.

He thought about the drawing of the dog in Henry's

hallway and grimaced. Perhaps he was just bowled over by her talents? Once he got to know her better – once his work began to outperform hers – the attraction would surely fizzle and die. In the meantime, he'd do whatever he could to steer clear.

'She's my goddaughter,' the older woman explained.

'I see,' Alex said as Ella's bloodhound, who'd been sitting beside her, suddenly noticed him. Alex watched as it stood and came galloping to Mae's side. Then the dog cocked its head and bent to sniff Alex's boots, taking his time to ensure he'd smelled every millimetre before he wriggled his nose and began to growl malevolently.

'You seem to have made an impression there too,' Mae observed dryly, looking amused. 'Wyatt normally likes everybody, so you're quite the anomaly.' She clicked her tongue. 'Although I suppose you did try to run him down.' Her smile grew.

'That's not quite—' Alex started.

He was interrupted as a group of people on the other side of the room began to talk loudly and Mae grimaced as she turned around to watch. 'I'm so sorry, can you give me a moment, looks like there's trouble afoot,' she said. 'If you're looking for the eejit artist, he's over by the stage.' She wafted a hand to her left.

'Pardon?' Alex asked, surprised by the insult and intensity of her tone.

Mae didn't respond. Instead, she walked quickly across the room to where the crowd had grown and the chatter had reached a feverish pitch. Even Aggie, Hunter, Ella and the two men she was with went to join in.

Alex watched them for a moment before he headed towards the stage. Henry was sitting beside it on a chair with a sketch pad balanced on one knee. As soon as Alex approached, Sprout shot from his haunches and trotted over to sit at his feet. Alex found himself reaching down to pet the tuft on the terrier's head before he caught himself and stopped.

'Is everything okay?' he asked when the older man didn't look up.

'Why wouldn't it be?' Henry growled, glaring across the room towards the crowd which was even larger now. He sighed. 'Something must have happened – if we stay for long enough, I'm sure we'll find out what it is. It's certainly got everyone lathered up.' He raised an eyebrow. 'Mind you, it's probably nothing more than one of the lads stealing another one's lass... or someone getting uppity about not having enough lines in the panto.' He huffed. 'It's a small village and that happens more often than you'd think.'

Henry stood and stared into the crowd looking unconcerned. Then he offered Alex the pad he'd been working on. The page featured a sketch of the stage with a series of rectangles surrounding it, each showcasing a different scene. The drawings were tiny but perfect, and Alex recognised the precise strokes of Henry's style. If someone tried to sell this rough drawing on eBay, he knew it could fetch thousands of pounds.

He wondered how it would feel to have this much talent, to be so admired. Alex studied the image, trying to imagine it, but couldn't.

One of the pictures was of a simple bedroom complete with a basic dressing table and unadorned bed. A few threadbare dresses were piled on a chair and a cat sat in the corner of the room staring out; on another Henry had drawn a garden with a large fountain and some lush bedding plants behind which he could see the front door of a large house. A pumpkin and a couple of mice were lounging beside it on the ground; he'd also sketched what looked like a palace ballroom with a glass chandelier that was similar to the one in Pinecone Manor. Alex could almost visualise the way it would glitter in candlelight and even now, he imagined he could hear an orchestra playing somewhere close by.

The final rectangle hosted a smattering of small creatures,

including more mice, this time wearing dungarees. Beside them stood a chunky lizard with bulbous eyes and a plump goose. There were a couple of candlesticks lying on the ground beside another pumpkin, only this one was squashed.

Alex guessed this was an illustration of the aftermath of Prince Charming's ball, after everything had returned to normal once midnight had struck. Indeed, in the far background he could just make out a castle complete with a large clock with both hands pointing to the twelve. All the drawings were brilliant, and he was beginning to look forward to helping to recreate them. Perhaps being involved with this project wouldn't be such a waste of his time, after all? He might even send his father some pictures when it was done.

'I'm designing some of the backdrops for the pantomime which you'll be helping me to paint,' Henry explained needlessly as he stuck a pencil behind his ear. 'I assume you know the Cinderella story?'

Alex nodded. His mother had died when he was two, and he'd had a series of nannies from that point until he'd gone to boarding school. One of his favourites had read to him every evening and she'd particularly enjoyed sharing fairy tales. Alex had loved listening to those stories – although they'd stopped once his father had found out. After that he'd been subjected to serious non-fiction tomes, in particular biographies from entrepreneurs, politicians and business gurus. He'd hated them all. Not that he'd ever admitted it.

'Don't worry, lad; I won't be asking how you feel about any of these sketches.' Henry chuckled, plucking the pad from Alex's hands just as Ella wandered up to join them, her face pale.

'What's happened, lass?' Henry asked, patting her arm. 'Is everything okay?'

Ella stroked hair from her face, her eyes shining. 'Andrew

Finn's been injured,' she whispered, sounding upset. 'He's playing Prince Charming in the pantomime,' she explained to Alex.

'How did he get hurt?' Henry asked, looking concerned.

Ella sighed as she glanced over her shoulder to where Mae was currently disengaging herself from the crowd. The older woman nodded in their direction and began to make her way across the room with Aggie and Hunter following. 'He was messing about in the snow apparently and got hit by a snow-plough last night,' Ella explained. 'His girlfriend just came to tell us about it.'

'Is the lad okay?' Henry shot back.

'Aye, he's fine – but he's broken both ankles.' She winced. 'He's been in the hospital for most of the day and he's just been allowed to go home – but apparently he won't be back on his feet for at least two months.' She pulled a face.

'But the show's going to be on in three weeks!' Henry gasped, looking back towards the crowd. People had peeled off and were now talking frantically in small groups.

Mae, Aggie and Hunter joined them. Mae's lips thinned when she glanced at Henry and then she deliberately averted her eyes. Hunter immediately trotted up to Alex and gazed up at him. What was it with the kids and animals in this village – had he been smothered in a multi-species catnip they couldn't resist?

'That's what we've been discussing,' Mae responded, turning towards Ella.

'Aye,' Aggie said. 'It's a disaster – there's no one who can take over from him.'

'He was really good too,' Hunter interjected, still goggling Alex. The child looked pale, but when Alex looked closer, he realised he'd been wearing white makeup which someone had obviously attempted to scrub off. He could just make out whiskers at the edges of his cheeks. 'I don't think anyone could be as good.'

Mae hugged the clipboard tightly to her chest looking unhappy.

'No one can take over?' Alex asked, surprised.

'There are only two lads of the right age who don't have a big part or important job backstage already,' Mae explained, her forehead tight with worry. 'One of them has a wife who's going to have a wee bairn any day now and the other's the midwife who's going to deliver it – so that means he needs to be available too.'

She shook her head. 'Both of them already have smaller parts in the chorus, which means the show can still go on if they're not here, but... there's no one else who can play Prince Charming.'

She sighed and squeezed her eyes shut. 'All the work we've already put in, I've sold tickets, started advertising. We do this show every year and people come from across the whole of Scotland to watch it, even tourists book – if we don't find a Prince Charming, we might have to cancel. It would be the first time Mistletoe hasn't put on a panto in over fifty-five years...'

'You can't cancel,' Hunter gasped. 'Da's promised he's going to come to watch.'

'Don't worry yourself, lad,' Aggie soothed, patting the boy's shoulder, but she looked worried too.

'There must be somebody who can stand in.' Henry's eyebrows met. He tried to catch Mae's eye again, but the older woman still refused to look his way.

Something had obviously happened between them. Alex could almost see the tension rolling off them both, but when he looked in Ella's direction, she discreetly jerked her head. He'd have to ask her at one of their lessons – if she ever actually turned up.

'Ach, we all know you're a talented artist, but unless you can paint me a lad from the village who hasn't already got a part, I think our panto is over before it's really begun.' Mae's voice cracked, and Alex saw Ella move closer so she could give the older woman's arm a squeeze.

'There's one lad who could do it – no painting required,' Henry said suddenly, his eyes lighting as they shifted to Alex.

Alex didn't understand and waited for Henry to explain. Then the penny suddenly dropped, and he felt the blood drain from his face.

'Oh, I don't think that's a good idea,' Ella snapped, clearly understanding too – Alex wasn't sure whether to be insulted or pleased that she was so against him taking the part.

'Ella's right. I'm not an actor,' he agreed. He hadn't come to Mistletoe Village to be in a village panto. At least helping to create the scenery made sense.

'He's really not,' Ella echoed forcefully.

'It's hardly Shakespeare, you two,' Henry said dryly, as the director's dull expression suddenly brightened.

'It could work,' Mae considered, allowing herself one silent nod in Henry's direction before she took a step towards Alex. She studied him silently as if he were a Christmas tree she was sizing up before getting out her axe.

'He's too tall and much too broad,' Ella said, sounding desperate. 'None of Prince Charming's costumes will fit him.'

'Ach, lass,' Aggie said, chuckling quietly. 'We can easily fix that.'

'It won't work,' Alex tried again. 'I really don't think I'm the right person to be on stage.' If his father found out, he'd never forgive him for embarrassing the family name. Besides, he wasn't an actor and Alex never did anything unless he knew he was going to excel.

'What about chemistry?' Ella asked, glancing at him and pulling a face.

Alex frowned – why was Ella so worried about him playing the part?

Mae's gaze shifted between them, her expression confused. 'Ach, lass, I'm sure that won't be a problem.' She winked.

Hunter tugged eagerly at Alex's sleeve. 'You'd get to wear cool costumes and makeup, and sometimes you'd even be on the stage with me! We can talk about art and all kinds of things. You'll meet my best friend Maxwell Wallace too – he's playing Perry, the other mouse.' He beamed, looking excited.

'Um,' Alex gulped, out of his depth. He didn't want to upset the boy or anyone else for that matter – but what the hell was happening here? He might be known as the iceman at work, but he wasn't looking to alienate an entire village by saying no. How was he going to get out of this nightmare?

'He's got the looks all right,' Mae continued as she looked him up and down. 'Ella's right, though. He's taller than Andrew, broader too, so Aggie, are you sure you and your sister can alter the costumes you've already made?

'It'll be our pleasure,' Aggie said.

'Then it's settled.' Mae looked at Alex again, her green eyes wily. 'I know you're going to be in the village until the show's over, so we don't need to worry about you disappearing when it's on.' She rubbed a hand over her heart-shaped chin, looking relieved. 'Just stay away from snowploughs, please...'

'Don't worry, lad – we'll be able to paint the scenery in-between rehearsals,' Henry said blandly.

'That's not what I'm worried—'

'The show must go on – and it won't if there's no one to play Prince Charming,' Henry pressed, his tone letting Alex know there was no point in arguing.

'But there are lots of men here, they can't all be busy,' Alex said desperately as his eyes skirted the room and fixed on the two young men Ella had been talking to earlier. 'What about them?' He pointed them out.

'They're my stepbrothers and they're playing the ugly sisters,' Ella told him. She turned to Henry. 'I really don't think this is a good idea. Surely Alex hasn't got the time to learn the part?'

'Ach, lass,' Henry soothed. 'He's only in the second half of the pantomime, and there are very few words for him to learn, so he doesn't have to worry.'

That wasn't what Alex was worried about. His heartbeat wasn't accelerating and he hadn't started to sweat because he was afraid of remembering a few words. He could recall every currency in the world, knew each of their values from one hour to the next. His memory wasn't the problem. He just didn't want to embarrass himself.

'It's not that,' he said, taking in a long breath. 'I'm supposed to be here to work on my painting. This is about improving my work and learning from one of the best watercolour artists in the world – it's not about being in a pantomime.'

'Ach, lad, you'll have plenty of time for your art.' Henry gave him a stern look. 'You've been struggling to access your feelings. My guess is a couple of days up on stage will help with that.' He raised an eyebrow. 'You're already more animated. You'll learn to understand yourself better by pretending to be somebody else. Besides.' The older man's face turned serious. 'I own your time for as long as you're staying with me, and I think a stretch playing Prince Charming will do you the world of good.' He grinned suddenly. 'You've got the right name for it.'

Alex wilted. He knew when to fight his corner and when to throw in the towel – and it was clear he'd already lost this battle. Even Ella had stopped arguing, although her expression was dark. If Henry really wanted him to play Prince Charming, then he'd have to do it. He just hoped his father would never find out.

'As long as it doesn't take up too much of my time,' he grumbled. 'When do we start?' He looked around. 'And who's playing Cinderella?'

If he was going to do this, he'd do it properly. That meant getting to know the cast – figuring out their strengths and weaknesses so he could understand how to make the best of his part.

He looked up when the others fell silent.

'That would be me,' Ella murmured, and Alex's heart sank.

# 8

## ELLA

Ella checked her watch for the fourth time as she finished mopping the kitchen floor in her client's three-storey mansion. She'd been working here all morning, doing a pre-Christmas deep-clean, which had been booked and confirmed months before. Her stepmother had come to help too, but so far, she hadn't even picked up a duster in between making a dozen urgent calls.

Ella hadn't been scheduled to work on the house, but Dane had called in sick first thing, so she'd agreed to step in. Ella had only just managed to fit it in because she'd gone to her previous clients' house three hours early – which had only been possible because the couple were away. But the early start combined with both cleaning jobs had left her feeling bone-tired and weary.

'Are you almost done?' Her stepmother, Lucinda McNally asked, sweeping into the room waving her phone. 'Because I really need to get on, Ella. I can't help out all morning.' She sighed, sounding put out.

Ella sighed and nodded, too weary to mention that she hadn't really helped. 'It won't be long now,' she said, trying to smile. 'Did you want me to make us both a cup of tea before we leave?' Ella wouldn't normally take a break, but she was parched and needed a hit of caffeine.

Her stepmother bunched her lips, which had been painted dark red. 'I really don't think we have the time,' she said. 'Your attitude to work has become increasingly lax, Ella. You need to be more committed to the family and Magic Mops.' She shook her head.

'Yes, Lucinda,' Ella said, because she knew it was expected.

'Talking of family.' Her stepmother sucked in a breath. 'I'm so busy keeping up with the boys' illnesses that I'm not going to have time to do the Christmas shopping this year. I've made you a list.' Lucinda dug into the pocket of her jeans and pulled it out.

She stared meaningfully until Ella realised what her stepmother wanted and took it. 'Thank you, Ella, I know it won't take you long.' Lucinda smiled.

Ella grimaced at the list which was extensive. 'I'm—'

'Don't tell me you don't have time,' her stepmother snapped, reading her expression. 'Honestly, Ella, you've got to start doing your fair share.' Her blue eyes grew icy, and Ella held her breath. 'Being a parent is hard work and I barely have time to myself most days. All the calls I just made were to consultants about your brothers' health. I'm exhausted. You know your father asked you to stay in Mistletoe to help out. You're not going to go against his wishes, are you?' Her stepmother's accusatory glare had all the air in Ella's body leaking out.

'Of course not.' Ella lowered her eyes back to the paper. Lucinda was right, she had made her da a promise, one she intended to keep. But at times like these, she wondered if she'd ever escape her obligations; if she'd ever be free to do as she pleased.

She pushed the thought away as her stepmother's mouth stretched into something resembling a smile. Lucinda pointed to the carrying case filled with sprays, cloths and polishes that Ella had placed onto the white marble breakfast bar when she'd arrived. 'I'm afraid I need to get going soon, so you're going to have to finish by yourself. I'm meeting a couple of my friends for lunch – it's been booked for months; otherwise, you know I'd have cancelled when I heard from Dane.'

She frowned. 'I've just remembered he was supposed to be spring-cleaning some of the bathrooms and bedrooms for Aggie this afternoon. It wasn't on the schedule, but she mentioned it to him at rehearsals.' She shrugged. 'I was supposed to tell you, but what with the boys being sick, I forgot.' She gave Ella an apologetic smile. 'I've had so much on my mind – what with them and the pantomime rehearsals. Playing the stepmother is a huge responsibility and I want to get it right.'

Ella didn't bother to mention to Lucinda that her part was important too, especially since she was on stage for almost every scene. But in her stepmother's world, everything was always about her. It was one of the things Ella's father had teased her about.

'Can't Clyde clean Pinecone Manor?' Ella asked hopefully.

Lucinda frowned. 'You know today's his day off,' she said apologetically. 'It's really not fair for us to ask him to give that up.'

'I've got a lot of things I need to do,' Ella said tentatively.

Lucinda's eyebrows danced. 'We *all* do, Ella. That's why everyone in the family has to pull their weight.' Her tone softened. 'This is only temporary, lass. As soon as the boys are back on their feet, you'll have a lot more help. Then you can take some extra time off if you like?'

Ella nodded. 'That would be nice,' she croaked, feeling guilty for making a fuss. Her stepbrother wasn't well, and Lucinda was doing her best. 'And yes of course I'll clean Pinecone Manor.'

Her stepmother's face immediately brightened. 'Thank you,

Ella. I'm so grateful that we can always rely on you.' Her pretty brown eyes grew troubled. 'Dane sounded so awful when he called this morning. The poor lamb gets the most awful back-aches...' She fluffed a stray strand of blonde hair out of her face. 'It's unlucky the twins have so much trouble with their health. I'm sure it's because of all the time they had to spend in hospital when they were wee. They were so sick, I had no idea if they'd be okay.' Tears shone in her eyes as she gazed at Ella. 'Not everyone is as lucky as you. You never get ill.'

Probably because she didn't have time, Ella thought and immediately felt bad. 'They do get very poorly,' she agreed.

'Aye.' Lucinda's face creased. 'And their aches and pains haven't improved at all despite their trips to the chiropractor and the painkillers their doctors have prescribed. I do worry about them. They need time to recover...'

Ella was worried about them too. She only hoped they'd be back on their feet soon.

'I doubt Dane's been mobile enough to cook.' Lucinda finally picked up a cloth and absently began to float it across the kitchen side that Ella had spent twenty-minutes cleaning. 'And Clyde's not much of a chef – even if he did think about feeding his brother.'

Her forehead squeezed and she continued, 'I want to get Dane a lasagne... You know the one you make that he loves?' Ella nodded and her heart sank because she'd mentioned to her stepmother earlier that she'd cooked one for herself. 'I've no idea how I'm going to fit that in today what with lunch. I would buy one, but I know nothing would ever compare to your recipe, Ella; you're a genius when it comes to Italian food.' Lucinda gave her a pleading look.

'Oh, well...' Ella swiped sweat from her forehead as she unplugged the steam cleaner and wound up the cables before walking into the hallway and placing the machine by the door. Magic Mops used all their own equipment to guarantee a superior clean, but it meant she had to transport the larger items to every job.

'You're such a kind lass. Your da always used to say that about you – my Ella, she'd do anything for anyone.' Lucinda paused and studied Ella for a moment. 'I wouldn't expect you to give it up, only your stepbrother is sick,' she repeated.

'Of course.' Ella swallowed, suddenly feeling selfish for not offering straight away. Her brother was unwell, and it wasn't Lucinda's fault that she already had a lunch booked so couldn't make something. 'Of course you can have mine. If you want to drop by my house, the lasagne's in the fridge. It only needs heating up.'

'Ach, lass, you really are an angel,' Lucinda said, beaming.

'Of course.' Ella smiled, but inside fought a rush of tiredness. Families pulled together when they were in need – and she knew Lucinda wouldn't relax until she'd taken care of her boys. 'I probably need to get on.' She glanced around the kitchen. 'I've got a lesson at the manor in two hours. If I pick up Wyatt on the way, I should have time to do the cleaning there before I meet with Henry.'

It would be tight, and she'd have to miss lunch, but Ella knew she could do it if she worked fast. Just so long as the van started. It had needed a lot of extra coaxing this morning when she'd left home.

'You'd better get going then.' Lucinda waved towards the door as Ella went back into the kitchen and grabbed the vacuum. She carried it to the front door and took off her slippers and housecoat as her stepmother pushed on her high-heeled boots and gripped the handle on the large front door.

Lucinda's eyes warmed and she gave Ella a cheery smile as she opened it. 'I'll let you get on, you don't want to be late for Henry,' she sang before sweeping outside.

'Aye.' Ella sighed as she shut the door feeling weary, wondering how she was going to find the energy to take a

lesson and then get on stage after cleaning Pinecone
Manor too.

   She let herself wallow for a couple of moments before
opening the door, and picking up both the vacuum and steam
cleaner. Then she stumbled into the snow. She'd figure it out –
it was all about having the right attitude. Hadn't her da always
told her that?

# 9

## ELLA

'You're late,' Henry said gruffly as Ella and Wyatt finally made their way into the attic studio at Pinecone Manor three hours later. Ella was so tired that her feet were scuffing the floor, and she wasn't entirely sure how long she was going to be able to remain upright. She'd walked the dog before charging around the west wing of the large house, cleaning as many of the bathrooms and bedrooms as she could, but even with Aggie helping she hadn't been able to finish them all. She knew she'd have to clean the rest once the lesson was over – hopefully by which point she'd have enough energy to drag herself there.

'I'm sorry, I got held up.' Her stomach growled and Alex – who'd been staring glumly at the blank canvas on his easel – glanced over at her and narrowed his eyes. He wore a pair of expensive-looking jeans, which drew attention to his muscular frame, and a casual-looking powder blue shirt that made his brown eyes pop. His gaze had Ella's long-dead hormones reanimating as if he'd just performed telekinetic CPR.

Ella's insides pitched as their eyes met and she forced herself to look away, surprised by the power of her response.

She'd been so busy working over the last year, trying to keep the family business afloat, that she'd barely had time to notice a man, let alone respond to one. Perhaps that's why her reactions to him were so extreme? The fact that she found Alex attractive despite his obvious disapproval of her was baffling.

'Didn't you have enough time to eat again, lass?' Henry asked as Ella's stomach grumbled again, louder this time. 'How are any of us supposed to concentrate if you're making a racket like that?'

'I'm fine,' Ella said as her tummy let out another loud protest and she pressed her hands flat on her belly trying to pacify it. 'I'm sorry. It's been a busy morning.' She sighed, too weary to make a better excuse. She should have eaten, but just hadn't had the time.

'Did you spend it with Mae?' the older man asked, his eyes brightening.

'No, I was working. I think she's in the art gallery today.' Henry's expression dimmed. 'Shall I say hello from you the next time we talk?' she offered, taking pity on him.

'Nae.' He shook his head. 'She doesn't want to hear what I've got to say.' He nodded curtly and pointed to the top of the stairs. 'I'll go and ask Aggie to heat you some soup.' His tone brightened again. 'She made some kind of carrot concoction, and you'll be doing me a favour if you can finish it up. Carrots –' His large frame shuddered. '– are my *least* favourite vegetable, and that's saying something.' He sniffed. 'Sprout, are you coming, lad?'

Henry bent to peer into his dog's face. The terrier – who was wearing a Christmas tree-shaped hat – was lying at Alex's feet gazing up at him, his expression adoring. He whined before rising slowly and reluctantly followed Henry down the stairs, giving the younger man more longing looks as he left.

Wyatt, who'd been glaring at Alex since they'd arrived in

the studio, took the opportunity to slowly meander across the room so he could take Sprout's spot – his usual amiable expression morphing into something more sinister. Ella saw Alex stiffen, but he didn't look at the bloodhound. Instead, he glanced over at Ella again, his gorgeous face a picture of annoyance.

'Do you actually own a watch?' he asked stiffly. 'We've been waiting for over an hour. Henry might not want to say anything, but do you realise he refused to begin our lesson until you arrived?'

Ella shook her head, feeling guilty.

'Some of us have better things to do than wait around.' Alex waved a hand towards his blank canvas. 'I've got limited time here and a lot I need to achieve.'

Ella exhaled as she slumped into one of the wooden chairs. 'I'm sorry, I had—' She hesitated. Did she really need to explain herself to him?

'You didn't even eat. Which means Henry's now got to waste even more time making sure you've got lunch. It's simply not good enough,' Alex continued – his usually cold expression animated. 'What could possibly be more important to you than studying with one of the country's foremost landscape artists?'

'I... I had a lot of things to do,' Ella muttered.

Alex put his hands on his hips as his glittering eyes bored into hers. 'You do understand what a great honour it is for us to be in this studio?'

Alex stared at Ella for a long beat, and she wondered why he seemed so angry. Sure, there had been a delay in their lesson, but did it really warrant this much emotion? Was something else bothering him – what in the world had got him so riled up?

'I was working,' she said, trying to inject a little warmth into her tone. He'd understand if she told him why she was late. She wasn't looking to fall out, Wyatt was harbouring enough resentment towards Alex for the both of them. Besides, her life was difficult enough at present without painting – and performing – alongside an adversary so she wasn't looking to stir things up more. Everyone had problems, perhaps Alex did too?

'I—' Ella hesitated, trying to work out how best to explain things without making her stepmother or stepbrothers look bad. She scratched a hand through her hair attempting to untangle it – perhaps if she did, her mind would start to function properly again? 'My family own a cleaning business,' she began because that seemed like the best place to start. 'And—'

'Henry told me that already.' Alex's eyebrows furrowed and he waved her words away impatiently as he twisted to face her, ignoring Wyatt as he let out a warning growl. 'We all have day jobs which we manage to work around. I had to attend a meeting with Tokyo this morning. It started at five am and I wasn't late – after that I had to deal with a tranche of important emails, but I still managed to turn up to this lesson on time.'

'Well...' Ella was taken aback by this information, and she wasn't sure whether to commiserate or apologise.

'I'm just asking you to do the same.' Alex's perfect mouth pinched. 'Isn't it possible for you to schedule your day more efficiently?' He tapped his Rolex which Ella realised wearily was probably pure gold and would pay off the company debts three times over. 'Perhaps you should consider getting up an hour earlier? I'm sure if you did, you'd find the time to take a lunch break too.'

Ella felt her temper stir as his mansplaining and unwillingness to hear her out got the better of her. Not only had she had to work additional shifts yesterday and today to cover for her stepbrothers – she was now being lectured by someone who knew absolutely nothing about her circumstances.

She stared at him, ignoring the traitorous wave of tingles as they journeyed up and down her spine. This man was obviously so privileged that he had no idea how the real world worked. He might have answered a few emails this morning, but what did he know about the pull of family obligations, or working until his fingers bled?

Ella had met a lot of people like him over the years. She doubted Alex Forbes-Charming could switch on a vacuum cleaner if his life depended on it, let alone manage back-to-back shifts like her. He was here, wasn't he? How many people could afford to take a month away from the office just to follow a dream?

The sudden longing at the idea engulfed her and she felt momentarily overwhelmed. 'I take my art lessons very seriously,' she said, swallowing; at least she would once her stepbrothers were both well. 'We've had some... issues with staff at work. Sickness. It happens.' She pursed her lips. 'When it does, I need to muck in.'

'Meaning what?' Alex shot back, his voice as tense as a rubber band.

Ella sighed. 'I've had to cover a lot of extra shifts over the last few days because my stepbrothers – Clyde and Dane – have both been unwell,' she said, wondering why she was explaining herself. It was doubtful he'd either care or understand.

'Weren't they both at the pantomime rehearsal last night? They looked fine to me,' Alex asked, and Ella stiffened.

'They weren't well during the day,' she insisted. 'But they were feeling a lot better by the evening. That happens too.' She knew the justification sounded weak, but when he raised an eyebrow, she had to fight a flood of irritation.

'Yet, despite that, they're off sick again today?' Alex checked, his tone dry.

'Clyde's fine,' Ella snapped. 'But unfortunately, Dane—' She winced. 'He gets a bad back from time to time.'

'He's got backache?' Alex's tone signalled what he thought about that. 'And that's why you're late? Surely there must be someone else who can cover these *emergencies* when you have important plans?'

'It's a family business.' Ella bristled. 'Which is made up of a very small team.'

Alex let out a long sigh. 'I see.' His tone indicated that he wasn't impressed with her excuses and for a moment, Ella wasn't either.

But she banked the flash of guilt and rose from her chair. 'You don't know me and you don't know my family,' she said quietly. 'I know I've been late a couple of times, but working with Henry *is* important to me.' She paused, hoping Alex would see she was telling the truth. 'It's just... sometimes it's impossible to be in two places at once. That doesn't mean I don't want to be, or that I'm not trying my best.' She slumped wearily back into her seat, exhausted.

'Okay,' Alex said, his tone more contrite as he studied her.

Ella puffed out a breath, determined to meet him halfway. 'I'm sorry my disrupted schedule has had an impact on your lessons.' She looked down at her hands and frowned. 'I can't promise anything, but I'll have a word with my stepbrothers about trying not to take any more time off.' Or perhaps she'd ask Lucinda to speak to them instead?

'That would be... great,' Alex said stiffly. 'Hopefully, tomorrow we'll be able to start our lesson promptly.' He paused, perhaps realising his response was less than polite. 'I appreciate you trying.' He looked awkward.

Henry suddenly appeared at the top of the stairs carrying a large blue flask and spoon. 'Aggie's gone to pick up Hunter from school, but I found the soup. You look hungry, lass, so I heated the rest up. Try to finish it,' he said eagerly. 'I don't want any leftovers. Here's something to help mop up the taste.' He reached into his pocket and pulled out a bag filled with chunks of bread, then put the food on a small wooden art table cluttered with paintbrushes, charcoal and pots of paint. He watched Ella as she opened the flask and dug in a spoon. She ate a mouthful, and her stomach let out a grateful growl.

Henry glanced at Alex. 'Is everything okay, I thought I heard raised voices when I was passing through the sitting room?'

'It's fine,' the younger man said flatly, his cheeks flushing.

The artist pursed his lips as he glanced between them. 'From what I heard, things aren't fine at all. I wonder if you're both just in need of some fresh air. Why don't you take a walk together after Ella finishes her food?'

'I don't think—' Alex started.

'On the contrary.' The older man's voice hardened. 'I'm not going to get the best work from either of you if you're not getting on.' He regarded them both with a sombre expression. 'Take a stroll around the grounds with the dogs. Get to know each other. I'll warrant there's at least one thing you'll find to like. What is the world coming to when Cinderella and Prince Charming can't get on?' He grinned, amused by his own joke.

When Alex opened his mouth to argue, Henry put up a palm. 'Besides, I'd like some time in my studio by myself. I have a germ of an idea which I'd like to think about.' He narrowed his eyes at Alex. 'Perhaps while you're walking and talking with Ella, you'll find a way to access more of those elusive feelings of yours? You certainly appear to have plenty of them when it comes to the promptness of my lessons – and from what I over-heard, you don't have a problem with sharing those.'

When the younger man frowned, the artist snorted. 'I've always appreciated the power of a good argument. It gets the juices flowing.' He hesitated. 'Not that everyone feels the same way.' Henry looked unhappy and Ella wondered if he was thinking about Mae.

'But I do agree with you, Alex,' Henry continued. 'Ella could definitely do with sharing her workload and responsibilities. But she's got to come to that conclusion by herself. Now finish your soup so you can take that walk.'

Ella winced. No matter how long she and Alex would be out together, it was unlikely they'd find any common ground. Despite his obvious love of art and the fact that they were starring together in the pantomime, they were as different as two people could get – and from the look on his face, Alex felt the same way.

# 10

## ALEX

A storm outside rattled the windows of Pinecone Manor as Alex stood in the large hallway. He watched Ella zip up a sparkly white coat and pull a pink hat over her multicoloured hair without looking at him. Then watched as she opened the front door and proceeded onto the porch, leaning forward when a gust of wind blew into her face.

'Unless you want to end up flat on your face and covered in snow, try not to let either of them get under your feet,' Ella advised as she stood back and let both dogs leap out front. The terrier stopped as soon as he got to the edge of the porch, obviously preferring to stay close. Then he let out a happy bark and rubbed himself against Alex's leg.

'What is wrong with him?' Alex growled, leaning down to scratch Sprout's head, and was taken aback when the creature immediately began to lick the back of his glove. Did his clothes smell of food? Perhaps that would explain all the continuing adoration? He pressed the glove to his nose and sniffed, catching the scent of fabric conditioner and fresh air but nothing edible.

'I think he just likes you,' Ella said, her tone signalling exactly how misguided she thought the dog was.

'I've no idea why,' Alex muttered.

'Oh, believe me, we're on the same page there,' Ella said dryly as she walked onto the driveway. Alex had to swallow his smile. He wasn't used to people expressing their feelings so openly – duplicity and repression were more common in his circles. But he liked that she said what she thought. If he was going to have to spend time with Ella, at least it meant he'd know exactly what made her tick.

'Do we need leads for the dogs?' he asked as their charges suddenly ran onto the driveway and began to frolic together in the snow.

'It's not necessary. They can't get far and the only car we need to worry about is parked over there,' Ella said, pointing to Alex's Volvo, making him want to laugh all over again.

'Wyatt!' Ella yelled as the large dog suddenly stopped playing and dropped his nose into the snow before changing direction. A couple of seconds later, Alex realised the bloodhound was heading for his car. 'Wyatt, come here!' Ella tried again, her voice a little panicky. But the dog either couldn't hear – or wasn't interested in following orders.

Alex frowned as Wyatt reached his destination and began to sniff excitedly at one of the wheels. 'What's he doing?' he asked. Perhaps the animal had a strange fascination with high-performance tyres?

'You don't want to know,' Ella said grimly, and she broke into a run and began to wave frantically when Wyatt slowly cocked one of his hind legs. She reached him just before he did the deed, managing to drag him away, all the while admonishing him.

'Was he really going to—?' Alex asked as he caught up. The dog turned its head and offered a toothy grin, confirming Alex's suspicions. 'Seriously?' he muttered, glaring.

'He's still upset about the other day,' Ella explained as she pulled a sparkly red lead from her pocket and clipped it onto Wyatt's collar.

'He's got a long memory,' Alex said. In some ways the dog reminded him of his father. He never forgot either, and had been known to hold grudges for years.

'You've no idea,' Ella said. She gave her dog a thoughtful look. 'Shall we head into the hills? Wyatt will be able to do a lot less damage there.'

'As long as you're not planning on losing me somewhere,' he joked.

'No promises there.' Ella shrugged nonchalantly, making Alex's lips almost quirk again. Damn she was funny. He watched her march right, in the direction of a narrow pathway. Then she suddenly stopped and frowned. 'Dammit!' she groaned.

'What is it?' Alex asked, watching Ella head towards a white van parked under a tree at the far end of the circular driveway.

The vehicle had a pink logo adorning the side panel that read, Magic Mops – it looked old and a little battered. The front tyre on the driver's side was flat, and the van dipped low at the front.

'That tyre was fine earlier,' Ella hissed as Alex caught up and she dropped to her haunches to get a better look. The bloodhound began to sniff at the flat tyre. Was he planning to pee on this one too?

'I need to put the spare on now or I won't make it home. I don't want to wait until later because it'll be dark by then,' she said wearily. 'I've got a cleaning job at six am tomorrow, so I can't leave it and I don't want to arrive late.'

Alex ignored the irony and watched Ella rise and turn, which gave him a full view of her expression. There were dark shadows under her eyes, and she looked shattered. Perhaps she'd been telling the truth about her work? For the first time, Alex began to feel a flicker of sympathy – a softening towards her, which he fought to ignore. He wasn't looking to make friends with her.

'If you call your car rescue service now, there'll be plenty of time for them to sort it before you're ready to leave,' he advised.

After the walk, Alex knew they'd have at least a couple of hours with Henry – and from what Ella had told him earlier, she still had cleaning to finish before she left. He glanced at the rolling white hills in the far distance. He was sure they'd be beautiful to walk across, but he was looking forward to getting back to their class. Ella had to get the van fixed now so they could get on.

'I'm not a member of a breakdown service,' she said dully, dipping her hand into her pocket and drawing out a set of keys before tramping to the back of the van. 'My membership expired and I...' She shook her head as if trying to dislodge the reason from her memory. 'It's a long story.'

'Surely you have someone who can help?' he asked.

She glanced back at him, her expression tight. 'There's no one to call. My family are unavailable.'

She sounded so sure, Alex decided it was best not to argue. Besides, he didn't want her life story. He needed to stay focused on why he was here.

'What about a garage?' It was a simple problem with dozens of solutions.

Ella's cheeks flushed, but she didn't drop her gaze. 'I can't afford one. It's okay, I can do this myself,' she said brightly. She frowned as she glanced into the distance. 'Why don't you take the dogs for a walk and we can catch up again in say, half an hour?' She ignored Wyatt's growl.

'I don't think your animal is happy with that idea,' Alex said warily as he watched Ella unlock the large doors at the back of the van. Then she tugged out a long pink canvas bag which matched the company logo and dropped it on the ground.

'Ough, that's heavy,' she muttered.

Wyatt went to sniff the bag and Alex decided to move it before he or Sprout got any ideas. He heaved it into his arms and put it beside the flat tyre – then decided to stand guard.

'I'm sorry, I know we're supposed to be getting to know each other, but I have to do this before it gets dark,' Ella said, her tone edgy.

'Then why don't I change the tyre and you can tell me about yourself while I do?' he suggested, unzipping his coat and shrugging it off, ignoring her protests. 'That seems like the most efficient use of our time,' he insisted.

Alex shivered when a sudden gust of wind seeped through his jumper – and considered putting the coat back on. It was cold, but he didn't want his jacket to get covered in dirt or oil. It was the only one he'd brought with him, and as his father always said, appearances mattered. 'Will you hold it?' He offered the coat to Ella and she stared, the groove in her forehead deepening. 'It won't bite.'

'You want to change my tyre? Why does this feel like a trick?' She glanced around, perhaps hoping someone else would magically appear. When they didn't, her gaze returned to him.

'Are you wondering where your fairy godmother is?' he asked dryly.

Ella grimaced.

'Look, I'm all about getting this done and I'm your best bet.' He watched her qualms transform into annoyance.

'I'm perfectly capable of—'

'I'm not saying you can't change a tyre. I'm sure you can.' Alex wasn't sure of anything – but he wasn't going to say that to her. 'But—' He hesitated, glancing at the flat. 'I've done this more times than I can count, and I'll be quicker than you. In case you haven't noticed, it's minus zero degrees out here. I'm purely thinking of myself because I'm not going to leave you. I don't think Henry would be very impressed if I did.' Nor would the rest of the village – and after the incident with Wyatt, Alex knew news here travelled fast. 'He's waiting for us, and as I mentioned earlier, I'd like to get started with our lesson. I've got a lot of work to do.'

He made a point of checking his watch. 'We should have started our lesson over an hour and a half ago.' Alex was expecting Ella to object, but instead, the groove in her forehead deepened. 'Do you have a spare?' he asked, detecting she might be softening to the idea of letting him help.

'Of course I do.' She jerked her chin, still looking unsure. 'It's under the van, I've got some of my work clothes in the back, if you can just give me a second, I'll change and get it for you.'

'Take the coat, Ella,' Alex said, offering it to her again. 'Please,' he added when she didn't move. 'This isn't a slight on your independence, I simply want this done.' He waited patiently while she stared – then her mouth bunched and she took the coat, clumping it between her gloves.

'Are you sure you know what you're doing?' she asked gruffly, as Alex took the cufflinks off of his shirt and rolled up his sleeves. Ella held out a hand for the jewellery and he handed them to her. Then he went to grab a waterproof mat and dropped to his knees, leaning to look underneath the van so he could locate the wheel. Once he had, it didn't take him long to unhitch it from the undercarriage.

'I'm sure,' he said blandly, rolling the tyre to where Ella was standing and tugging off his gloves so he could easily search in the pink bag for the right tool. Wind whipped around them and Alex shivered, working hard to stop his teeth from chattering. It might sound stupid, but he didn't want Ella to think of him as vulnerable – she might use the information to get the better of him.

'Are you okay?' she asked, and Sprout barked again and

came to hover by Alex's legs, unnerving him. What did the strange creature *want*?

'I'm fine,' he said roughly, pulling on the gloves again because it was too cold to keep them off. 'Tell me something about yourself.' He positioned the jack and began to ease the van upwards, putting his back into it because it was heavy.

Ella sighed. 'Are you sure I can't help?'

'I'm sure,' Alex said tightly. 'But I'd appreciate it if you'd talk to me – Henry set us a task,' he reminded her. Once the driver's side of the van was off the floor, he repositioned the mat on the snow so he could kneel on it. Then he began to unscrew the first bolt, stopping to swipe snowflakes from his eyes as they hammered into them. The storm was definitely getting worse.

'What do you want to know?' Ella finally relented, brushing a wisp of green hair as it escaped from her hat.

'Tell me about your family.' As Alex talked, his breath created smoky curls, making him think of dragons and damsels in distress, unnerving him further because his head was usually filled with assets, financial markets and bonds.

'There's not much to tell,' Ella said.

'I know you have two stepbrothers, what about your parents?' he pressed, gritting his teeth as he fought with the first bolt which was rusty and difficult to turn.

Ella took a moment to respond, and Alex looked up and stared. When he did, she nodded. 'Fine.' She blinked and he noticed for the first time that her eyes were the same colour as the sea he'd painted in Skye. He'd never seen irises that colour. His fingers tingled as he imagined mixing watercolours to create an exact match. Ella flushed and looked away and Alex realised he'd been staring. 'I suppose I could tell you that my mam died when I was a bairn, and my da followed her a year ago,' she said roughly. 'My da remarried, though.'

'So you've got a wicked stepmother for real?' he asked, raising an eyebrow.

'Nae, not really,' she said, flushing. 'Lucinda, his new wife, is... well, she's a dedicated mam and... well, she loves my step-brothers.' Something passed across Ella's face, and Alex wondered what she hadn't said.

'Clyde and Dane,' Alex confirmed as the first bolt finally relented and he put it on the mat and began to work on the second. 'The unreliable twins.'

Ella grunted. 'They're not that bad.'

'Tell me something else,' he said, realising he wanted to know more.

Why was he pushing her? Then again, it was what Henry had tasked. Alex knew he was beginning to warm to Ella. Learning that her lateness was due to work was something he could relate to, and it was difficult not to be impressed with a good work ethic. Plus, she'd lost both of her parents – even he could have sympathy with that.

'There's not much to tell.' Ella frowned. 'I've lived in Mistletoe my whole life. Aside from when I was at art college for two years.' Her expression dimmed. 'I run Magic Mops, which is the family business. I spend most of my time cleaning, or when I can, painting and drawing – and I'm playing Cinderella in the village pantomime, which you know.' She sighed. 'I'm always in the show because Mae – my godmother – is usually the director. She was my mother's best friend—' She paused, her voice softening. 'And now she's mine.'

Ella's genuine candidness surprised Alex, and he let her talk. He forced his attention away from her to the second bolt which was proving just as difficult to take off as the first.

'I live on my own– but I spend a fair amount of time at home, helping my stepmother and stepbrothers,' Ella said, hesitating suddenly, perhaps realising how much she'd shared.

'You were at art college?'

She shrugged. 'I dropped out when Da got sick. I nursed him for a while, and when he died, I...' She took in a deep breath. 'Stayed on to help with the business. My stepmother was very upset. She needed my help. Still does...'

There was a lot to unpick, but Alex didn't get a chance to ask more.

'Now tell me something about you,' Ella said. She leaned down so she could watch Alex work. He caught a whiff of eucalyptus and wondered if it was her perfume or a leftover from when she'd been cleaning. He liked the scent; it was crisp and fresh and reminded him of long walks outside. He puffed out a breath, suddenly frustrated – he was beginning to sound like Stan.

'There must be something you can share,' Ella pressed, jerking Alex back to her question. 'Tell me what the drawing on your cufflinks means?' She held them up. Inside a white enamel circle, three dogs faced each other: a German Shepherd, a Great Dane and a husky. 'Is there some special meaning here?'

Alex shrugged. 'It's the logo for Charming Capital Management. Dogs symbolise prosperity and the breeds are all known to be powerful and resilient.'

'In that case I'm surprised you haven't taken to Sprout yet,' Ella joked as she continued to stare at the cufflinks before looking back at him. 'Tell me something else.'

Alex's mind went blank and after a long moment of silence, she made an irritated huffing sound.

'Okay,' he relented just as the second bolt moved and he spun it until it came off. 'It's just me and Da – Mam died when I was two, so I suppose that means we have one thing in common.' He didn't look at her.

'I suspect that might be the only thing, unless you count our love of art,' Ella said. Alex might have been offended, but there had been humour in her tone. 'I'm sorry about your mam. I know it was a long time ago, but it's still tough.' She swallowed and Alex felt a hit of pure emotion in his chest, fought to contain it. He didn't think about his mother much. His father had often told him he was like her – but he didn't mean it as a compliment. She'd been an artist. Talented apparently, but too emotional and too concerned with other people's feelings. She'd smiled too often and had lacked the killer instinct for success.

Alex had spent his life trying to supress any hints of her. The only thing that had leaked through was his love of art. His father only tolerated that because he saw Alex's talent as a potential income stream.

'Where did you grow up?' Ella asked, studying his face.

Alex paused, considering what he wanted to share. 'I lived at home with Da in our main house in Edinburgh until I went to boarding school.' He began to work on bolt three, which was as rusty as the last.

'How old were you?' Ella asked.

The question was unexpected, and Alex found himself telling the truth. 'Six.'

'That's young.' He could hear the frown in Ella's voice but decided not to react to it. This nut was looser, and he made quick work of undoing it.

'Not for me. I loved it there, and I was self-sufficient and mature for my age,' he said flatly. The school had been a lot homier than any of the family houses – which he still considered cold and austere.

He'd enjoyed the consistency of waking in the same place every day, of having the same people to talk to at breakfast and dinner, of meeting Stan. 'I made some good friends and got an excellent education.'

Alex was pleased when Ella remained silent. He wasn't sure what else he'd want to share about his childhood. Most of the time he didn't think about it. Life was all about looking forward and moving up. Making your name and impressing people. He unscrewed the fourth nut, which was loose too, and placed it on the mat.

'Tell me how you know how to change a tyre,' Ella asked,

perhaps sensing his reluctance to pursue the subject of his family. 'I'll admit, I'd have expected you to be clueless. Don't you normally have people for jobs like this?' Ella injected her voice with warmth, perhaps in an attempt not to offend him.

Alex stopped so he could gaze up at her. People often underestimated him, especially when it came to doing anything practical. Probably because he'd been raised with servants and people to see to his every physical need. His father had once told him that he should use those low expectations as a weapon. *'If they're not expecting you to knife them in the back, they won't see it coming'* was another of Michael Charming's rules of success.

'I'm sorry if that's rude, but...'

Alex gave Ella a tight smile. Her assumption shouldn't have grated, and he wasn't sure why it did. He didn't care what she thought, she couldn't matter to him. He let out a careful breath and began to pull the wheel off.

'When I was nineteen, my father bought me a vintage sports car – it was beautiful.' He'd named the car Ernestine and she'd been the first female love of his life. Perhaps the only one in retrospect, aside from his mother who he barely remembered. He'd had girlfriends, but no one he'd allowed himself to connect with – no one he'd ever wanted to let himself have feelings for. Or be vulnerable with.

'Nice,' Ella muttered, and Alex could hear something in her tone. He guessed she wasn't impressed by the information. 'But that doesn't really answer my question.'

'Aye, that's true.' Alex finished taking off the wheel. His fingers were stiff despite the gloves, probably because the rest of him was freezing. He fought to stop his teeth from chattering. He hated showing weakness and wasn't going to let the weather get to him.

'A few months after I got the car, I was driving and got a flat. I tried to call a recovery service, but I didn't have a phone signal, and I was too impatient to wait for someone to drive by and help.' He also suspected he wouldn't have asked for help even if someone had offered. He'd been raised to solve his problems for himself. 'I decided I could change the tyre myself. I thought it would be easy.' He absently rubbed his palms on his jeans and then picked up the spare and easily slid it onto the van before picking up the wrench.

'I was so sure I knew what I was doing, I just went ahead. I put the jack under the frame, but because it was in the wrong place, it ripped through the undercarriage.' He swallowed. It had felt like a part of him had been ripped out with it.

'My father threatened to take the car away.' He'd threatened a lot more than that, but Alex didn't share. He could feel his cheeks flush even now, because just talking about it made him relive the feelings of humiliation, the sense of failure. Michael hadn't spoken to him directly for months. 'I was embarrassed – but it also taught me a lesson about being helpless. It wasn't a feeling I liked.' He picked up one of the bolts and began to screw it back on.

'What happened?' Ella asked, edging closer.

Alex cleared his throat. 'I went to our local garage and asked them if they'd teach me about car maintenance and what to do in emergencies. They laughed at first, but—' He shrugged. 'I can be persuasive, and I offered to work for free.'

'Impressive,' Ella said, and Alex felt something inside him flicker and immediately snuffed it out.

He jerked his chin. 'They got me to clean up after them and to take money from customers and in return they let me watch them work. It took all summer, but I learned what I needed to keep a car on the road,' he said flatly. 'I still have the sports car, but it's locked in a garage on my father's estate.'

'Because?' Ella asked.

'I prefer driving more practical cars.' Cars he didn't particularly like, Alex realised, thinking how much of that sentiment applied to the rest of his life. If you don't allow yourself to care, you won't get hurt. Alex frowned as the nut stuck again and he had to put more weight into it. 'You need to go to a garage tomorrow and get yourself a new spare,' he said as he finished attaching the wheel. He pumped the jack again, easing the vehicle to the ground before putting all the tools back into the pink bag. 'Finished.'

Alex rose to his feet and swiped his gloves on his jeans. 'Do you want to take that walk?' He glanced back at the hills. The snow was thicker now, and he couldn't see very far.

Ella shoved the cufflinks and his coat at him, and Alex gratefully put everything back on. This time when his teeth began to chatter, he couldn't make them stop.

Ella watched him for a moment before pursing her lips. 'How about we take a quick walk to the porch and go back inside? I think you're cold enough and we've done what Henry asked.' She looked reflective. 'I feel like I know you better. Perhaps I might even like you – just a bit.' She grinned as she indicated exactly how much with her thumb and index finger – and the gap was tiny.

Then Ella picked up the mat and pink bag and walked slowly to the back of the van, refusing help when Alex tried to take them from her.

He shook his head and followed, rolling the damaged wheel out in front. Wondering what Ella had meant about liking him – and whether he'd inadvertently given away something important about himself.

# 11

---

## ELLA

'Did you get a chance to talk?' Henry asked eagerly as soon as Alex and Ella had made their way back into the studio with the dogs. Ella watched as Alex pulled off his coat and gloves and began to shiver all over again.

'Aye.' Ella nodded as she eased off her coat, still watching the younger man who was now rubbing his arms and large hands, trying not to give in to her growing awareness in case she embarrassed him. She wanted to offer him a blanket but suspected he'd be offended. She couldn't figure out why, but Alex being cold made her feel unexpectedly protective.

Something between them had changed since their conversation by the van. Ella had been surprised by Alex's competence – she'd made some assumptions about him since they'd met, and it was clear she might have to rethink at least some of them.

In turn, he seemed to have grown more relaxed around her since their chat. He'd waited patiently by the front door of Pinecone Manor while she'd taken off her boots and had even offered to carry Wyatt's lead when she'd unclipped it. Although he'd also commented on what a ridiculous colour it was.

From what Ella had surmised from their first meeting, she

would have expected Alex to take his walk alone and leave her to deal with the tyre. When he'd insisted on taking over from her, she'd been suspicious at first – but he hadn't used the problem as a chance to get one up on her. Instead, he'd calmly fixed her tyre and hadn't asked for anything in return beyond a conversation. He hadn't commented on the state of the van, or tried to make her feel guilty about the further delay.

Ella sighed and tried not to stare as Alex began to pace the studio – going to rest the back of his legs against a radiator in the far corner and discreetly warming his hands. After hearing more about Alex's life, she felt like she understood him better. The details he'd shared on his background might explain his initial unfriendliness – which Ella guessed was a defence mechanism. Despite the man's obvious wealth and privilege, it was clear he'd had to deal with heartbreaks.

Ella understood about those too. Her life was filled with them – she sighed as her attention drifted back to Alex. At least she had family, though. From what he'd told her, he didn't have anyone, aside from a father who sounded distant and unloving. Nothing like her own. Her da had had a huge heart and his life had been devoted to making others happy. He'd always been the first to volunteer to help out at the panto, had offered discounts to struggling clients, or done odd jobs for them for free.

Ella watched as Alex wriggled his legs against the radiator, his cheeks now flushed. She still wanted to offer a blanket or to tell him to put his coat back on, but guessed he wouldn't appreciate the interference – and she didn't want to upset their tentative new truce which she already suspected wouldn't last long. Was it odd that she wanted it to?

Henry perched onto one of the stools by his easel and turned his gaze to Alex. 'Your father called while you were walking.'

'He did?' Alex stiffened. He pulled his mobile from his pocket and stared at the screen, his forehead knitting. 'There are no missed calls, so he didn't try to speak to me,' he said. 'Is something wrong? What did he have to say?'

'It's all fine, lad,' Henry soothed, looking at him oddly. 'He didn't say much. Mostly he wanted to check in and find out how hard you were working.' The older man ran a hand over Sprout's ears when he wandered up to nuzzle him. 'I told him you were walking in the grounds with Ella and the dogs. I also told him you'd be busy this evening because you were helping at the pantomime.'

Alex winced. 'You didn't tell him I was playing Prince Charming, did you?' he checked.

'No.' Henry chuckled. 'I only mentioned the scenery and he didn't sound impressed.'

'What did he say?' Alex's voice was tense.

'Not a lot,' Henry said, and Alex's shoulders softened. 'Except it all sounded like a waste of your time. But I told him when it comes to my money, he's in charge – and when it comes to art, *I* make the decisions.'

'Right,' Alex muttered. 'And how did he take that?' Was it in Ella's imagination or did he seem a little buoyed by Henry's story?

'Not well.' The older man flashed a grin. 'But I said he has to trust me, and if he can't, then *you* –' He pointed to Alex. '– might as well go back to Edinburgh and your fancy job.'

Alex paled. 'Aye.' He swallowed. 'So, does that mean I need to pack?'

He looked unhappy, and Sprout immediately crossed the room so he could stand beside him, clearly offering support. Alex must have noticed because he gave the dog a baffled look before absently scratching his head.

'Nae. You're not going anywhere. Your da's far too clever to make you throw this opportunity away.' Henry waggled his eyebrows. 'I expect Michael will give you a call later to fill you in on his thoughts about my methods. In the meantime—' The older man stood so he could pace to the other side of the studio where his paintings had been piled face-first against the wall. 'I wanted to get your thoughts on this.'

Henry picked up one of the pictures and spun it around presenting them with a large watercolour. It was a picture Ella had never seen, a portrait. Ella had often been tempted to peek at his work when she'd been in the studio alone, but had always felt too guilty about prying and too afraid of being caught. As far as she knew, Henry had only ever worked on landscapes, so the content was a shock. Curious, she edged closer.

'It's Aggie,' Alex said softly as he moved nearer too. He wasn't rubbing his arms anymore and Ella hoped that meant the radiator had finally warmed him. He cocked his head as he studied the painting and stretched his back, drawing attention to his large, lean torso and the powerful arms he'd used earlier to replace the tyre. The movement highlighted a tiny spot of grease on his cheek – an imperfection that made Ella like him more. He was big and his presence seemed to suck the air out of the room.

Ella turned to face the painting as tingles of unwelcome heat flooded through her again.

It was a close-up of the housekeeper's face and showed every line and wrinkle that had burrowed into her skin over the decades. Her eyes were the perfect shade of brown and the bags resting under them had such intricate and lifelike shadows that the picture could have been mistaken for a photograph.

'Aye, it's her all right. She sat for me once, after I promised I'd eat her soup for a month without complaining.' Henry placed the painting onto one of the easels and moved, giving them more space. 'Take a good look and tell me what you see.' He scratched the white hairs peppered across his chin as he waited.

'Um.' Ella considered the image, trying to find the right words. 'It's brilliant of course. The brushstrokes, luminosity, the shadows...' She had to force herself not to stroke a fingertip across Aggie's cheek to check if it was warm.

Henry really was a genius.

'Aye,' Alex agreed. 'The colours are incredible. It's so life-like. I wouldn't be surprised if she started to speak.' He echoed Ella's thoughts exactly.

'She'd probably just say something about *broccoli*,' Henry said sourly, turning to face them, his gaze as sharp as a hungry bird's. 'But?' he snapped. 'Because I can hear it even if you're not saying the words.' His expression dimmed. 'This exercise isn't about you complimenting me. I know I'm talented because people pay obscene sums of money for my work.'

He shrugged as if admitting that was the most ordinary thing in the world. 'And I don't need adoration designed to swell my ego. I've been told on a number of occasions that it's already large enough.' He chuckled. 'I want to know how this picture makes you *feel*.' His tone sharpened. 'This is a lesson, not a fancy cocktail party where we all get to tell each other lies.'

Ella pulled a face. 'Um. I think it's amazing, I've got nothing else to add.'

Nothing she wanted to share anyway. She wasn't looking to offend her mentor. She just wanted to do her painting and finish the cleaning so she could get home. Ella wrapped her arms around herself, then unwrapped them when Henry's eyes followed the movement as if he were unpicking it, analysing what the gesture meant.

'I can still hear the *but* in your voice, lass – and you need to say it out loud.' His eyes glittered. 'I know there's a lot you don't share.' He stared at Ella, his message clear. 'A lot of feelings you keep hidden. Perhaps a few complaints you really ought to air. But what you do in your own time is your business.'

He paused as Ella took the hit from the observation. Henry was talking about her stepbrothers – about Lucinda. She hadn't realised he'd seen what was happening, probably should have guessed he would since she was late to class so regularly and he'd commented on her tiredness more than once.

'In my studio I make the rules, and I want honesty, Ella. Even if you find it difficult to express.' Henry took a step forward and she gulped. He was asking the impossible. Surely he knew that?

Alex cleared his throat. 'It's – perhaps a little too lifelike. It makes me feel uncomfortable.' He glanced at Ella and waited for her to nod before continuing, leaving her feeling grateful but confused. 'Could it be a little too honest? I mean, it's not very flattering,' Alex folded his arms, suddenly looking awkward. Ella wondered if he was already regretting stepping in to help her out.

'Well done. You've expressed what a lot wouldn't,' Henry breathed. 'But do you think flattering the model matters, lad?' He stared at Alex with all the emotion of a T-Rex studying its prey.

'It depends.' Alex shrugged. 'What did Aggie think when she saw it?'

Henry puffed out his cheeks and roared out a laugh. 'You think I'd show this to her?' He widened his eyes. 'I'm not a bampot. I still get served the odd haggis and shepherd's pie and I'm hoping for some turkey at Christmas too – I'm not about to jeopardise that. Not everyone wants honesty. For some it's simply too much.' His thick eyebrows met again and his face registered hurt.

'Has that happened to you?' Ella blurted.

'Aye, once.' Henry's eyebrows flopped – then his face went blank. 'But this isn't about me, it's a lesson and we need to stay on track.'

'If you knew the picture might upset Aggie – why did you paint her like that?' Ella asked.

Henry frowned. 'How can you feel anything real if you're

living in a world that wants to mask or hide the truth?' he asked, sounding frustrated. 'We spend our lives covering things up, making them pretty. Living in fairy tales. What we fail to realise is there's beauty in the flaws. Why would we want to hide them?'

He paused and glanced at the sketch on Ella's easel. 'I love the whimsy of your art, I'm not saying that it isn't good – even brilliant sometimes – but we have to know what's at the core of what we see, in order to develop how we show it. I don't think either of you have learned to do that. I think you're both still showing the surface. Perhaps because you're afraid of what you're going to find?'

Ella rocked on her heels, feeling uncomfortable. It was the first time Henry had shared these thoughts with her, and she wasn't sure she liked them. She loved her drawings, enjoyed escaping into another world. One where everything was beautiful, where everyone was kind and even animals were your friends. In her art, no one was mean, the people you loved didn't die – and everyone did their fair share. She swallowed the hot knot of emotion as it rose in her throat. She wasn't sure she was ready to face the truth. Wasn't sure she ever would be.

'By honest, do you mean truthful, real?' Alex checked.

'Aye.' Henry let out a long exhale looking pleased. 'Good work, lad, I knew you'd get there. We need to learn to love what's underneath the veneer. In order to do that we have to show and accept it in all its glory – warts, lines, wrinkles, curves, all of it.' He frowned.

'So, what do you want us to do?' Alex asked, looking confused.

He shrugged. 'I want you to bear it in mind when you start to work. Practise sketching what you see. I don't care what it is. Dig deep, expose what's underneath those sparkles, festive cakes and glittery faces.'

He stared at them, his wizened face serious. 'You'll be at the pantomime rehearsals tonight, take some time to notice and sketch the cast – or each other.' He studied them. 'You're both going to start working on your new project tomorrow, and I want you to bring the truth to your work.'

'I...' Ella swallowed. 'I'm not sure I can. I mean in my work, my animals, they're—' She paused, struggling to express herself. 'When I'm drawing them, I imagine them talking to me. They're not real...' Her work was pure fantasy, an escape from the drudgery of her life.

'The animals *are* real, lass,' the artist said kindly. 'Just think about that when you're working. I'm not asking you to change your style, I want you to deepen it. I want to believe I can see what those creatures of yours are thinking. I want to know what's about to come out of their mouths. You're so close, but I want to see their flaws too.' Ella opened her mouth to disagree, but the words wouldn't come.

'I understand,' Alex said, stepping in again. 'We can do it.' He glanced at her, his expression a mix of expectation and sympathy.

Ella sighed and nodded. She'd try, although she really wasn't sure she was ready to face the truth.

# 12

ALEX

'I hope you're working hard,' Michael Charming asked as soon as Alex answered his mobile. He pulled the Volvo to a stop just ahead of Mistletoe Village Hall and squinted into the darkness.

It was snowing again, the flakes so huge Alex could barely see. 'I've been painting every day,' Alex assured his father, because he knew that's what he'd want to hear. No embellishment or colourful details – just cold, hard facts.

'You sound like you expect me to congratulate you,' Michael growled. 'When that's the only reason you're there. I expect brilliance, remember. That, and a tangible return on your time.'

'Aye,' Alex said because it was expected. 'How's work?'

'Fine,' his father said stiffly. 'A little busier without you – but nothing I can't handle. No one is irreplaceable, not even you.' Alex nodded, numb to the 'pep talk' which was designed to make him feel insecure.

Michael's particular brand of motivation ran to ultimatums, threats and warnings. Touchy-feely was anathema to him. For many years, Alex had wondered if his father simply hated him, but time had taught him it was just his way. An inability to approve of anything with a pulse seemed to be hardwired into his DNA. 'I trust you're keeping on top of your emails?'

'I am.' Alex had been up at five this morning to make sure he'd worked his way through anything urgent and he'd already earmarked the emails he'd have to reply to tonight. Although being out of the office was making him nervous. He might be related to the boss, but he knew his father would have no qualms about firing him if he didn't keep up. 'I'm out at the moment, but I'll check them again when I get back to Pinecone Manor,' he promised.

His father sighed. 'I suppose you're helping at that foolish pantomime this evening?' He sounded irritated. 'Henry always was eccentric – talented but he has some strange ideas. Don't waste any more of your time than you have to – in fact get out of it if you can.' His tone suggested that Alex helping with the scenery was all his own fault.

'Aye,' Alex said again, tapping his hand on the steering wheel and checking his watch. 'I'll do my best, but I don't want to alienate Henry.' Like his father, the artist was difficult to refuse.

'Your mam always had a soft heart. She cared far too much about others' feelings. My parents never approved of my choice.' Alex stiffened trying not to let the implied criticism get to him. 'Do you have any important news to report?' his father asked sharply.

'No,' Alex said. Michael wasn't interested in personal details. *How do you feel, are you okay, what do you want?* were questions that had never been asked. Even as a child, his father's expectations had trumped every want, need or human emotion. Alex couldn't imagine what he'd make of the people he'd met in Mistletoe so far. He thought of Ella and his lips curved, startling him.

'I'm calling to let you know that I've given the go-ahead to

HR to start interviewing for a replacement for Stanley.' His father's tone was cool, and Alex's smile disappeared.

'I thought we agreed to give him six months?' he insisted.

'We can't wait forever, Alexander – I've told you before. There's no room for sentiment in business, anyone who tells you different is after your job.'

'Stan told me he's going to book his flight home soon,' Alex lied. 'Can you give it another few weeks?'

His father remained silent for a beat. 'Two weeks, and only because Stanley is one of our best. After that, he's gone,' he snapped.

'Can we wait for longer? He's worked with us for almost ten years. What about loyalty?' Alex said, regretting the words the instant they left his mouth.

'Mr Bailey has been paid handsomely for every day that he's been with us. Remember it was *his* choice to leave and *his* choice to stay away. We don't owe him anything,' his father shot back, and Alex swallowed the words that were on the tip of his tongue: who would have chosen to have a heart attack?

'I spoke to one of my clients today.' Michael swiftly changed the subject before Alex could make any more fuss. 'He was impressed that Henry Lockhart has agreed to work with you.' His voice had warmed, but Alex couldn't summon the glow that it would normally elicit. 'How's my painting going?'

'Still work in progress,' he said flatly.

A phone buzzed in the background. 'I've been waiting for this call. Make sure you keep up with your emails and report back on Stan,' Michael said stiffly before the line went dead, ending the conversation as abruptly as it had begun.

Alex stared at the mobile and let out a long breath. His father never changed – but for the first time in a long time, Alex allowed himself to wonder what would happen if he did.

.   .   .

'You're here!' Mae pounced on Alex as soon as he stepped into the entrance of Mistletoe Village Hall. 'It's time for you to get measured up for your costumes,' she said excitedly, guiding Alex through the noisy hall which was filled to heaving with people dressed up in a variety of dazzling outfits and wearing glittery makeup.

A few waved their scripts trying to attract Mae's attention – but she ignored them, charging ahead. 'I'll be back soon,' she cried, flapping a hand.

'Where's Ella?' Alex asked as he followed, sweeping his gaze back and forth across the room, trying to pick her out from the crowd. He'd been thinking about her all afternoon, even before the call with his father.

When he'd gone back to his bedroom to change for the evening, he'd even pulled out his sketch pad and found himself doodling her until he'd caught himself smiling. When he had, he'd ripped out the page and put it in the bin.

'She's trying on one of her costumes,' Mae explained, sweeping them out of the hallway through a set of red velvet curtains into a narrow corridor. 'I've got Prince Charming,' she yelled as they reached a door. She knocked once and opened it without waiting. Alex took a step inside and stopped as his heart tripped and stuttered in his throat.

Ella was standing in the centre of the well-lit room wearing a stunning silver and blue dress with a sweetheart neckline that showcased the pale shimmer of her skin. She looked beautiful, like something out of a fairy tale – which Alex supposed was the point. Although that didn't explain why just looking at her made his chest pulse. He rubbed a hand over his jumper, trying to swipe the sensation away.

Someone had already done her makeup and styled her hair, piling it onto the top of her head, from where brown, red and green tendrils waterfalled around her neck in delicate swirls. Her waist looked tiny, especially since the material had been pinned to accentuate it. She stood ramrod straight, making her appear taller than Alex remembered.

An unwelcome current of electricity sparked through him, and he let out a noisy breath trying to relax as he silently repeated another of his father's rules: *'attraction is a weakness, stamp it out at the first sign.'* Although it might be too late. There was just something about this woman, something that drew him in.

An older woman, who looked almost identical to Aggie, appeared from the back of the room and bustled towards them, holding a jar of pins.

'Alex, meet Blair McBride, Aggie's sister,' Mae said as the woman approached.

'Blair runs The Snug Tea Room in Mistletoe Village and we're working together on the costumes for the panto,' Aggie told him. 'Blair is also providing refreshments for the cast.'

'Pleased to meet you,' Alex said as both women looked him up and down. 'I'm Alex Forbes-Charming.'

'Oh, I know,' Blair declared in a strong Scottish lilt, chuckling girlishly as she fanned a palm in front of her chest.

'I need to get back to the main hall,' Mae said, looking worried. 'From the looks I was getting on the way here, I have to speak to some of the cast. Alex, when you and Ella have finished being fitted for your costumes, please join me by the main stage. When you're ready, just head outside this corridor and take the first right.' Before anyone could say a word, the door swung shut behind Mae and the room fell silent.

'Oh, you're a handsome one. Then again, I've always been a sucker for a broody expression!' Blair said, holding out a hand. Alex took it, noticing her long ringless fingers and red and green festive nails. 'And if I were twenty years younger...'

'You'd still be married to husband number three,' Aggie said dryly. 'I know you like them young, Blair, but I think the lad would be better suited to someone who was born a little closer to his own decade.' She looked stern.

'Aye, I suppose.' Blair winked at Alex before her attention swept towards Ella again and she waggled her eyebrows. 'In that case, I'd love our next project to be a wedding dress. I'm thinking an ivory silk gown and a long lace train...' Her eyes rolled over Ella again.

'Oh, really—' Ella started, her cheeks flushing bright pink. 'I'm not looking for... neither Alex nor I feel...' She swallowed. 'We barely know each other, we're just classmates nothing more.' As her embarrassment grew, her words ground to a halt. She folded her arms and shook herself, making the long skirt and pretty petticoats swing around her ankles. Alex caught himself watching until he realised what he was doing and forced his attention away in case the women noticed his interest.

'Don't forget, lass, you're playing Cinderella to this lad's Prince Charming – one of the greatest love stories of all time.' Blair winked. 'Ach, and it's Christmas, so we're all in the mood to watch a real romance bloom, especially since none of us are falling in love at the moment.' She shrugged as she glanced between them, taking in their expressions. Even Alex was taken aback by Ella's look of pure dismay. 'No mind, we'll make do with watching you on stage I suppose.' She looked disappointed.

'That's good,' Alex said stiffly.

Aggie swung her gaze towards him again, her eyes sharp. 'What's wrong with Ella, lad – are you married, or do you have a significant other?'

'No...' Alex said slowly, feeling tongue-tied. 'I'm just— Ella is obviously beautiful.' He saw her cheeks were now burning, and wondered if his were the same shade. 'But as she says, we're working together.' He cleared his throat. 'So it wouldn't be appropriate...' The look on their faces told him he was making things worse. 'I'm not looking for a relationship.'

Alex had faced down intimidating CEOs in the company boardroom without blinking, but in this room, he felt completely out of his depth. He glanced across the room at Ella again, but now she held a hand over her mouth, obviously trying to hold in a laugh.

'Ignore my sister, she loves winding people up,' Blair said, eyeing him critically. 'You could do with some meat on those bones. I like my heroes a little chunkier. We'll be putting refreshments out in the hall soon, so make sure you eat – and I'll be expecting to see you in my tea room soon. Hunter's in there most afternoons and the lad's taken a shine to you.'

'Aye,' Aggie agreed, looking happy. 'Poor thing's usually with his mam and when she's working, he's with us – he hasn't got much in the way of positive male role models because his da's, well...' She swallowed. 'The less said about him...'

Alex wasn't sure if anyone should be modelling themselves on him – especially not a child. He'd come to Mistletoe to improve his artwork, not get involved with a village of strangers – and he had no intention of befriending anyone. He had no experience with children, no clue of how to connect – what would he say?

'You'll see him later when you're out front,' Aggie told him. 'He'll be with his friend Maxwell who really wants to meet you too.'

'Enough small talk.' Blair suddenly clucked. 'I need to measure you so we can start to work on your costumes.' She clapped her hands. 'You're going to be so much fun to dress.' She grinned as she gazed at him. 'You're better-looking than poor dear Andrew, I think there'll be a lot of hearts fluttering at the panto, which will be good news for ticket sales.' She studied Alex and a wrinkle appeared in her forehead. 'We might want to replace Andrew in the pantomime posters if there's time – I'll speak to Mae about it.'

Alex shut his eyes, absorbing the full horror of that. He had clients spread across the whole of Scotland. What if someone recognised him? His father would be appalled.

Aggie hiked up her sparkly red top and swiped a tape measure from the pocket of her dark green trousers, taking Alex's arm and guiding him to where Ella was standing. She moved out of his way.

Then Aggie slowly spun Alex round until he was facing a long mirror illuminated with lights. Beyond it were four rails where dozens of shimmering costumes dangled from hangers. In the other corner of the room, he could see a small table with a black and gold sewing machine and a half-open box containing cotton, scissors and pins.

'We'll need your measurements before we can start. I'm thinking you'd look adorable in silver and blue.' Aggie studied Alex.

'Adorable?' he repeated. He could imagine Stan laughing at the inappropriate description, while his father stood with his arms folded, shaking his head.

'He'd suit red too, he's got the right skin colouring,' Blair said.

'I think the lad will look gorgeous in anything we make,' Aggie agreed.

'Can you just...' Blair indicated that Alex should spread his legs by widening her own.

Alex did as he was told and tried not to move when she began to angle the tape measure downwards. He glanced across the room at Ella who was watching, her shoulders shaking as she gave into her laughter. Sighing, Alex allowed the corners of his mouth to twitch up too and met Ella's eyes as the two women worked.

'I need your inside leg measurements first and Aggie will

want to know the size of your feet, head and chest,' Blair explained as someone suddenly lassoed Alex with another tape measure from behind, capturing his arms before shifting it down.

'Oh, dear God.' He shut his eyes again for a moment.

'Sorry to startle you, lad,' Aggie whispered as she loosened the tape. 'As I thought, a little skinny, but we can work on that. Can you put your hands up so I can get a proper measurement?' Alex untangled his arms and did as he was asked as the housekeeper shouted a series of numbers to Blair who dutifully scribbled them down. After what felt like hours, she yelled. 'That'll do!' and stepped away. 'You're going to make such a bonnie Prince Charming.' She grinned.

Alex cleared his throat, embarrassed. He could hear a voice in his head – and he knew it was his father's. He was asking what the hell Alex was doing, telling him he was embarrassing himself. He stiffened, refusing to admit, even to himself, that he was having fun. It had been so long he almost didn't recognise the feeling.

The door to the room swung open and Hunter appeared, closely followed by another boy. Both had red hair and freckles – and each wore a headband with mouse ears flapping at the top.

'Alex!' Hunter yelled excitedly, trotting across the room. 'This is my best friend Maxwell.' He turned and swept a hand towards the younger boy. 'Mae told us you were here – I knew you'd want to meet him.' He beamed, his small cheeks shining.

'Ach, lad. We don't need to measure you both yet,' Aggie said. 'You should get back into the hall in case you need to practise your parts.'

'Mae said it was okay to pop in for a moment,' Maxwell said. His eyes rounded and he gazed at Alex. 'Is running over dogs really your hobby?' he asked.

'Pardon,' Alex gaped.

'Nae!' Ella laughed. 'That's just a misunderstanding, lad. Wyatt loves Alex now – it's mutual, even though they're both good at hiding it.' She winked as she nodded in Alex's direction and the young boy grinned.

'I drew you a picture,' Hunter told Alex, reaching into the pocket of his jeans and tugging out a piece of folded white paper. He handed it over as a hush fell across the room.

Alex unfolded the drawing and stared at it. He might not have had any experience of children, but he understood his reaction mattered. 'Wow,' he gasped, a little taken aback by how much he wanted to please the child. It was a picture of two mice playing by a fountain, with a castle in the background. 'This is really good,' he said, feeling something inside him warm when the boy's chest puffed to twice its normal size.

The door opened again, and Mae entered. 'I'm sorry to interrupt, but Aggie and Blair, we need you on refreshments now,' she said, her voice a little panicked. 'Your brothers are getting a little overexcited, Ella, and the rest of the cast is threatening to revolt. I think coffee, tea and a couple of your magnificent Christmas cakes might help to avoid a riot.' Her attention shifted to Alex and Ella. 'How are you getting on?'

'We're mostly done. I'll have something for you to try on in a few days – you can pop into the café at lunchtime when it's ready,' Blair said to Alex, putting her pad back into her pocket. 'Ella, take off the costume before you come out front, lass, and hang it up. I'll get it later so we can make the adjustments.' With that, she and Aggie followed Mae and the two boys into the corridor, slamming the door shut.

Ella pulled a face as the room fell into an awkward silence. Alex watched as she twisted round, trying to peer at where Aggie had secured the material on her dress.

'I should go.' He edged towards the exit.

'Do the pins look like they'll be easy to remove?' Ella shuffled closer to the mirror and bent one arm, unsuccessfully attempting to grab the top pin. 'I need to change. This dress is getting uncomfortable, and I can feel the pins coming loose.'

Alex watched as she changed tack and began to tug at one of her sleeves. 'I don't think Aggie or Blair realised I might not be able to do this by myself.' She sighed as she turned towards the door. 'I'll need someone to help.'

'I can do it,' Alex said as his tongue finally unstuck itself from the roof of his mouth. 'If you want,' he added awkwardly. What was wrong with him?

'If you're sure?' She looked embarrassed.

'We probably shouldn't disturb Blair or Aggie, especially if the cast are really going to riot,' he joked. 'Could you turn around please?' Alex moved closer as Ella did as she was asked. 'Do I just take out the pins?' His attention caught on a wispy red ringlet curling down the back of her neck. He took in a deep breath and smelled eucalyptus which stirred his blood – making it pump faster and harder, making his ears strain to pop.

'Can you take the pins out and put them back in the same place so Aggie and Blair will have a guide to work from?' Ella asked. 'I know Blair took down my measurements, but I think it'll be easier to work from the actual pins.'

Was it Alex's imagination or did Ella's voice sound husky, and had the room somehow shrunk to half its normal size?

Alex cleared his throat and leaned in so he could see the tiny silver slithers better. It took a couple of tries to undo the first because his normally dexterous fingers had grown gawky and uncoordinated. When he finally succeeded, the top of the dress sprung open exposing a creamy triangle of skin.

Alex let out a shaky breath and glanced at the door, praying one of the Blair sisters would return.

When the door didn't open, he knew he'd have to commit – winners didn't give up, even if they did suddenly feel like they couldn't breathe.

He tugged at the collar of his shirt and popped open the top button before carefully undoing the second pin on the dress. The material sprang open, revealing another inch of rosy flesh. Ella's skin was so smooth, Alex had to stop himself from running a finger over it. Instead, he steeled himself and continued. By the time he reached the fourth pin, he suspected Ella was only wearing underwear beneath the top half of the dress. He tensed.

*Did she know – did she care?*

'Are you okay?' Ella asked as Alex hovered his fingers over the next pin. An energy seemed to hum in the air, and he tried to fill his head with his father's voice, imagining what he'd say if he were here. Ella was his colleague, a competitor – the person he had to best.

'Of course,' Alex croaked as he undid the next pin and the silky material bounced open again, revealing another inch of silky flesh. He tried to take in a steadying breath, but it clogged at the top of his throat, making him want to undo another button on his own shirt so he could breathe.

But he didn't.

Instead, Alex leaned closer. There weren't many pins to go until Ella would be able to step out of the costume – he could do this. His eyes skimmed across her exposed back, and he realised her skin had grown rosier while he'd been working. He went to take out the next pin, but his hands were shaking so much that he accidentally touched the tip of his finger to the imprint of her spine. Ella inhaled sharply and goosebumps erupted across the surface of her back.

'I'm sorry,' Alex said as Ella's breath stuttered. He jerked his chin to meet her gaze in the mirror. She was watching him, her mouth slightly parted, her cheeks glowing. Was she as affected by this as him?

Alex swallowed an unwelcome wave of desire, an unexpected need to kiss her. 'Are you okay?' he asked, ignoring the unsteadiness in his voice. He *never* showed his feelings, and he would not show them now.

Ella stared at him looking uncertain. 'Yes, of course,' she said, and her body quivered next to his fingertips, proving she was lying.

'Do you... do you want me to undo all the pins?' Alex's voice sounded wrong, and he cleared his throat.

'Aye.' Ella let out a gentle gasp when he undid two more, exposing a thin strap of white lace and the edges of two straps.

'Okay, I think we might almost be there.' Alex ignored the way his body tightened.

He'd undressed plenty of women in his life, but he'd never been so turned on by something so ordinary. 'I've unpinned the dress as far as your bra strap,' he said still staring because his eyes refused to budge. 'Do you want me to find you a T-shirt or something to put on?' He hovered his hands over the next pin and waited.

'Oh *crappity crap*.' Ella jerked forward. 'Of course. I forgot I undressed.' She swallowed. 'I've got something.' She grabbed the front of the dress and almost tripped over her petticoats in her haste to move. Alex watched her rummage through a bag before she dug out a black T-shirt, jumper and jeans. 'Can you just undo the pins to my waist?' She asked as she returned. 'I'll be able to step out of the dress and then I can put on these clothes.'

'Sure,' Alex said, taking in a long breath. He didn't speak as he worked on the remaining pins, but he could feel Ella's body trembling and an insane part of him hoped it was because of him.

'All done,' he said roughly when he thought he'd unfastened enough.

'Please can you turn your back?' Ella circled a finger.

'I should probably just go,' he said gruffly as he turned to face the door. Only instead of leaving, his feet remained stuck to the floor. Alex shut his eyes as he heard the telltale sound of silk dropping to the ground. Then he gripped his hands into tight fists and filled his mind with his father's face: the angle of his chin, his dark eyes and permanent frown.

As he did, Alex tried to imagine sketching his father sitting behind a desk. But instead of Michael Charming's sharp jawline, all Alex's mind would conjure was Ella's heart-shaped chin.

His eyes sprang open when he heard the sound of a zip.

'You can turn around...'

When Alex did, she'd already disappeared into the racks of costumes, and he saw the blue Cinderella dress draped on a hanger ready for the McBrides to finish off. 'I'm just finding my bag,' she shouted.

Alex stood where he was and listened to her moving. His lips were tingling, and he knew with a certainty he couldn't explain that if he stayed in this room for a moment longer, he was going to ask Ella if he could kiss her.

'I need to go, I've got somewhere I have to be,' Alex said roughly, heading towards the door and jerking it open, then following the long corridor.

He heard Ella's bark of surprise – her shout that she wouldn't be long. But he couldn't trust himself. *Wouldn't* trust himself to be alone with her.

Ella McNally was dangerous. He was here to paint a picture, to impress his father and to stay focused. And he had to stop anything – especially her – from getting in the way of that...

# 13

---

## ELLA

When Ella finally emerged from the dressing room, Alex was nowhere to be seen. She glanced out from the stage, hoping to spot him in the crowd of chatting cast members tucking into cake. But he'd clearly been eager to race out of the building. Ella wondered if it was their chemistry that had spooked him – the strength of it had caught her off guard too. When he'd been unpinning her dress, she'd had to force herself not to give in to the impulse to turn and kiss him, to let the heat between them run its course.

Alex kept surprising her, turning her initial opinion of him on its head. Those small acts of kindness earlier – like when he'd been speaking with Hunter and had taken the time to admire his drawing. How, instead of being irritated, he'd indulged Aggie and Blair when they'd teased him about falling for her. The way he'd unpinned her costume, even though it affected him. She knew she hadn't imagined the way his hand shook – or how her body had trembled in response. She just wasn't sure what to do about it.

She took a step further into the room and immediately saw that Blair and Aggie had set up a long table beside the

Christmas tree to the left of the stage. They were serving refreshments, and a queue of eager cast members stood waiting their turn. Most were dressed in their costumes, their faces shiny with glitter and rouge – she could smell makeup powder and the lingering scent of chocolate cake, and her mouth watered.

'Where have you been?' Lucinda approached from Ella's right wearing a gothic style dress with long, flowing skirts. The costume was crimson, and the matching lipstick made her step-mother's mouth stand out, drawing attention to the frown aimed in Ella's direction. 'No one's been able to do a thing without you,' she accused.

'I was trying on my costume,' Ella said. 'I'm here now,' she added brightly.

Lucinda sighed. 'I'm sorry, lass, but you need to stop putting yourself first all the time. Clyde and Dane have been waiting to rehearse with you for almost an hour. You know they've both been poorly again today?'

'Aye.' Ella nodded – she knew because she'd had to cover for them. They'd had a dose of the flu. Something particularly virulent apparently. 'I'm sorry,' she added, feeling guilty.

Lucinda's lips pinched and Ella braced herself for another onslaught. She tried her best, but never seemed to measure up. The only reason she kept trying was because of the promise she'd made to her da.

Inexplicably, her stepmother's eyes lit and she smiled. Ella smiled back, confused as Lucinda straightened, drawing attention to the curves she worked so diligently to preserve. 'Prince Charming, I presume?' she purred at a spot above Ella's right shoulder.

Ella felt her skin start to tingle as she realised Alex was standing behind her. The slow roil of her stomach signalled her relief that he hadn't left.

'Aye,' he rumbled as he moved until he was beside her.

Lucinda grabbed his hand and squeezed. 'I'm Ella's step-mother, Lucinda McNally. I know what you're going to say, I'm far too young.' She giggled, fluffing her hair. 'I've heard a lot about our handsome new visitor. Clearly no one's been exaggerating.'

Alex's eyes widened. 'Er. Nice to meet you,' he said stiffly, claiming back his hand.

'Ella, perhaps you could get us both a hot drink so Prince Charming and I can get to know each other?' Lucinda said.

'I don't want one,' Alex said as Ella heard a crash and loud shouts from the other side of the hall.

'Oh, Clyde,' Lucinda yelped as she turned and saw her son lying on the ground. As Ella stepped closer, she could see Dane standing over him. He was holding up the skirts of his costume, exposing chunky hairy legs which were half obscured by red and white striped socks. 'Are you okay?' Lucinda rushed towards them looking panicked.

'I'd better—' Ella turned to Alex and nodded in their direction.

'Aye,' he said as she quickly followed her stepmother, weaving her way through the cast members who'd gathered to see what was going on.

By the time Ella arrived, Lucinda was kneeling beside Clyde, stroking his head. His blonde wig had flown off, exposing flyaway brown hair. A couple of chairs lay on the ground, their legs broken in half. 'Is he okay?' Ella asked, kneeling too and spotting a long tear in her stepbrother's costume, which she knew the McBride sisters would be furious about.

'There's no blood,' Hunter, who'd come to check on Ella's stepbrother, said, sounding disappointed. 'So it can't be that bad.'

'Thank goodness!' Lucinda exclaimed. 'What were you doing, Clyde?'

'We were just messing around, trying to see if the skirts on these dresses worked as parachutes. We got bored,' Dane said from where he was still standing. He picked up one of the chairs and tried to put it upright, but it immediately toppled.

'Of course you were. It's not a surprise when you had to wait so long to rehearse,' Lucinda said grumpily, making Ella feel awful. 'Have you got a concussion, darling?' she asked, gently stroking a hand over her son's head. 'I can feel a bump!' she yelled.

'I've got a headache,' Clyde groaned.

'I thought your brothers were supposed to be sick?' Alex asked as Ella rose to find him standing beside her. 'Or was that yesterday?'

'Well.' Ella sighed, embarrassed. 'Unfortunately, they were both ill again today.' She glanced at Dane who was now kicking one of the broken chair legs. 'Clyde told me he thought they had flu this morning – looks like a twenty-four-hour thing.' He'd sounded awful, and she'd immediately offered to cover the shifts.

'Flu,' Alex snorted as he paused for long enough to take in the scene. 'More like hypochondria. Don't you think it's time you considered that they're not telling the truth?'

'They, well... I...' Ella frowned as she considered his question. If Alex had asked the same thing a few weeks ago, she'd definitely have said they were. But looking at her stepbrothers now...

'I don't know,' she admitted slowly. Had they been lying to her about their ailments? Had Lucinda known? The idea of them tricking her made her blood run cold. Ella shook her head – it wasn't possible, they wouldn't and besides, surely she'd have known?

'How old are they?' Alex asked more gently.

'Twenty-two. They've both just finished university. They've only been working with me for a few months. They're still finding their routine. They were really keen when they started.' She watched Dane help Clyde to his feet. Her step-brother rubbed his head and winced, then began to limp towards the refreshment table as Mae came charging over.

'What happened?' She took in the broken furniture.

'An accident,' Lucinda soothed. 'We'll pay for the chairs of course.'

'Of course,' Ella agreed because it was easier, and she had kept her stepbrothers waiting. Besides, what were a few more pounds of debt?

'Don't worry, lass,' Mae said. 'I'm sure we can get them fixed. There are a couple of carpenters in the cast, after all.'

Lucinda smiled sweetly. 'You really are our fairy godmother, aren't you?' she said, before following her sons.

'I'm all for taking on responsibilities and stepping up,' Alex said to Ella as Mae winked and went to speak to someone waving at her. 'But I wonder if it's time you faced the fact that your stepbrothers are taking advantage of you.'

'I know it looks bad, but I don't think they are...' Ella sighed. Clyde and Dane knew how hard she worked, they wouldn't be so cruel. 'They've always been sickly. Even at university they kept missing deadlines because they had to go to the doctor and hospital so much. This isn't new.'

Alex watched her dismiss his concerns – but when her eyes met his, they were filled with sympathy. He nodded once, before turning on his heels, leaving Ella wondering if he thought she was a fool – and if perhaps he was right.


Four days later, Ella tentatively knocked at Clyde and Dane's house and pressed her ear to the wooden surface. She'd imag-ined she could hear music blaring inside when she'd been walking up the narrow pathway from the gate, but by the time she arrived, the house had grown quiet.

The Christmas lights she'd helped Dane string around the facade of the building when Clyde's back had been bothering him were twinkling so she suspected her stepbrothers were inside. She leaned against the door and took a moment to scour the garden and frowned when she noticed a fresh snowman and some large boot prints leading towards the back of the house.

Confused when no one answered the door, Ella stroked the top of Wyatt's head and leaned down so she could push a fingertip into the silver letterbox, prising it open so she could see. The hallway was dimly lit, but she could just make out Christmas lights sparkling through the open doorway that led to the sitting room – and flickering shadows which suggested someone was watching TV.

'Clyde!' Ella shouted. 'Dane!' She pressed her ear to the door, but it remained silent. 'Lucinda told me you think your flu's returned?'

Both her brothers had returned to work the day after the incident at the pantomime, although Clyde had complained of a headache since. They'd managed to work for three whole mornings, but today they'd both called in sick. For the first time, Ella had begun to have doubts about their illness.

It wasn't just because of what Alex had said at the pantomime rehearsal. Her stepbrothers had been skiing yesterday afternoon and it seemed suspicious that they'd both already been struck down again. Ella felt guilty for doubting them, so she'd decided to check on them after her first shift. If for no other reason than to prove herself and Alex wrong.

Ella let out a breath as she pressed her mouth to the letterbox. 'Your mam asked me to bring you some food because she was worried you'd get hungry.'

According to her stepmother, the lasagne Ella had sacrificed had lasted less than a day. Lucinda had requested that she deliver another, but Ella hadn't had time to make any – so she'd stopped off at The Snug Tea Room to pick up a couple of pots of Aggie's famous chicken soup.

'It'll help you feel better.'

Ella heard a faint moan from somewhere in the house. 'Are you there?' she yelled again, concerned. Were her brothers too sick to make it to the door. She almost shouted again, but then she heard the heavy tread of footsteps and pressed her face to the letterbox. She sighed in relief when she spotted a pair of socked feet heading towards the door.

'Hello,' Dane croaked as soon as it opened a crack. His cheeks were ruddy, and his eyes looked tired. 'I'm sorry I didn't hear you before, I had a terrible night, so I was trying to catch up on some sleep.' He yawned, his mouth contorting.

'Are you okay? You look like you've been sweating,' Ella said as she rose to her feet and stepped closer so she could study him. He wasn't pale exactly, but his cheeks were an uneven shade of red. The colour reminded her of a blusher the makeup team used at the pantomime which had made her cheeks look more spotty than flushed.

'Do you have a temperature?' Feeling even more guilty for doubting her stepbrothers, Ella tried to touch Dane's forehead. But he shook her hand off and took a step back. 'You look awful,' she sympathised.

'Thanks a lot,' Dane said dryly.

'I'm just worried.' Ella sighed. 'Can I come in?'

He looked unsure but jerked a shoulder and stepped back when she continued to stare. Wyatt scampered in ahead of Ella and dived for the two pairs of snow boots that had been left in the hallway. They looked wet.

'I haven't dried them up from yesterday.' Dane coughed and shoved the bloodhound away from the boots before tugging his dressing gown tighter around his large frame. It looked odd – a little too bulky, almost like he was wearing clothes underneath. 'I've got a blanket under here,' he explained, clearly noticing her interest. 'You and Wyatt shouldn't get too close,' he warned gruffly, changing the subject. 'I don't want you to catch this too.'

'I'm sure Wyatt and I will be fine. He's unlikely to pick up a human bug and I'm not as prone to getting sick as you and Clyde.' Ella took another couple of steps along the hallway until her brother blocked her path.

Ella heard a loud wheeze from the sitting room and then Clyde appeared from inside, his brawny body wrapped in a thick brown dressing gown. It looked chunkier than usual – was he hiding a blanket under his too?

'Did I hear you brought lunch?' Clyde asked, eyeballing the pots Ella had pulled out of her bag. 'Dane's right, you mustn't stay.' His face looked as flushed as his brother's – did he have a temperature too? 'You can't afford to get sick as well,' he croaked. 'There'll be no one left to cover for us at work if you are.'

'Aye,' Ella said as she shut the front door before leaning against it as doubts nagged at her and she fought them. 'I'll go in a minute – can I heat up this first and bring it to you in bed?'

'I'll do it,' Dane shot back, glancing at his brother. 'Don't worry, we can look after ourselves. We've got everything we need, especially now you've brought food.'

He put his hand over his mouth and began to cough. Great hacking whoops that took a few minutes to subside. 'Sorry,' he rasped once they were under control. 'I really think you should go. But thanks so much for lunch – and for covering for us again. You really are a lifesaver, sis.' Ella felt a twinge of guilt at her stepbrother's kind words.

Clyde nodded and grabbed the pots from her hands before she could stop him. 'Let me put this in the kitchen and we'll heat it up later. I'm not very hungry at the moment and I'm beginning to feel *really* tired.' He yawned and rubbed a fingertip on his temple. 'This headache is killing me,' Clyde complained. 'I'm guessing you've got places to be.' He disappeared from the hallway into the kitchen.

'Are you sure?' Ella asked.

Dane began to cough again and then pointed towards the door. 'Don't worry about us. We're going back to bed now. I'm sure more sleep will do us good. We should be back at work in a few days.'

'A few days...' Ella echoed as her temples began to throb. 'What about the pantomime rehearsals tomorrow?'

'We'll definitely try to be there,' Clyde shouted from the kitchen.

Ella nodded as Dane barged past and opened the door before practically shoving Wyatt onto the porch. Ella followed, but when she turned to say goodbye, the door slammed in her face. Then she heard the click of a lock and slide of a bolt, and frowned all the way back to her van.

# 14

---

## ELLA

Ella spotted Alex as soon as she stepped into The Snug Tea Room on Mistletoe's high street. It was warm and welcoming inside and 'We Wish You a Merry Christmas' was playing giving the space a wonderful festive feel.

The whole room glittered and there were multiple streamers hanging from the ceilings and bauble-laden Christmas trees wedged into each corner of the space, all twinkling with a multitude of fairy lights. Ella knew Blair McBride always went full out at Christmas, but this year she'd surpassed herself. Ella wandered towards the counter which was positioned at the far end of the room. She'd been here once today to collect her stepbrothers' soup, so had seen the mouth-watering array of cakes, biscuits and sandwiches already. This time, her stomach grumbled, reminding her she hadn't found time to eat.

She dodged past one of the many tables that were heaving with customers and waved at a couple of kids who were singing in the pantomime and were sitting in the café with their parents eating cake.

All the while Ella studied Alex from the corner of her eye.

He was sitting upright in a booth to the right of the room, sketching. He looked completely engaged. His mouth quirked charmingly in one corner which made Ella want to leap across the rest of the tables so she could see what had put that dreamy expression on his face.

'Ach, what a surprise!' Blair said, clapping her hands as soon as she spotted Ella approaching the counter. 'Our Cinderella is here just in time for lunch with Prince Charming.' She winked, nodding in Alex's direction. 'I'm happy to see you in here again, lass. Did the two of you cook up a date?' She waggled her eyebrows, her eyes glittering hopefully.

'Nae, I think me being here will be a surprise – hopefully a good one.' Ella chewed her bottom lip nervously. She'd come on impulse, but hoped Alex would be happy to see her. She wasn't really sure why she'd decided to pop in, but Blair had mentioned earlier that he was supposed to be heading to the tea room at lunchtime and she'd felt compelled to see him again. She rarely gave into her desires – her life was too busy – but her feelings for Alex confused her and she wanted to see him to clarify them.

'I'll be late for my next cleaning job,' she admitted, checking her watch and wincing. 'But I'm starving.' As if in agreement, her stomach grumbled again.

'Then you're in the right place,' Aggie declared, appearing from the door to the kitchen, which was positioned behind the counter, carrying a couple of bowls of steaming soup. 'Sit yourself down in the corner booth with Prince Charming,' she ordered. 'I've promised the lad a sandwich and some of my special soup, so I'll bring you the same. Oh, and you left your cardigan at the village hall the other night – I've got it in the back. I'll bring that over too. You'd forget your head if it wasn't screwed on,' she teased.

'Thanks for bringing it,' Ella said.

'As soon as Alex has eaten, we're going to get him to try on one of his costumes in the back room,' Blair told her.

Ella nodded and then glanced over to see if Alex had noticed she was here. He was still sketching, clearly oblivious to everyone in the room.

'Aye,' Blair tutted. 'The lad hasn't stopped working like that since he got here this morning.'

'I swear he doesn't sleep,' Aggie whispered, still standing beside them holding the steaming soup. 'When I went into the Andy Warhol suite this morning to make his bed, I realised it hadn't been slept in. It was the same when I popped in yesterday too.' She looked concerned. 'Henry told me he's seen light under Alex's door right into the early hours – and he's sure the lad took Sprout for a walk at four am.'

She shook her head, her forehead wrinkling. 'He's going to make himself sick if he doesn't give himself a break. I've no idea what would drive someone to work himself into the ground like that. Go and join him.' She shooed the bowls in Alex's direction, almost spilling some of the soup. 'Get the lad to talk, make him laugh. You could both do with a little time off.' She glanced down at the bowls suddenly and gasped. 'Ach, I almost forget about these, he's got me in such a lather!'

She turned and marched away in the direction of one of the tables and Blair folded her arms. 'Off you go then, lass,' she said sternly, waiting until Ella nodded and made her way across the tea room.

Ella's heart was in her throat as she drew closer to the booth and Alex glanced up. Red swept across his cheeks, and he immediately slammed the top of the sketch pad shut.

'Can I join you?' She slid onto the bench opposite. 'Are you working on something?' She pointed to the pad.

'I'm just playing around with a few ideas. Doing what Henry asked,' he said, looking uncomfortable. He picked up the sketch pad and placed it on the bench beside him before absently drumming his fingers on the top. 'Aren't you working today?' He glanced around. 'You haven't made it to our lessons for the last couple of days. Have your brothers been off sick again?'

Ella flushed.

'Okay. That wasn't a criticism.' Alex held up a palm. 'Aggie mentioned your brothers were ill today, so I assumed you'd been covering.' His voice was gentler than it had been when he'd complained about her absences before.

'They've been fine until today. But I've had—' She paused, thinking about Lucinda's shopping, which was the reason she hadn't had time to visit Pinecone Manor. 'Some other things to do. I'm sorry I've not been around.'

He shrugged. 'It's fine.'

Alex's nonchalance bothered Ella. After their almost-kiss at the pantomime, she'd begun to fantasise that he'd want to see her. 'You're not upset?'

'Well.' Alex pulled a face. 'Henry agreed to continue to teach without you since you're rarely around.'

She frowned, absorbing the full punch of his words. Work was out of control, but she'd get back to her art soon... wouldn't she?

'But...' Alex said awkwardly. 'You should try to make the next session.' His forehead squeezed and he looked pained. 'You're naturally talented.' He cleared his throat. 'You shouldn't waste your abilities. That's just my opinion.' His cheeks grew pink.

'Um, thank you,' Ella said, touched. It had been a long time since anyone had complimented her and she drank it in. She'd needed to hear those words; she just hadn't expected them to come from Alex. But the fact that he'd said them meant a lot.

He shrugged, still looking embarrassed, and looked down at the black coffee sitting in front of him before absently picking it up. 'Ergh,' he spluttered as he sipped. 'It's cold.'

'I should think so,' Aggie said, sweeping up to their table carrying a tray. 'I left it there almost two hours ago, but you've barely looked up from that sketch pad, lad.' She tutted.

Alex winced. He looked tired, and his cheeks were pale. Was the housekeeper right about him not sleeping?

'I hope you're both hungry,' Aggie said as she quickly handed Ella the cardigan she'd misplaced and then put large bowls of soup in front of them, adding plates of sandwiches decorated with lettuce pieces in the shape of holly. 'The soup is split pea.' The older woman smiled wickedly. 'I dropped in a saucepan for Henry earlier, and he didn't look pleased.' She chuckled. 'Oh, I do enjoy torturing him – he deserves it, after what he did to Mae.'

'I wish they'd sort things out,' Ella admitted.

'All in good time,' Aggie said quietly. 'They're both stubborn, but things have a way of working out.' She winked. 'The sandwich is cheese. When you've finished, I'll bring some cake.' She glanced between them. 'You both look like you're losing weight which would be very inconvenient because we've almost finished your costumes. Speaking of costumes—' She waggled her eyebrows at Alex. 'After you've eaten, you need to try yours on.'

'Good grief,' he murmured as the older woman spun on her heels and headed towards the counter. 'I've no idea how to say no to those women and that's usually my favourite word.' He stared down at the food. 'I'm not really hungry.'

Ella picked up her spoon. 'It'll be easier if you just eat. Look at Henry, it doesn't matter how much he complains about soup, Aggie insists on feeding it to him.' She grinned because she secretly enjoyed watching the playful battle of wills. Aggie was the only person who'd ever won when it came to Henry – aside from Mae, who barely spoke to him now.

Wyatt whined as Ella sipped soup from her spoon, then he

dropped to his haunches, and stared at them, his expression accusing.

'Damn.' Ella shuffled through her handbag. 'I'm so sorry, I forgot to bring snacks. I wasn't expecting...' She glanced up and saw Alex watching her. 'I mean, I wasn't planning on coming here today.'

'We'll go back to the house for your lunch before we head to the next job,' Ella told Wyatt. Another detour would make her even later and she already felt frazzled.

'I might have a solution.' Alex reached into his pocket and pulled out a couple of carrot sticks. 'They're for the dogs. I got them for Sprout,' he explained as his cheeks turned a brighter shade of pink. 'I needed something to bribe him with when he kept following me.' He looked embarrassed. Wyatt sniffed the carrot suspiciously before glancing at Ella, clearly garnering her opinion on their safety. 'They're not poisoned.' Alex sounded offended.

'Aye,' Ella said as her insides melted. She suspected he'd got the treats for Sprout because he was falling for him, despite insisting Henry's pet was nothing more than an annoyance. She nodded at Wyatt who immediately gobbled them down.

'Don't read anything into me buying those. I still don't like dogs,' Alex said sharply to Wyatt. 'But I promise to give you more if you agree to stop peeing on my car. Let's call it a gentle-man's agreement.'

Wyatt made a snuffling sound which could have been a promise and Alex jerked his chin. Then he grabbed his spoon and scooped up some soup.

They ate in silence, but every time Ella glanced up, she caught Alex watching her.

'How are you getting on with your picture?' she asked even-tually, her voice strained.

He shrugged. 'I think I've found what I want to work on. There's a lochan about a mile from Henry's stables. I spotted it when I went for a walk with Sprout.' He frowned. 'I don't really know how I feel about the view, but Henry's agreed I can make a start.'

'This painting is really important to you,' she said.

'I suppose.' He took another sip of soup.

'Why?' Ella didn't think Alex would tell her, but she really wanted to understand. Learn why he was here and what was driving him to work so hard...

Alex fell silent. 'My da wants me to paint a landscape,' he finally said. 'He wants it to go in the reception area of our company's head office.' He paused and she saw something flicker behind his eyes. 'I'm not sure why I told you that.' He put the spoon down and picked up the sandwich and bit into it. It was obvious he was hungrier than he thought.

'Perhaps you want me to know the picture matters to you?' she guessed. 'Because it obviously matters to him.'

He studied her as he swallowed. 'Aye. I'm not sure there's anyone else I know who'd "get it" like you.' He narrowed his eyes, and Ella could see he wasn't comfortable with that thought.

'I *do* understand,' she said, leaning closer. 'What my father thought always mattered to me.'

He let out a long breath. 'Does your art *really* matter?'

'Aye.' Ella hesitated. 'I know it doesn't look like it at the moment.' She leaned back on the bench and folded her arms. 'I'm just being pulled in too many directions. I miss learning. I miss painting. It's all I ever wanted.'

It was all her father had wanted for her. He'd been so proud. Her next breath came out as a hiccup and Ella rubbed a palm over her chest, aware Alex was still watching.

'I'm not sure it's exactly the same,' he said sadly. 'What do you think your da would say if he could speak to you now?' he asked.

'I...' Ella swiped her tongue over suddenly dry lips. 'I

honestly have no idea.' She wondered if she should. 'Before he died, he asked me to stay in Mistletoe to take care of Lucinda, Dane and Clyde and that's what I'm doing. I think he'd be happy with how things are going. The company is still going.' *Just.* 'My family are content.'

Alex's forehead squeezed. 'So he wanted you to live the way you are now?'

Ella shrugged. 'Well.' She thought about her stepbrothers' behaviour earlier, about how rarely she got to paint. 'Probably not. We didn't get a chance to talk about the future or what should happen long term.' She'd been happy to stay and help out, had always intended to return to her art course at college. They hadn't formed a plan beyond the immediate. 'Dad died so suddenly.' He'd been here one moment and gone the next. Ella had been so focused on getting him well, on willing him to be okay, she'd refused to consider a different outcome.

But everything had suddenly changed and instead of getting better, her father had died. She looked up and caught Alex's gaze. 'What would you do – if your da asked you to do something for him?' she whispered.

'I'd do it,' Alex shot back. 'Whatever it took. Whatever I had to give up.' He frowned as he gazed at her. 'Making him happy is the thing that matters to me most.'

'Why?' Ella asked.

'Because... I...' He looked surprised. 'He expects it.' There was a shout at the other side of the tea room, then suddenly a dog was barking and Henry was barrelling towards them with Sprout hot on his heels.

'Aye, I heard you were both here,' the artist said thoughtfully, glancing between them as he indicated to Alex that he should shift up on the bench. 'I thought I'd come and join you.' He eyed their pea soup and shuddered. 'That way I can eat what I want for lunch, and I get to see my elusive student while

I do.' He slid in next to Alex and raised a reproachful eyebrow at Ella.

'I'm sorry,' she croaked, just as Hunter came running towards them too. When he arrived, he eyed Wyatt and Sprout, before dropping to his haunches to give both dogs a boisterous stroke. 'Nana said I should sit with you.' He rose and glanced between Alex, Henry and Ella looking unsure.

'Of course you should,' Ella said, shuffling up the bench until she was facing Alex again, acknowledging her relief that their conversation had been cut short. He'd raised too many questions – questions she'd spent the last year trying to avoid.

The small boy climbed up beside Ella and carefully put his blue satchel in between them on the bench. Then he stared owlishly at Alex.

'Aren't you supposed to be in school, lad?' Henry barked. 'You'd better not be sick because I've got no time for bugs and neither have they.' He eyed Alex and Ella.

The boy blinked and dragged his gaze from Alex towards Henry. 'I'm not ill. School finished early today,' he told him before focusing on Alex again. 'I've been drawing more pictures. They're in my satchel. Have you been drawing?'

Henry picked up Alex's sketch pad which was sitting on the bench in between them and placed it on the table. 'Looks like it, lad,' he said gruffly. 'Why don't we take a look at what he's working on now? I have to admit, I'm curious to see if any of my lessons have taken yet.'

'It's not ready!' Alex flushed as he grabbed for the pad. But before he could wrap his fingers around it, Henry flicked it open and everyone fell silent.

It was a picture of a woman. Ella heard Henry clear his throat and leaned down so she could get a better look.

'That looks just like you, Ella,' Hunter said, sounding impressed.

Ella studied the figure with a feeling of delight that quickly turned to dismay. The woman in the picture was around the same height as her and the curves on her body an almost perfect match. Alex had got the exact shape of her chin and nose – and her mouth was full with the same top-heavy lip. He'd even added the dimple she'd inherited from her da, the one that usually appeared from nowhere whenever she laughed, although she wasn't laughing here.

There were signs of strain around the woman's eyes and dark shadows underneath them suggesting she was exhausted. The hair was about the right length, although it lacked any lustre or bounce. It had been shaded darker in pencil where Ella had streaked it for Christmas in red and green, but even that didn't lift it. Instead, she looked flat and thoroughly miserable.

'Wyatt's there too.' Hunter pointed to a huge dog with floppy ears sitting in the background glaring at a Volvo. 'And look, this woman's wearing your uniform. I can see the words Magic Mops here.' He pointed to the logo Alex had doodled on the collar of the woman's jacket. Only...' The boy paused, his forehead smooshing as he leaned in closer still. 'It looks just like Prince Charming's costume, not Cinderella's because she'd be wearing a dress.' He bobbed his head at Alex clearly expecting him to explain.

When he didn't, Ella leaned closer. The picture was teaming with details, all brilliantly crafted and devastating.

'I think that's Clyde and Dane,' Hunter said excitedly, pointing to the two young men Alex had sketched in the background who were obviously supposed to be Ella's stepbrothers. They were laying on the ground, eating grapes and they were laughing at her.

'It's really good,' the boy added, but Alex just frowned.

'Aye, I'd go as far as saying it's brilliant and better than anything in that portfolio of yours,' Henry said, glancing between them. Although his triumphant expression dimmed when he took in Ella's face. 'In fact, I think you've caught the lass perfectly – and I can see a lot of truth in this.' He nodded at Alex, his expression sombre. 'You've taken my lessons on board, lad,' he said gruffly. 'Well done.'

'That's not me. I mean it looks like me, but...' Ella gulped as she gazed at the image taking in all the minutiae Alex had sketched – and the full implications of what they implied. Is this what he thought of her? She thought they'd connected, thought he respected her.

She tried to pull her gaze away, but couldn't, so gave in and took in the woman's billowy jacket and long, elegant gloves, the fitted trousers with the wide stripes up the sides and the tall, ridiculous boots. 'I'd never wear that outfit at work,' she said, her voice wobbly as she tried to ignore everything surrounding the woman who obviously *was* supposed to be her. Deliberately missing the point because she didn't want to face it.

'I think it's a metaphor, lass,' Henry said kindly.

'But what's the thing she's holding supposed to be – it looks like she's waving a sword. But it's not a sword, is it?' Hunter asked innocently, pointing to the duster the woman held which was topped off with an abundance of feathers. Out of the corner of her eye, Ella saw Alex wince and she *knew*.

'Nana's got one of those and she uses it to dust away cobwebs,' Hunter continued. 'Is that because Ella has a company that cleans houses?'

'Ah, it's... not exactly...' Alex choked, but clearly couldn't bring himself to explain the full horror of what the drawing meant.

'It's clever. I think it means our Ella is fighting a kind of battle with herself when she goes to work,' Henry explained delicately, confirming her worst fears.

She'd hoped she was wrong, that the meaning she could see was only in her imagination. But there was sympathy in Henry's gaze, compassion from a man who believed in showing the truth – and Ella felt like a blind eejit. Is this what everyone thought of her? Her wayward brain shifted to Dane and Clyde this morning – to her suspicions and eventual dismissal of them – and she shoved the image away.

'She's the heroine in this picture. Fighting to deliver whatever needs to be done, despite the fact that it's a job that's far too big for one. And despite the fact that it's not all her responsibility and doing it is making her stressed and tired. Keeping up with it also means she's having to give up one of the things she loves most. The thing that could become her future.' Henry fell silent.

'Wow, that's a lot,' Hunter said, his tone hushed as he gazed at it. 'Clever...'

Henry nodded.

Hunter let out a sigh and remained silent while he continued to study the drawing, looking confused. Ella could feel the burn of embarrassment as it rippled across her skin, searing her to the bones. She grabbed the cardigan Aggie had given her and twisted it in a fist, her eyes darting towards the exit as she contemplated how she could make her escape. But Hunter was sitting on the bench, trapping her – and she couldn't leave without asking him to move. If she did, everyone would know exactly how much the sketch had affected her. So she just sat in place and smiled, hating herself.

'What's the wastepaper basket mean?' the boy asked suddenly, and Ella sank into the cushions, realising she was going to have to endure this agony until the very end.

Henry glanced at Alex, and Alex looked at Ella; his cheeks were pale, and she knew he hadn't meant for her to see the drawing but couldn't bring herself to feel any sympathy for him.

'You might as well explain,' she said, trying to keep the smile in place even though her teeth were gritted so tightly the enamel was probably filing off. 'Finish what you started. It's all there in black and white anyway.'

Ella could feel tears pooling at the back of her eyes and

schooled her expression to remain impassive. She wouldn't cry and she definitely wouldn't let Alex – or Henry or anyone else in the tea room – see how much the picture had hurt her. She just had to let this run its course, until it was over; then she could make a dignified escape.

After that, Ella had no idea what she was going to do. Her world as she knew it had just cracked wide open – and she wasn't sure if she'd ever be able to put it back together again.

# 15

### ALEX

Alex felt like his head was going to explode. From the moment Ella had sat in the booth opposite him, he'd had a bad feeling. He'd been drawing her for the last two days. It hadn't mattered how many times he'd tried to portray Henry, Wyatt, Sprout, Stan or even his father, the person in his sketch had always morphed back into Ella.

His head was filled with her – so in the early hours of this morning, he'd finally given in. Deciding to just go with it and let the images run free. She'd never see the picture. Even if he showed it to Henry, he'd ask if they could keep it between them. He was doing what his mentor had asked, drawing the truth in all its glory – warts, lines, wrinkles, curves, all of it. And *fuck it*, hadn't he done exactly that?

'What's the wastepaper basket mean?' Hunter asked again, and Alex felt his whole body go rigid. He searched his mind for one of his father's rules, one that might help to justify what he'd done. Then he remembered.

*It's a dog-eat-dog world out there – make sure you're the one who eats.*

Which roughly translated meant do whatever the hell you

need to make sure you succeed. Which Alex had done – why then did he feel so awful about it?

He shut his eyes for a beat. He was going to have to explain, to lay bare everything he'd been thinking – but he didn't want to. He admired Ella, was attracted to her too and the thought of hurting her was...

'There's lots of rubbish,' the boy continued – his questions like fingernails scraping across a chalkboard. 'It's like when I'm trying to draw something and it keeps going wrong. I rip out the picture, screw it up and throw it away.' Hunter's nose creased, the cute freckles along it rippling.

'It's my art, isn't it?' Ella asked, her voice raw. She'd obviously been trying to hold her smile in place, but the effort must have become too much for her, because it had disappeared and her face was now pale and drawn. 'You're trying to say it doesn't matter to me, or maybe you think my pictures aren't very good.' She nodded and her shoulders seemed to sag. '*That's* why the artwork is in the bin.'

'Ah!' Hunter said his expression brightening as the puzzle got solved. 'So that's why you've thrown all your drawings away.' The boy frowned, looking confused. 'I don't understand. Ella draws animals. Nana has one in her house and they're really good...'

'That's not exactly what the picture means,' Alex said quietly, wishing he hadn't drawn anything.

It had come to him in the early hours when he'd been so tired he could barely think. Ella had been swimming around his mind. The fact that he'd wanted to kiss her in the changing room, would have asked if he hadn't come to his senses in time... And he'd been annoyed. Angry that she'd hadn't come to her lessons, that every time her stepbrothers told her they were sick, she dropped everything and stepped in. It was so obvious to everyone they were taking advantage – and she was letting them.

The picture she'd almost finished had been taunting him from her easel in the studio. She was so talented and seemed so happy to give it all up. But he hadn't known about her promise to her father then – hadn't understood anything when he'd started the sketch.

He gazed across the table, Ella looked pale and a little sick, and suddenly he felt ill too. He knew he shouldn't – his father would say he hadn't done anything wrong. But his mother's blood flowed through his veins – and it was telling him in no uncertain terms that he should have kept his opinions to himself. That he was an arrogant eejit for judging this woman so harshly.

'Your art comes last, Ella,' Henry said, his voice kind but firm. 'I don't think the lad meant to be cruel.' He looked between them, and for the first time, Alex wondered if he was regretting the lesson he'd set. The older man reached out a hand intending to close the sketchbook, but Ella placed her palm over the picture so he couldn't.

'You don't need to hide it. There's no point,' she said flatly. 'I've seen it now and—' She lifted a shoulder. 'There's a lot for me to think about here. Plenty of truth and what did you say?' She lifted her eyes. 'Warts. I can see those in the picture too.' She nodded. 'Perhaps even some I have to finally consider.' Her chest heaved.

'The drawing's good, though, isn't it?' Hunter asked, looking between them, his face registering confusion and a touch of distress.

'Of course it is,' Ella said, stroking the back of her hand across his cheek, her voice soothing. 'It's brilliant. Alex is a wonderful artist. I can't wait to see what he draws next. I'm *so* sorry.' She made a point of checking her watch. 'I've got to get to work. My stepbrothers are sick again.' Her voice cracked on the last word, and Alex saw the way she heaved in a breath, gathering herself. 'I've got to cover a cleaning job and I'm going to be late.'

'You haven't eaten your lunch,' Hunter said, staring at the bowl of soup and sandwich sitting in front of her. She'd only had a sip of the soup and the rest was untouched.

'Aye.' Ella rubbed her hand across the boy's head, ruffling his hair. 'Don't worry, I'll ask your nana to save it for me.' She gave him a dim smile.

'I'll try and make it to the next lesson,' she said to Henry, her voice a little raspy. 'Would you mind letting me get out, lad?' she asked Hunter.

Then without looking at any of them again, Ella slid from the bench, grabbed Wyatt's lead and fled.

## 16

ELLA

The Art House was empty of customers when Ella arrived. Still out of breath after her run from The Snug Tea Room, she flipped the sign at the entrance to closed and heaved in a breath. Hot wet tears bubbled down her cheeks as she finally allowed them to flow, letting all her feelings of shame run free.

'Mae!' she cried, trying to keep her voice even as she made her way across the gallery.

'Ella?' her godmother asked as she appeared from the back room. She was dressed in an immaculate, bright blue suit and her white hair was styled back from her face. She looked cool, curvy and absolutely stunning. 'What's wrong?' she asked as she took in Ella's expression. 'Come into the back.' She pointed to the entrance. 'I'll shut up shop.'

'I've already done it,' Ella croaked and then allowed Mae to lead her into an office that was just as elegant and airy as the main gallery. Ella slumped into a white leather chair in front of Mae's glass desk and Wyatt sat on the floor beside her looking perplexed.

'I assume you've got bad news.' Her godmother carefully opened her desk drawer and drew out a bottle of single malt and two delicate glasses, before pouring them each a small shot and taking a seat. 'This is medicinal, designed to loosen tongues and make things seem a little less awful,' she said kindly, taking out a box of festive chocolates from the drawer as well. 'From the look on your face, I'm guessing we need these too.' She ripped off the wrapper and offered the sweets to Ella, plucking one from the box without looking. 'Are Lucinda or your stepbrothers to blame for your tears?' Mae asked.

Ella chewed the lump of chocolate – she could barely taste it so swallowed quickly, following it up with a slug of whisky. 'In a way it's all three of them. But mostly it's me...' Ella finally told her. 'Am I a total eejit?' She brushed hair from her eyes and then swiped at her cheeks, mopping up the tears feeling angry. 'Scratch that, I know I am,' she said as the picture Alex had drawn swam into her mind. It had been a shock, a moment of awful clarity – one she'd been doing her best to avoid. But now it had all been laid out for her, she couldn't ignore it.

'What's this all about?' Mae asked gently, picking up her glass and downing her shot before stashing the bottle back into her desk.

'Clyde and Dane,' Ella said, glancing above Mae's desk and taking in the framed drawing of Wyatt that she'd gifted her godmother last Christmas. Her tears started up again. 'They're making a fool out of me,' she croaked. 'And Lucinda's letting them. I don't know if it's deliberate on her part, but she's always been—'

'Far harder on you than on them; happy to let you take on the responsibility for Magic Mops and do all the work; willing to forgive them for every transgression because they're her *boys*?' Mae asked dryly. 'Aye.' She shrugged. 'Well, that's not a secret or a surprise, lass. I've been trying to tell you as much for months. It's got worse since they joined the business.' She leaned closer. 'What made you finally see the truth?'

'I don't know. I went to see them this morning – they're off sick again. I had a feeling they were lying.' She pressed her fingertips into her eyes. 'I knew it really, I just didn't want to believe it. Then I saw this sketch...' Ella sighed, thinking about it again. Had Alex done it to hurt her? Now she'd had a chance to calm down she realised he'd looked upset when Henry had flipped open the pad. And he'd winced each time Hunter had asked a question, as if he'd been just as upset by it as her.

Alex was talented, there was no doubt about that. She'd known immediately that the woman was her. But every stroke of his pencil had made something inside her bleed.

'A sketch?' Mae asked, leaning back in her chair and folding her arms. 'One of Henry's I assume?'

Ella shook her head. 'It was Alex,' she croaked. 'Henry asked us to draw something or somebody and show the truth.'

Mae's lips thinned and she shook her head. 'The man is far too obsessed with showing the truth – as *he* calls it.' Her eyes flashed. 'What's wrong with softening things or looking at them through rose-tinted spectacles? The truth *hurts*. That's why we all enjoy pantomimes and fairy tales. *That's* why we celebrate Santa Claus coming at Christmas. It makes us feel good – none of us need to disappear into the rabbit hole called *truth*.'

She sucked in a long angry breath, clearly making an effort to calm down. 'Tell me,' she snapped.

Ella frowned. 'It's difficult to explain,' she admitted. 'It just...' She shrugged. 'The picture implied that I try to fix everything by cleaning it up, that Clyde and Dane are taking advantage and I put all of that before my art. It was really clever actually.'

She could admit that, now she'd had some space, now her feelings weren't threatening to overwhelm her. 'It was brilliant, but I didn't like what it showed. I know I'm tired, I know I've been doing too much, but it's the first time I've let myself admit that my stepbrothers have been making a fool out of me. What's worse is it's obvious now that everyone knew.' Ella sighed. 'The trouble is, I promised Da—'

'To set your family on the right path,' Mae said sternly. 'I've told you before that you didn't promise to give up everything so they can live the way they want. Do you really think he'd have expected you to give up on your dreams?' Mae shook her head, her frustration showing in the jerky movement. 'Or your talent – wasn't he so proud when you went to college? He was your biggest cheerleader.'

Ella shrugged.

'I'm sorry you're upset, lass, but I'm not sorry you've finally seen the truth. Prince Charming deserves a medal as far as I'm concerned.' Mae paused. 'Or perhaps a crown would be more fitting.' Her smile was wry. 'You've been living as Cinderella for real for too long and it's way past time you wised up and changed something.'

She pointed to the sketch Ella had drawn which was hanging above her head. It was a picture of Wyatt laying in a meadow in the sunshine with butterflies and bees fluttering around his head. 'You're talented and you're wasting it. Living a life you don't even want. You've no idea how many of my clients have admired your picture – I'm talking to a few dozen at least.' She wafted a hand.

'Have they?' Ella asked as Mae's words seemed to snap something inside her, releasing a flood of warmth.

'Aye.' Mae nodded. 'You're good enough to make a living at this. You've just got to—' She lifted a shoulder. 'Learn to put yourself and your art first.'

Wyatt made a woofing sound and got up and wagged his tail making his big body shake.

'Even the bloodhound agrees,' Mae joked as someone began to hammer on the door at the entrance of the art gallery. 'The sign on the door says closed. Sometimes, I wonder if people can read!' Mae huffed, rising from her chair. 'Wait there,' she ordered, disappearing out of the office towards the front of the gallery.

Ella slumped back in her seat and gazed up at the picture of Wyatt again. She'd drawn it on impulse one evening when she'd missed another of Henry's lessons. She'd been frustrated and Wyatt had been gazing at her with his big reproachful eyes – so she'd just picked up her pencil and started to sketch. She could still feel the way the energy had flowed through her as she'd worked with the pencil. She'd barely slept that night and she'd been so happy with the result that she'd framed it for Mae.

Ella frowned. How long had it been since she'd had the time to find that flow? How many of Henry's lessons has she missed while she'd been dusting or mopping a stranger's house in place of her stepbrothers?

'I've no idea what you're doing here,' Mae snapped as she marched back into the office, and Ella spun round and saw Henry and Sprout. 'Haven't you upset the lass enough?'

The older man sighed and shoved his hands in the pockets of his battered jeans as he stopped and silently looked around Mae's office before his attention came to rest on Ella. 'I came to see if you were okay,' he said, scouring her face and wincing.

'Where's Alex?' Ella asked, glaring behind Henry into the gallery, feeling something pitch inside her chest as she imagined he'd followed.

Henry snorted. 'In the back room with the McBride sisters and young Hunter, being tortured with pins and scissors I expect.'

'Seems fitting,' Mae said lightly.

'The lad's got your cardigan with him,' Henry told Ella. 'You left it behind and he was reluctant to part with it when I offered to give it to you.'

Ella frowned. There would be no way of avoiding him now.

'What were you thinking setting them a task like that?' Mae suddenly barked at Henry, narrowing her eyes.

He shrugged. 'I didn't tell the lad to draw Ella,' he muttered, looking upset. 'The intention wasn't to hurt anybody,' he said quietly. 'The purpose was for them to draw the truth as they saw it.' He winced.

Mae's eyes flashed. 'I've heard that one before,' she ground out, putting distance between them as she strode to the other side of her desk and sat, her back straight and her chin tilting as she glared at him. 'Only sometimes the truth *does* hurt.' Her eyes burned into Henry's, and Ella saw him sway on his feet.

'I still don't understand why,' he said faintly, and Ella could hear an ache in his voice, perhaps even a hint of regret. 'I've told you a million times, the truth celebrates what's *there*,' he insisted, his forehead pinching. 'It doesn't hide or pretend; it honours and acknowledges.'

'Or it eviscerates,' Mae snapped back. 'Showing every fault and flaw, every line, wrinkle and extra layer of flesh in pencil and paint for people to study and analyse is cruel.' The words were delivered with such venom, Henry flinched.

Ella leaned back in her chair as her attention flipped back and forth between the older couple – did they remember she was here?

Her godmother was obviously furious – but not just that, she was hurt. Ella didn't know all the details of what had happened between them. It had been obvious from the minute their relationship ended that her godmother didn't want to share. Ella only knew it had something to do with a painting Henry had done of Mae. But now things were falling into place. Ella could only imagine how upset Mae would be if the older man had painted a picture as truthful and detailed as the one he'd done of Aggie. Or as devastating as the one Alex had done of her.

Mae had always been concerned with her looks – perhaps a hangover from her days as a model. She was terrified of her emerging lines, wrinkles and what she often called '*too much*

*Mae'*. Had her mentor drawn attention to those on canvas, had he shared that with her godmother too?

'Aging can be beautiful,' Henry said rapidly, and Ella got the feeling this was an argument he'd already used because her godmother made an angry tutting sound. 'I simply drew attention to what I thought was worth celebrating. To all the things that I lov—' He stopped and swallowed. 'I never expected...' Henry looked down at his hands. 'I've told you I'm sorry, I've no idea what I can do to put it right,' he said unhappily.

'Maybe you can't,' Mae snapped. 'Or perhaps you could if you could see beyond your ego and figure it out.'

Henry looked shocked, and Ella thought she could see something clicking in his mind. Then he frowned and shrugged before his eyes rested back on Ella and his expression was blank. 'I'm sorry that you were upset by Alex's picture – but even if I could, I wouldn't want him to take it back.'

He ignored Mae's curse.

'I know the truth can hurt, but I also believe it can set us free.' He shrugged. 'You've been doing lessons with me for almost a year. In the time I've been trying to teach you, you've missed more hours in my studio than you've turned up for. The lad helped me to really see that. I think he did the same for you?' He raised an eyebrow and Ella nodded.

He drew in a long breath. 'I came here to make sure you were okay, but I also need to add my weight to what we've both realised today. Ella – you *have* to commit to your art,' he insisted. He pinched his lips and took a moment to study the picture of Wyatt above Mae's head.

'I only have one protégé a year – and that's Alex this time – which, until you, was always a hard and fast rule, designed to stop me from being pulled away from my own painting.'

His forehead creased. 'I made an exception for you because you're so talented and you were keen to learn. But...' He sighed. 'If you're not going to give me your absolute best – I'm going to start thinking that I'm wasting my time. Which means unless you start turning up to my studio *every* day, I'm not going to be able to teach you anymore, lass.'

'What?' Ella blurted as her heart began to beat rapidly. 'You can't...' She stopped because Henry Lockhart could do whatever he wanted.

'It's for your own good,' Henry said quietly.

Ella looked at Mae, her eyes wide, but her godmother just shrugged. 'For once, I'm in agreement with the old man. I'm sorry, Ella,' she said kindly. 'It's way past time you learned to put yourself first.'

'I can't,' Ella said as her head swam with the promises she'd made to her father. If she did what Henry wanted, she'd be letting her da down. But she didn't want to give up her art either. She had no idea what to do.

# 17

---

## ALEX

'You're here!' Hunter shouted as soon as Alex made his way into Mistletoe Village Hall later that evening clutching Ella's cardigan tightly under his arm. Henry had sent him ahead because he wanted to work on a painting in private, but he'd insisted that he would join with Sprout later on. Alex had offered to wait, or to take the terrier along to the rehearsal with him, but the older man had waved him away.

'And you're here,' Alex said self-consciously to the boy as he studied the pantomime cast, some of whom were already sitting in huddles busy running through their lines. A lot were dressed in costume, and in the corner of the room, Alex could see Ella's stepbrothers, who were wearing wigs and dresses, spinning each other around and sending chairs flying.

'Aye, Aunt Blair said I had to come early because she wanted me to try on my costume. I think she's got another one for you too,' Hunter said excitedly.

Alex cleared his throat. The older woman had been unhappy with the sizing of his suit when he'd tried it on in the tea room earlier so had promised to adjust it and bring it here tonight.

'Has Ella arrived?' he asked. He hadn't spoken to her since she'd run from the tea room, and he wanted to make sure she was okay. Wanted to apologise.

'I think she's trying on one of her dresses,' Hunter told him. 'I brought you a picture to look at while you're waiting for her, I've been working on it all afternoon, I thought your drawing in the café was really good and I wanted you to see another one of mine.'

The long sentence was delivered in one breath, and the boy gulped in air when he finished. Then he beamed up at Alex and swiped a piece of paper from his back pocket before waving it. Alex took it and unfolded the work carefully, studying the image.

'I drew it earlier,' Hunter announced proudly. 'It's a picture of Pinecone Manor.'

'Aye,' Alex hummed his approval – it was similar to the last picture the boy had given him. A decent representation of the content, if a little childish in style. But some of the smaller details – including the herd of deer, fir trees and the building's unique turrets – indicated signs of an emerging talent. He scoured the sketch, making appropriate approving sounds as he tuned out the voices in the background and the building anxiety of seeing Ella again.

Which was madness, because usually nothing fazed him. He had a reputation for being heartless at work and had begun to believe that were true. Especially since Stan had gone travelling – because the one person who insisted on telling Alex that he did have feelings was gone.

But he'd upset Ella earlier and that hadn't been his intention. She shouldn't have seen the picture, and it had obviously offended her far more than he'd expected it to. Perhaps because she hadn't been ready to face the truth? Or maybe the sketch had simply been too harsh. There had been nothing to indicate Ella's kindness, selflessness or talent, nothing positive at all. In retrospect, the whole thing had looked like a criticism. Although a part of him – the rational part – didn't understand why he cared.

Alex had hoped Ella would be at Pinecone Manor this afternoon so he could apologise or at least explain. There had been no official lesson planned, so he'd just begun to sketch the landscape he was intending to paint, and he'd overheard Aggie telling Henry that she was expecting a visit from Magic Mops. But no one had arrived – and Alex was sure it was because of his picture.

For the first time ever, he felt bad because he'd hurt someone's feelings, and he wanted to put things right. Which probably meant he'd been in Mistletoe for far longer than he should have – because his mother's genes were beginning to emerge.

'What do you think?' Hunter asked, gazing at Alex looking hopeful and nervous.

Alex cleared his throat, searching for the right thing to say because he wasn't looking to wound anyone else today. 'I think your picture is really good. There are signs of real talent here,' he said honestly.

The boy frowned as Alex handed the paper back. 'I phoned my da earlier and showed it to him on the camera. He says I could do better.' His small eyebrows met, forming an expression Alex had seen on his own face many times. 'He thinks the trees don't look real and the deer are too big. He said I need to tear this up and draw the whole thing again.' Hunter's lips pinched as his young face tightened further, and Alex experienced an unexpected wave of solidarity. 'I'm going to start again tomorrow, but I don't want to rip this one up.' He flushed. 'It's not really lying because I didn't tell Da I'd throw it out.'

'Is your father an artist?' Alex asked, curious.

'Nae.' The boy shook his head. 'Da's too important to spend his time just drawing,' he said absently, and Alex suspected the words had come straight from the man's mouth. His father had said similar things to him over the years, at least until he'd realised Alex could make money from his *hobby*. 'Mam was annoyed about what he said, but Da told me he knows his own eyes and he knows what's good and what isn't.' The boy's shoulders sagged. 'I've been practising and practising drawing trees at school, but I can't make them any better. Have you any advice?' The boy looked desperate.

Alex scratched his chin as Hunter shoved the drawing back into his hands and he took it and gazed at it for a moment before glancing around.

Where were the McBride sisters, and why had this boy taken such an interest in him? Aggie had talked about Hunter needing a male role model, but Alex had barely got his own life together and he certainly wasn't equipped to influence a child's. Even if a part of him suddenly wished he could.

'I...' Alex puffed out a breath, torn because he wanted to say the child's father clearly had no idea how good this picture was for someone of Hunter's age. Only he didn't want to upset the boy. He knew how important a father's opinion was and it wasn't his place to interfere. 'Maybe try to draw something else. Does your da like dogs? Mine likes them so much he put them on our company logo.' He bunched up the sleeve of his jumper and showed the boy one of his cufflinks.

'Cool,' Hunter said, looking closer. 'Yes, my da does.' Hunter's face transformed and suddenly he was beaming. 'Good idea. Thank you. You can keep that picture if you want and put it in your bedroom at Pinecone Manor.'

'It would be an honour to hang this in my room,' Alex said solemnly, earning another shy smile which had his insides warming. It felt good to make someone happy. It wasn't something Alex experienced often in his world. He carefully folded the picture and put it into his back pocket just as Ella emerged from the back room. She carefully stepped onto the stage, and he found himself staring.

She wore an orange and green dress that had been crafted to look like rags. It was tight around the bodice and strikingly simple in style. It hugged her waist and moulded the curve of her hips before flaring out and falling around her knees in jagged triangles. A simple white apron completed the outfit, and someone had put Ella's hair into a high ponytail. Even from where Alex was standing on the other side of the room, he could see the style of the dress suited her. It brought out the colour of her skin, the pink of her cheeks, and flattered the delicate angles of her slim body.

'Wow,' Hunter gasped as he turned to check where Alex was staring. 'Ella looks bonnie.'

'Prince Charming, why aren't you with Cinderella?' Mae asked sharply, appearing from behind them. 'I want to get you both up on stage this evening and time's running out.'

She marched in front of him, waving her script before her eyes narrowed and she took a moment to glance around. 'Where's the eejit artist? He's supposed to be showing me his scenery plans.'

'Henry will be along soon, he got caught up working,' Alex told her.

'Aye, that'll probably be him trying to find his *truth* again,' she said darkly, wagging the script towards the stage. 'Come on, you might as well come too, Hunter.'

'Oh good. Can I help with the scene?' he asked, excitedly skipping ahead. 'Maybe I can wave your wand. Should I give Cinderella some magic flowers?'

'I'm sure you'd be brilliant, lad, but that's not in the script,' Mae said, giving the boy an encouraging smile.

Ella flushed as Mae guided Alex towards the stage. She avoided his eyes as the older woman handed them both a set of scripts. 'I thought we'd start by doing a run-through of one of the final scenes,' she said, flicking through hers until she was closer to the back. 'The one where Prince Charming gets Cinderella to try on her slipper.'

'And it fits!' Hunter told Alex tugging at his sleeve. 'And then they kiss, which is pretty yuk.' He pulled a face. 'Maybe I could do some magic instead?'

'I think we should stick with the kiss, the audience will expect it.' Mae chuckled. 'But Cinderella has to try on the shoe first. Ella already has a pair that we gave back to Aggie earlier so she could make sure they work with the ballgown.' Mae gave the young boy an indulgent wink as Aggie suddenly came charging from the back of the stage carrying a pair of glass slippers – she handed one to Ella and the other to Alex.

'You left them in the changing room, lass,' she said.

'I know you might not know all your lines yet,' Mae said to Alex gently. 'But that doesn't matter. Tonight is about getting you comfortable with each other and that means you might want to start by putting a few of your issues aside.'

'What are issues?' Hunter asked, glancing between them. 'Can I have some?'

'Nae, lad. Issues are misunderstandings. That's not something many of us want.' Mae raised an eyebrow at Ella, and Alex realised she'd confided in her godmother – and felt another wave of guilt.

Mae guided them both towards the set of stairs that would lead them up to the stage and Alex felt his stomach sink. There was almost no chance of Ella getting comfortable with him after seeing his sketch. At least not until he'd had a chance to talk to her, to apologise and try to explain.

'We've not got all the props, and you'll have to imagine how things will look,' Mae said, looking around. 'But take a few minutes to get comfortable.'

Hunter raced ahead and sat cross-legged in the middle of the stage. 'I can help with props, what do you need?' he asked, shooting up and heading towards a cardboard box. He pulled out a pirate hat and a sword before scooting back to Alex and handing them to him. Alex put on the hat. He felt ridiculous, but he wanted to make the boy smile. Perhaps Ella would too?

'It looks silly,' Hunter giggled.

'Hunter lad, Aunt Blair wants you to try on your costume again and this might be a good time,' Aggie said, and the boy pulled another face.

'Okay. But don't worry, Alex, I'll come back soon to help with your scene,' he promised, skipping down the steps and away with his nana as Mae turned back to them looking sympathetic.

'I realise you might feel awkward,' she said. 'So I'll leave you for a moment so you can talk. If you've got things that you need to air, I'd like you to do that now. I'll give you half an hour – and make sure we keep Hunter busy so you're not interrupted.' She walked to the edge of the stage and activated the pulley that shut the curtains. They swept down and the billowing red velvet blocked out everyone in the main hall.

Mae looked between them and her gaze was intense. 'Deal with what you need to before you move onto your scene. When you have – assuming you're still alive.' She gave Alex a tight smile. 'Start with Prince Charming arriving with the slipper.'

'Oh, and before I go, let me help you get a feel for where we are in the story. Ella, your stepmother and stepsisters have been doing everything they can to make sure the Prince doesn't see you today. Dane and Clyde have already tried on the slipper, but of course it doesn't fit. Perry and Patch – your mice friends, Ella – have managed to sneak you into the gardens. Alex.' She nodded at him.

'When you see Ella, I want you to look smitten. Cinderella is beautiful – but you don't recognise her from the ball because she's dressed in rags. Get her to sit on the bench.' She looked around. 'Except we have no bench,' she grumbled. 'I should have kept the lad, he'd have found one. Ah.' She went to pick up one of the stacked chairs before plopping it in the centre of the stage.

'This will be your bench for now. Alex, get Ella to try on the slipper. Obviously, we already know it's going to fit, but try and look surprised when it does.' She gave him a tentative smile. 'Once you realise Ella is Cinderella, then I'd like you to kiss. Don't forget, you need to be comfortable with one another before you start working on any of this.' She looked between them and grimaced. 'Don't worry about the kiss too much today – a quick peck will suffice.'

Alex glanced at Ella – she was staring at the floor.

'Does that sound okay, lass?' Mae pressed.

She raised her head and met Alex's eyes. 'Of course,' she said. Mae gazed at her for a few moments and then she nodded.

'Give me a shout if you need anything.' Mae glanced at Alex looking worried before she headed from the stage.

'I'm sorry,' Alex said the moment the older woman had gone. 'You were never supposed to see that sketch. I wouldn't have drawn it if I'd known you would. I had this idea for a picture of my friend, Stan, but—'

'What happened, did your pencil slip?' Ella asked tersely.

'I have no excuse,' he said gently. 'You need to know the drawing wasn't meant to hurt you. I admire how hard you push yourself, the things you're trying to juggle, all the people you're helping.'

'Admire?' Ella snorted. 'You think I'm an idiot.'

Alex folded his arms. He wasn't used to explaining himself, but he had to find the words today. 'Not everyone puts themselves out for others like you.' He paused, mulling his words. 'That's the issue here. Not whether they deserve it. In my world, people are inherently selfish.' He sighed as he tried to think of one person that he knew in Edinburgh – aside from Stan and including himself – who would go out of their way for someone and came up empty. 'It honestly wasn't intended as a criticism.'

Ella stared at him for a long moment, her face a picture of confusion. 'I didn't expect you to say that. I thought you'd tell me I deserved what you drew – that I'm a fool.'

Alex stiffened. 'I realise I may not...' He swallowed. 'I don't always come across as sympathetic.' He wasn't used to apologising or articulating himself and this was difficult. 'That's not what I meant by the sketch,' he said finally. 'I felt sorry for you.' His whole body hummed with discomfort. But had his words been enough?

'I don't want people to feel sorry for me.' Ella studied him, her expression softening, and Alex's insides untwisted. 'But I know why you do. I'll admit, I've been thinking about the picture all afternoon.'

He winced. 'I'll rip it up—'

Ella stopped him by holding up a hand. 'I didn't like your drawing.' Her forehead pinched, and Alex steeled himself for more. 'I hated everything it was trying to say. But it made me think.' Her eyebrows met. 'I talked to Mae who told me she thinks you might be a genius, and Henry basically threatened not to teach me anymore unless I start to take my art seriously.' She looked tense.

'I could talk to him?' Alex said roughly. The picture had obviously set off a domino effect – one that could make Ella's life worse. As if he didn't feel bad enough... 'I never meant—'

'I know,' Ella interrupted. 'I don't want you to talk to anyone. I'm not sure what I'm going to do about it yet.' She sighed. 'Or what to do about Clyde and Dane.' There was a sudden loud clatter behind the curtain and then Mae shouted both of Ella's stepbrothers' names.

Ella sucked in a breath. 'I do know I have to change something because my art matters to me. And if you hadn't drawn that picture, if I hadn't seen it, then I'm not sure how long it would have taken me to accept the truth. So, perhaps I should thank you.'

'You don't sound like you mean that,' Alex said dryly. 'I still want to apologise. In retrospect, the picture was cruel.' His cheeks flushed as he acknowledged that, and that it mattered to him.

'I'm not trying to make you feel bad, Alex,' Ella said gently. 'And you've apologised enough. I don't hold on to grudges, life's way too short.'

'But I *do* feel bad. The only way I'll feel better is if you agree to draw me,' Alex said. 'It's what Henry asked you to do. At least he asked you to draw the truth about somebody.' He stepped closer to Ella just as someone brightened the lights above them, illuminating her face. She'd been crying, Alex could see that now. Her eyes were red and a little puffy, and something in his chest felt like it was going to shatter with shame.

His whole life had always been about winning, about gaining his father's approval. People's feelings didn't count – at least that's what he'd always been led to believe. But for some reason, this woman's did matter – and the fact that he'd hurt her made him feel awful. 'I'd need you to be brutal,' he said seriously. 'If I've got any chance of being able to sleep again.'

Ella met his eyes. 'Tit for tat? I don't play that game.' She hesitated, her expression curious. 'What would I draw?'

Alex shrugged. 'You tell me,' he said. 'You don't know me really, but I'm sure you've picked up enough to be able to sketch something... the devil perhaps?'

Ella's lips twisted into a knot. Then her eyes dropped to Alex's arm, and she looked surprised. 'You have my cardigan?' she said.

'You left it in the tea room.' Alex glanced down; he'd forgotten he was still carrying it. 'I just picked it up.' He handed it to her.

'Thank you for taking the trouble. I'm always losing things.'
She frowned.

'Perhaps there's so much to remember, you forget the stuff
that's not important?' he suggested. The words felt odd in his
throat. Being kind was unnatural, but when Ella nodded and
smiled, Alex felt something glow inside him – like something
dormant had just been zapped. It felt good and that was a wake-
up call.

'Perhaps.' She put the cardigan on the chair. 'Picking that
up and bringing it for me tonight was a nice gesture. Perhaps
you have a heart – a small one anyway.'

Alex shook his head. He wanted to smile, to acknowledge
her teasing, but the truth was – he didn't have a heart. Not one
he'd allow himself to show or share.

'So if I was going to draw you, in all your truthful glory...'
Ella hesitated and began to pace the stage, the pretty triangles
of fabric at the bottom of her dress swaying around her knees.
They were supposed to look like rags, but Ella made the scraps
of material look sensual, and Alex had to force himself to drag
his attention away before she noticed him staring.

'Go ahead. What would you draw?' Alex asked again,
steeling himself for Ella's observations, guessing he wouldn't
like what she thought of him. But it was only fair.

He tried to make himself cold, tried to block out his feelings
and turn himself into the iceman. It would help him cope with
whatever she came up with, it would stop the peaks and troughs
of emotion he didn't always understand.

'Let me start.' He kept his voice low. 'I don't smile much and
I rarely laugh, so in your sketch I'd definitely be frowning – I
might even be baring my teeth.'

'Oh, I don't see you like that,' Ella said quietly, shaking her
head.

'Why?' Alex asked, surprised.

She cast her eyes upwards as if searching for a memory.

'You get an odd look on your face when Sprout comes to see you. It's like you're trying to work out what he wants from you, and you're surprised by his attention because you don't think you deserve it. And you keep trying to work out why he likes you, but you're also secretly pleased that he does.'

'That's not true,' Alex snapped, taken aback by the accuracy of Ella's observation. He wasn't normally so easy to read. 'You could draw my car,' he said, flustered. 'How I drive too fast – show how little I care about the creatures or people I might run down.' He knew he sounded desperate – but he wanted her to see who he really was.

Ella shook her head again. 'I think we've already established that you didn't see Wyatt or me on the road that day. I'm not saying you were in the right to drive so fast, but I have noticed you're much more careful when you're in your car now.' She frowned as she studied him. 'You're hard on yourself, aren't you?' She sounded sympathetic.

Alex shuffled on his feet. 'It's best to acknowledge your faults, that way you can work on them,' he said, his voice stiff, echoing a conversation he'd had with his father at least a few hundred times.

Ella studied Alex for a while longer, her eyes dark but curious. 'I think I'd draw you near an easel, because I know art matters to you,' she said. 'Even more than your job I think, because when you talk about doing emails or meetings in the mornings, you always sound stressed.'

Alex jerked his chin because he was surprised. He waited for the arrow to pierce, waited for Ella to show him that she knew the awful truth about him.

'I'd put that sports car you spoke about in the background,' she continued. 'The one you got when you were nineteen. Because you loved it, but I don't think you let yourself drive it now.' Her eyes narrowed.

'How do you know that?' Alex asked roughly.

'You had a look on your face when you talked about it,' she said quietly. 'It looked like grief.'

Alex gulped and shoved his hands in his pockets, completely undone. 'I don't know, you're—' He was about to say she was wrong but couldn't bring himself to lie. He was supposed to be making amends.

She gazed at him, her mouth curling on one side and Alex steeled himself again. 'I would—' She hesitated. 'Now this is going to sound odd.'

'Say it,' Alex muttered. Hopefully, she'd finally come up with something he could agree with.

'I might put...' She pressed a hand to her heart and patted it. 'I'd want to find a way of showing that you've got a big heart but you don't want anyone to know. Or maybe you're embarrassed by it.' She screwed up her nose.

'What makes you say that?' Alex asked, shocked. The only person who'd ever insisted that he had feelings was his best friend, and it had taken Stan a lifetime to see through him. How had Ella seen so much in such a short time?

'The way you are with Sprout.' She glanced over her shoulder into the hall. 'And Hunter, you're so patient with that boy – you helped me with my tyre and despite the fact that you don't know me, you're really bothered I'm wasting my artistic talents.' She sucked in a breath, obviously poised to tell him more, and Alex wanted to tell her to stop but couldn't find the words. He didn't want to hear this.

But he did.

He just had no idea how to deal with the picture she was painting of him. It's the only reason he couldn't tell her to stop.

'You feel awful that you hurt me today. You don't want to, though – that bit I can't understand.' Ella's eyes blazed as she stared at him. 'And the picture was...' She winced. 'Okay it made me cry, and I was appalled by what it meant.'

She blinked away emotion, her blue eyes suddenly clear.

'But everything in that sketch was true. I wasn't meant to see it – I know that too. You're not cruel, Alex.' She folded her arms. 'In a way, I'm glad I saw it.' She sighed and stepped closer as there was another clatter behind the curtains and again someone shouted her stepbrothers' names. 'There were truths in it I finally have to admit.'

Alex could feel something burning in his throat, but he was too confused to know what it meant. 'That's good.'

'Shall we call a new truce, and let's make this one last?' she asked, gazing into his eyes, making Alex's chest expand to twice its normal size – which was such a contrast to his usual feeling of emptiness.

'Truce,' he repeated, but his voice sounded wrong. Ella offered a hand and Alex stared for a beat before he grasped it in his own. Hers was warm, and she squeezed it into his palm and shivered.

'Are you cold?' he asked, acknowledging his body was mirroring hers. He wasn't cold either and his shiver had nothing to do with the temperature of the room.

'Aye, I must be I suppose.' She nodded and dropped his hand before striding to the chair and scooping up the cardigan and pulling it on over her dress. 'Should we, um, practise our scene now?' she asked, her cheeks turning pink.

'Sure.' Alex nodded too many times.

What was happening? He was all over the place. Alex watched Ella pick up one of the glass slippers from the stage before handing it to him. Then she took her place on the chair, her pretty skirt fluttering around her legs.

He swallowed, acknowledging how much he wanted to kiss Ella. But there was a battle waging inside him – a war between his head and his heart – and he had no idea which of them he wanted to win.

# 18

## ELLA

Ella took in a deep breath as she watched Alex make his way towards her on the stage carrying the tiny slipper. He'd surprised her just now – his insistence that she should be eager to seek revenge on him. As if in the world he inhabited that was the only way to deal with an upset. To batten down the hatches and seek justice.

He'd obviously been shaken by her opinion of him, but Ella could see from the way Alex's cheeks had reddened and his eyes had darkened that he'd liked her version of him. Even if he was still denying it was accurate.

'So, what should I do?' he asked, standing in front of her, glancing around the stage. The lights in the ceiling were so bright now that she could smell the peppery heat from the bulbs. Their beams picked out the colour of Alex's eyes and the chiselled jawline that she'd imagined sketching and – who was she kidding – touching too.

Ella shrugged. 'I guess you need to get closer to the floor. You're not going to be able to get that slipper on my foot from all the way up there,' she joked, feeling awkward suddenly. She tugged the edges of her cardigan together as Alex did as she'd suggested, dropping onto one knee until his face was almost level with hers.

'What now?' he asked roughly.

'You know how the fairy tale goes. You're bowled over by my beauty.' Ella's words didn't make Alex laugh as she'd intended. Instead, he looked at her silently and her stomach did a somersault before landing in the top of her throat. 'Then –' Her voice sounded heavy. '– you ask if you can help me try on the slipper.' She glanced down at her feet. She was still wearing her shoes. She'd slipped them back on after getting dressed in her costume because she'd been worried about being cold. But the flames that were now burning through her limbs could probably heat the entire stage.

'May I?' Alex asked, gesturing to her foot.

'Or I can?' she offered, leaning down so she could take the shoe off herself.

'Let me do it, Ella,' Alex demanded, and whatever had somersaulted into her throat, vaulted again, landing low in her belly and flooding her with even more heat. 'You don't have to do everything,' he said, in a tone that made Ella think of rumpled sheets that had found their way onto the bedroom floor.

Ella gulped. 'Um, okay,' she said, the words almost sticking inside her throat.

Alex shifted closer and put his palm beneath her calf. Her insides increased the acrobatics and began to divebomb against her ribs. She shuddered and looked down at the same time as Alex looked up so their eyes collided. 'Is that okay?' he asked.

She nodded – because she couldn't trust herself to speak. Was it odd that just a few hours ago she'd disliked this man? Or at least she'd hated his picture. Hated the way he could see right through her and pinpoint every place in her life where she'd gone wrong.

How had they gone from there to here so rapidly? Why did

she feel like she knew him so much better after their short conversation?

She shuddered as Alex slid her shoe all the way off and let it fall onto the stage. His fingertips tickled the underside of her foot and Ella let out an involuntary humming sound.

'Sorry,' Alex murmured, although he didn't sound sorry, and when she met his eyes, they were full of heat – which proved he knew exactly what he was doing.

'It's okay,' she whispered, wishing she could ask him to do it again. Ella hadn't felt this turned on in, well, she didn't remember. There had been a few men in art college, but most of them had been more interested in their paintings or themselves than her. They'd never made her almost catapult off her chair simply from a touch...

Alex slid the glass slipper onto her foot and smiled charmingly. 'It's a perfect fit. Does that mean I should propose?' he asked, leaning back as if he was suddenly worried about crossing some invisible line.

'I think we should practise our kiss first?' Ella suggested, keeping her wobbly voice low and even.

Alex glanced at her, looking surprised. 'Mae said a peck would be okay,' he checked.

'It's up to you.' Ella shrugged, feeling self-conscious as she remembered they were on the stage and glanced around. The heavy velvet curtains Mae had drawn were still shut and gave them plenty of privacy. 'It's just we're here,' she said more eagerly now. 'We're supposed to be running through our scene and we've got no way of knowing if – when we kiss – we'll seize up. Because we're embarrassed,' she added in case she hadn't been clear.

'Seize up?' Alex's lips curved. He was smiling a lot for a man who always frowned.

'Aye, well. Stage fright, hysteria, performance anxiety, take your pick.' She shrugged. 'You never know what might happen on the night. Last year, I was Sleeping Beauty, and the prince, well.' She pulled a face. 'He almost fainted because his girl-friend was jealous and she told him she'd be watching his every move...'

Alex snorted. 'That's not something I need to worry about.'

She sighed. He was taking a lot more convincing than she'd have liked. 'The year before, I was Belle, in *Beauty and the Beast*. When the Beast tried to kiss me...' She shuddered. 'He almost had a panic attack when someone in the audience shrieked. The makeup department were particularly talented that year...'

Alex watched her face, his expression incomprehensible – although Ella was sure she could detect laughter in his eyes. At least she hoped she wasn't imagining it. She'd sensed him relaxing while they'd been talking and wanted to hold onto that.

'I had no idea that being in a pantomime was fraught with so much peril.' Alex shook his head. 'Well, in the interests of avoiding embarrassment, panic attacks or a fainting episode, I think you might be right. We should definitely practise our kiss.'

He rose to his feet and Ella found herself looking up.

'We can't very well do it down there,' Alex teased. 'Not properly anyway and I take my pantomime kisses very seriously. After all, Prince Charming's reputation is on the line.' His eyes twinkled, and Ella giggled, relieved that he hadn't been offended by her pushing.

He held out a hand and helped her up. 'How do you want to do this?' he asked, gazing at her mouth in a way that made Ella want to go up onto her tiptoes and grab him.

'I think kissing usually involves the pressing of lips together,' she said primly. She wasn't trying to tease Alex anymore – well, not much – but suddenly she was wondering if this was such a good idea.

She could already feel heat burning between them. It had been there since they'd met. At first it had been powered by dislike, then annoyance, but now it had transformed into appreciation, understanding and perhaps even liking him. She didn't want to fight it. Despite the fact that it wasn't a good idea. Didn't she have enough on her plate without catching feelings for a man like Alex Forbes-Charming?

She was probably going to get her heart broken, but at this moment, Ella really didn't care. She was fed up with doing the right thing, with worrying about everyone else. She was sick of cleaning other people's houses and dealing with her stepbrothers' constant absences, of Lucinda's demands and of worrying about a business that wasn't just hers. Weary of the thousand problems she couldn't share. She needed something for herself. A kiss with this man would be a perfect start.

'That sounds like it could work,' Alex said, shifting closer until Ella was staring at his chest. He was wearing a dark blue jumper, and she had a sudden urge to press her nose into the wool, to run her fingers up and down his sides, then rub them over his chest. 'Perhaps you should start by looking at me?' he suggested, sliding a fingertip under her chin. 'May I?'

'Aye,' she said huskily, and he tipped her face. Now they were closer she could see his pupils had almost blown. Her mouth felt dry, and she swiped her tongue across her lips.

'Good improvising,' he whispered as his eyes followed the movement. 'I'm feeling a little parched myself.'

'Must be the heat from the lightbulbs. But I've got an idea,' she said, and went up onto her tiptoes so she could press her mouth against his.

Alex had obviously been expecting the kiss – Ella could tell, because he immediately got into character by carefully wrapping his arms around her and leaning down so he could deepen it. Turning something that was meant to be playful – at least initially – into something far more real. This was no peck on the cheek, and it wasn't suitable for a PG pantomime either. But Ella just went with it, because there was no fighting this almost desperate craving building inside of her. She needed him now.

She let out a low moan in the base of her throat as the kiss grew hotter and thought she might have heard Alex echo the sound. Although it was difficult to hear anything above the buzz of voices in the main hall and rush of blood now pounding in her ears.

She reached her arms up and wound them around Alex's neck and pressed her body hard against his. He smelled really good up close. Of expensive aftershave with spicy tones of lemongrass and cardamom – which for some reason reminded her of Christmas. Or perhaps it just would from now on.

Alex tasted good too – and Ella tangled her tongue with his, marvelling at how quickly this day had changed.

It had already delivered a rollercoaster of emotions – from annoyance with her stepbrothers, to excitement when she'd gone to meet Alex at the tea room, to devastation when she'd seen the sketch.

But now she could only feel heat. And not just any heat. This was a searing, heart-pounding, pulse-accelerating, body-melting blaze. Desire like she'd never experienced. This was what the books, movies and Netflix series meant when they talked about chemistry.

Ella felt Alex pull back and tried to remain upright, although her knees weren't feeling cooperative, so she found herself leaning into him.

'Should we count that as a successful run-through?' he asked throatily, whispering into her hair.

'Well, you've definitely blown all the other princes out of my mind – and probably ruined me for the next one too,' she joked. 'We might have to tone it down for the opening night,' she croaked. 'There are going to be small children in the audience and grandparents too – I'm the only person who's supposed to swoon.'

'Do you think we should have another go, then?' he asked, his chest heaving.

'We could try.' She kept her face buried in his jumper. 'In the interests of getting it right. I'm sure Mae would appreciate us going the extra mile.'

Alex chuckled and the rumble of his body tickled her nose and sent a wave of warmth travelling downwards. 'That's one of my mottos, right up there with give everything your best.'

Ella pulled away so she could look into his face. 'You certainly did that.' She cleared her throat, wondering if her cheeks were luminous. Alex obviously didn't mind if they were, because he was looking at her with an expression that told her he was just as ravenous as she was – equally impatient to kiss again. 'Time for round two,' she whispered and went up onto her tiptoes.

This time, their kiss started soft which was calmer but still made Ella's stomach pitch and whirl like a Christmas carousel. She pressed her palms onto his shoulders and fought to stop herself from wrapping her arms around his neck again. Control was the order of this kiss, control and restraint, limitation and reserve. It wasn't about indulgence or need.

But the kiss deepened, and Ella found her arms winding their way around Alex's neck anyway, found herself pressing her body into his chest. Her heartbeat ramped up to wild and the kiss became hot, wet and fast – an exercise in urgency and abandon.

She was only glad they were on the stage because otherwise there was no telling what would happen – or how long her Cinderella dress and cardigan would remain in place. Her arms were already untwisting themselves and skimming down Alex's sides, intent on discovery – and he was obviously on the same page because his chaste grip on her waist had become an uninhibited exploration of her hips and the curvy globes of her rear.

Then suddenly someone cleared their throat, and Alex shot

away, grabbing Ella's arm to keep her upright as she twisted around to find Hunter, Aggie, Henry and Mae standing at the top of the stairs gaping at them.

'Yecch!' Hunter yelled, covering his eyes. 'Where's the fire extinguisher?' The boy trotted past them and shot towards the back of the stage.

'We will *not* be needing a fire extinguisher!' Aggie spluttered, racing after him.

'Well, the lad's right, I think I can still feel flames from here,' Mae said wryly, fanning a hand in front of her chest and arching an eyebrow at Ella.

Henry cleared his throat. 'Er, it looks like you've both sorted out your differences. Which is um, good,' he ground out, looking uncomfortable. While Sprout, who'd been watching them from beside his master's feet, let out a happy bark and then charged across the stage before hurling himself at Alex's legs as if he hadn't seen him for weeks. Alex leaned down to stop the dog from leaping up.

'Do you want us to run through it again?' Ella squeaked, hoping Mae would say no. Her whole body was trembling, and she wasn't sure if she could walk in a straight line, let alone do a chaste redo.

'Nae, lass,' Mae said, looking amused. 'You've clearly rehearsed enough.' She went to open the stage curtains as Hunter came running back holding the fire extinguisher.

'Don't worry, it's just a prop!' Aggie yelled as the boy pretended to douse Alex before turning the hose on Ella, giggling the whole time.

She couldn't help joining in, and when she glanced at Alex, he was laughing too. It looked good on him, and she wished she could help keep that look on his face.

'How about we all head down for a bite of something sweet?' Aggie suggested. 'Blair's just put out refreshments and we need Alex to try on his costume again. Oh, the lad's going to look bonnie.' She waggled her eyebrows.

'I need Alex to start helping with the scenery,' Henry grumbled.

'That'll have to wait,' Mae snapped. 'Although I'm impressed with the progress he's been making. Seems to me, he's a natural at the part.' Her gaze shot back to Ella, her eyes twinkling.

Then her godmother turned and made her way down the steps before signalling that they should follow. Ella let out a long breath before she went, wondering exactly what had just happened and how long it might be before they could do it again...

# 19

## ALEX

Alex stood back from his easel so he could study the sketch he'd been working on. The lines were almost there, and he was happy with the progress he'd made. He'd already used charcoal to sketch the outline of the landscape he planned to paint – and Henry had given him pointers on improving the perspective, helping him to establish darker and lighter shades for depth. Now it was time to start the real thing. But dread gnawed in the pit of his stomach. What if he got it wrong, what if his father hated it? Then again, why did he still care so much about his opinion? Alex didn't have an answer, but suddenly he wished Ella was here – maybe she'd have an idea?

He hadn't seen her for three agonising days. He knew she'd been working in the studio because her easel was covered in a long sheet, obscuring her new project. Also, a bag had appeared yesterday, which she'd left hooked over a chair – Henry had checked it and found a duster, coat, her glass slippers and a random sock. The artist had mentioned her coming in at odd hours, fitting in her art whenever she could, and Alex knew she'd been painting because the brushes on her table were sometimes still wet. He'd tried to catch her a few times –

arriving in the studio extra early or late after Henry had gone to bed, to no avail. Yesterday, he knew Ella had been in early because when he'd arrived, her cup of coffee was still warm. He'd gone to search for her in the kitchen, but Aggie had told him she'd had to leave.

Alex pressed his fingers to his lips, conjuring the kiss they'd shared on the stage the last time he'd seen her. They hadn't spoken afterwards – Hunter had been circling, and Blair had insisted they both try on costumes while Mae had wanted them to go through the ballroom scene. But he could still remember the feel of Ella's lips, recall the way his heart had pounded and how he hadn't wanted their encounter to end.

The feelings had surprised him, humbled him – and left him wanting more. Did she feel the same? And was he crazy for having such a strong attraction to someone he barely knew? To someone who made him feel vulnerable? His father would say he was.

He paced towards Ella's easel and reached for the sheet – perhaps her new painting would give him some answers? Some idea of what she was thinking and how she might feel.

'I don't think the lass wants anyone to see her work in progress.' Alex jumped and dropped the material as Henry suddenly spoke. 'She told me the picture is meant to be a surprise. I understand that. It's how I feel about my own,' Henry growled. Alex spun around as the artist emerged from the stairway, his cheeks splattered with paint. Henry wandered towards his own easel which was also covered in a white sheet. He stared at it, his expression pensive. 'Aye, some things aren't for everyone. Some work is private – meant for one pair of eyes.'

'Okay,' Alex said. Although he didn't have a clue what the older man was talking about. But if Ella's picture was only meant for one person, who was it?

Henry walked across the room and came to gaze at Alex's work. 'You've made good progress, lad, but you're going to have to get started on that soon or you'll be leaving Mistletoe before it's done.'

'I know,' Alex sighed. 'I'm just...'

'Afraid of getting it wrong?' Henry guessed. 'Aye.' He looked over at his canvas again and winced. 'I know that feeling. How do you feel about what you're going to draw?'

'Pretty good.' Alex took in a deep breath. He'd been waiting for Henry's question and already knew what he was going to say. Something had shifted since his conversation on stage with Ella – perhaps a result of all her compliments? How she'd made him feel like he wasn't a failure for the first time. His tongue had untangled itself and the reticence he normally felt about sharing his thoughts had eased. At least a little.

'I'm looking forward to seeing what my da thinks,' he admitted as he imagined his work enjoying pride of place in the reception of Charming Capital Management. 'He wanted something powerful, and I think I've got it right. The colours will be strong and vibrant, and the addition of snow makes me feel—'

He pursed his lips, because offering these insights was easier, but it still went against everything he'd been taught. How he shouldn't give anything away because it was like handing over ammunition. How keeping your feelings to yourself was the only path. He took in a long breath.

'It makes me feel like I want to build a snowman,' he said, letting the air out of his lungs as a memory flickered into his mind. Of icy mornings at boarding school when he'd sneaked into the gardens with Stan when no one was looking. He could remember building snowmen and the squeals of delight when one of them threw a snowball and the other retaliated, the subsequent battle of ice and laughter. He'd loved those days.

All that childhood innocence and sense of wonder he'd forgotten – all those emotions Alex was only starting to acknowledge now. He'd never be able to reminisce about any of it in front of Michael Charming, though. His father considered snowball fights – or play of any kind – a waste of time.

'Bravo, lad.' Henry winked. 'I knew you'd bleed eventually.'

Alex thought about Ella again, about the feelings she was helping him recognise and expose. 'I hope not,' he murmured.

The older man grinned before the smile dropped and he looked serious. 'I'd like to tell you that you're developing as an artist. I think meeting Ella and being in the pantomime has really helped to bring you out of yourself.' His tone was earnest, but Alex waited for the catch. 'I'm intrigued to see what you'll do with your painting.' Henry's attention strayed back to Alex's sketch. 'You have skills lad – I'm proud that you've been brave enough to let them show. That I had a part to play in that.'

Alex blinked as he absorbed the praise, shocked by the power of Henry's words, a little baffled at how much they affected him. 'Thanks,' he said eventually, his voice raspy as he realised it was the first compliment he'd received in a very long time – unless he counted the ones from Ella.

He couldn't articulate how much it meant, but Henry must have known, because he nodded once, then swiped his hands over his black Rolling Stones T-shirt as if scrubbing away lingering emotions. 'You're welcome, lad. Now enough with the compliments, you need to get on with proving me right.'

He indicated Alex's canvas and put 'Honky Tonk Woman' onto his mobile before connecting it to his speaker and ramping up the volume. Then Henry spun his easel all the way around until his canvas was hidden from view, swiped off the sheet and got to work.


Alex's mobile went off four hours later and he put his paintbrush to one side. The Rolling Stones were still playing, and he knew if he tried to talk, no one would be able to hear. He quickly trotted out of the studio and down the stairs, pausing when he reached the sitting room. He hadn't spent any time in this room, but it was a pretty space with a large Christmas tree to the right of the fireplace. Alex headed for one of the high-backed chairs beside it and answered the call as he slumped down.

'Iceman,' Stan said. 'Sorry we haven't spoken for a while.'

Alex smiled. 'I know how it is, so many shells, so little time...' he teased as he made himself comfortable. 'It's good to hear from you. I've missed our chats,' he blurted, the words rolling off his tongue before his brain caught up.

'It's good to speak to you,' Stan said slowly, sounding odd. 'Now can you tell me what you've done with Alex Forbes-Charming because he'd never say something like that?'

'Call it the Mistletoe effect,' Alex said as the fire beside him spat and he bent to throw another log onto the flames, marvelling at the colours. 'How's New Zealand?'

'The same as it was last week.' Stanley paused. 'You sound relaxed – or maybe drunk – so I'm assuming Michael hasn't mentioned that he fired me today?'

Alex sat bolt upright. 'He did what?' His insides churned. They'd only spoken a few days ago and his father hadn't mentioned a change of plans to him, but they'd been emailing constantly. 'He promised to give you at least a fortnight before he did anything. He mentioned he was thinking about replacing you, but... Well, you know what he said because I summarised every word?'

He'd mentioned his father's threats within hours of their conversation. Because forewarned was forearmed. And Stan had told Alex not to worry.

'Aye. I wasn't expecting my P45 yet, but I wasn't surprised. Your da is not a patient man.' He chuckled, but Alex didn't know why. It wasn't funny.

'What did he say?' he shot back tersely.

'The message was brief but decent and I've been given a

generous payout,' Stan told him, sounding relaxed. 'I'm happy –
I was ready for a change.'

'That's not the point!' Alex spluttered, rising to his feet so
he could pace. 'You've worked for our company for years. What
about loyalty to staff? My father promised me that he'd wait—'
The fact that he hadn't, that he'd ignored Alex's request was as
unsurprising as it was shattering.

'We both know Michael does what Michael wants and be
dammed with what anyone thinks.' Stan laughed. 'I'm not
upset, Alex,' he repeated. 'I called to see if you knew, but also
because I've got a proposition for you.'

'I'll speak to him. Get you un-sacked,' Alex promised in a
rush. Charming Capital Management would be an unthinkable
place without Stan. Having him leave wasn't an option. His
father *would* relent. He rubbed a palm over his forehead,
fighting the rush of disappointment and temper.

'I don't want my job back, Alex,' Stan said quietly.

'You'll change your mind,' he snapped. 'You're going to get
bored of travelling, of searching for shells.'

'I already am,' Stan said lightly. 'That's one of the reasons
why I'm calling.' He sucked in a breath. 'I've been thinking a lot
and today's news has made me decide. I want us to go into business together. To do the same as we do now, although we'll add
some heart. I've got money my grandpa left me, and I've already
spoken to some very wealthy people who are willing to work
with me. With us.' He paused as Alex absorbed his words.
'Don't say anything now. I'm going to put all the details in an
email. Speak to a lawyer. I dinnae know, maybe your artist can
give you his perspective. They're good at that I hear,' he joked.

'This isn't funny,' Alex said tightly, shaking his head.

'Read the email, Iceman,' Stan said quietly. 'Then we'll
talk.' With that, his friend hung up.

Five minutes later, Aggie found Alex staring into the fire
still trying to calm down. She was carrying a slice of Christmas

cake and a mug of tea. 'Ach, I thought I heard you talking in here earlier,' she said kindly, offering them to him. 'I want to ask you a favour.'

'Whatever you need,' Alex grumbled, trying to smile at her when he realised he'd sounded angry.

'Hunter's not feeling well, and I need to pick him up from school. Ella called to say she'd left some things in the studio the other day.' She shook her head. 'Again. She wanted me to drop them by her on my way home, but...' She stared at him, clearly wanting Alex to fill in the blanks.

'You can't,' he guessed.

'Aye. Could you go to her house for me please, lad? If I tell her I can't do it, I know she'll try to fit it in herself. Her eejit stepbrothers have been running rings around her all week.' She sighed. 'Clyde called in sick again this morning, even though I saw him in the café last night.'

'I thought she was going to speak to her stepmother about them?' Alex asked, rising so he could pace the room again, trying to burn off his irritation with his father and now his annoyance at Ella's relatives.

'Aye.' Aggie nodded, her face tightening. 'I believe she did, but the woman's not interested in anyone criticising her boys.' She grimaced. 'The lass has been running herself ragged all week, trying to keep Henry happy by coming to the studio every day, while Clyde and Dane keep calling in sick.' She blinked. 'It can't go on, lad. Someone's got to talk her into having it out with them.' She stared at him intently.

'You mean me?' Alex asked, reading her expression. 'Let me get her bag,' he said, thinking about his father. Ella was in a similar position – beholden to a family who never listened; underappreciated and confused.

He might not be able to fix his own life – but he was going to do whatever he could to help Ella McNally with hers.

# 20

## ALEX

Alex was walking along Mistletoe's high street when the heavy snowball came out of nowhere and hit the back of his head with a loud, *thwack!* Its remnants bounced off the window of The Snug Tea Room and shattered, while icy stragglers slid down his neck.

'Oy!' He yelled as he heard the thunder of feet and spun around, searching for whoever had thrown it. He immediately spotted two figures dressed in dark snowsuits with red and white lacy petticoats pulled over the top, sprinting away and laughing. They were both tall and had black hats pulled over their faces. Scraps of what looked like orange and blonde wigs poked from the bottom like octopus's arms. Despite the disguise – or perhaps because of it – Alex knew who they were. What kind of eejits wore their pantomime costumes to ambush people?

He cursed and narrowed his eyes as ice dripped down his back and watched as they followed the path of the Christmas lights that lined the pavement, before disappearing down a side street. 'I'm coming for you,' he muttered, taking a step, intending to follow, just as he heard a jangle from the café door.

'Did you just throw a snowball at my window, lad?' Blair McBride asked, sounding surprised.

Alex turned to face her and shook his head. 'Nae, but I saw the two culprits run down that street.' He pointed to the spot where they'd just disappeared. 'I know who they are—'

'Clyde and Dane McNally?' Blair's eyes glittered and she pursed her lips. 'Aye, lad. Were they wearing their ugly sister costumes?'

'Aye,' Alex said, intrigued. 'How did you know?'

She looked annoyed. 'It isn't the first time. They think they're being funny. Last year, when they were back for Christmas, they dressed up as a pantomime horse and cracked my window.' She shook her head.

'What did you do?' Alex asked, surprised.

She shrugged. 'Lucinda refused to accept it was them. Although the costume was still soggy the following day. She made up an *alibi* as she called it. The lads both had a bad toothache, which meant they couldn't go out apparently. Although I'm still not sure how toothache affected their feet. *Eejits!*' She grimaced. 'I doubt their mam would believe it was them tonight either, considering she told me earlier they were both at death's door.' She rolled her eyes. 'Those two have got more lives than a cat! They're just as lazy too.'

'Aye. I heard they've been sick again,' Alex said, shaking his head. 'Aggie told me Ella's been working all their shifts.' He took in a deep breath. 'I don't understand why she keeps covering for them.'

What was she waiting for? Ella *knew* her brothers were lying. She'd even accepted it the other day.

Blair's mouth pinched. 'The lass has a soft heart – and it's not always easy to take on your family – especially when it's the only one you have,' she said. 'Also, she made a promise to her da—'

'Aye,' Alex said, 'but don't you think she's kept that promise for long enough?' Blair shrugged. 'Although...' He could hardly fault Ella when he hadn't confronted his father about sacking his best friend yet. Sometimes, loyalty and expectation were harder to navigate than it seemed.

Blair stepped back into the tea room, signalling to Alex that he should follow. 'It's too cold to have the door open,' she said as she headed towards the counter without looking back.

The tea room was busy and the buzz of voices soothing. Being in Mistletoe was so different from Alex's usual world, and he was beginning to love it here – which made little sense. He should be missing the push and pull of the office. The high figure deals and adrenaline rush he got from winning. Should still be craving the scraps of approval his father occasionally delivered, the surge of gratitude he felt when he received a half-hearted compliment. Only he wasn't...

'Aggie called and told me she'd asked if you'd pop something in to Ella, so I've been looking out for you. I wondered if you'd take her some Christmas cake too – she's not been eating properly. Also, I've just written her Christmas card and the postman popped in earlier and forgot to take it with him.'

She disappeared into the back room before returning with a festive tin and a red glittery envelope. 'Here you go.' She handed them both over and Alex put them in Ella's bag. 'There's enough in the tin for you. Get the lass to eat if you can.' She frowned. 'And make her sit while she's doing it.'

'I'll do my best,' Alex promised, fully intending to feed Ella something while he encouraged her to see sense about her step-brothers. 'I'll catch up with you at rehearsals,' he said, realising he was looking forward to seeing the older woman again.

'Aye – you know you make a really good Prince Charming,' Blair said after a long pause. 'Probably even better than the original.'

She winked and Alex nodded, too touched by her words to respond. Still feeling tongue-tied, he headed out of the door.

. . .

Alex had to use Google Maps to find Ella's house. It was a couple of streets away from the high street, but the snowfall had grown heavier since he'd left the tea room, which meant it was more difficult to find. He paused at the front gate and checked the address twice on his mobile because the house looked smaller and shabbier than he'd expected. Also, there were no Christmas decorations anywhere and, considering Ella had covered most of Pinecone Manor with tinsel and lights, he was surprised.

He knocked and it took a few minutes until the door opened.

'Alex!' Ella exclaimed. She looked an endearing mixture of tired and shocked. She shoved her hands over her cheeks as if attempting to hide her expression. 'Are you okay?' She moved back into the small hallway as Wyatt bustled past and came to give Alex a sniff.

'I'm fine,' he said, stroking the dog. 'Can I come in?'

'Aye, sorry.' She moved and waited as he shut the door then made his way into the house, taking a moment to tug off his boots and coat before handing her the bag. 'Aggie asked me to bring your things. There's cake in the tin and a Christmas card from Blair too.'

Ella stared at him. 'That was kind,' she said. 'Of you I mean.'

Alex felt the punch of the words hit deep. He wasn't used to compliments, but he'd received more today than in the last year and he wasn't sure what to make of it. Couldn't bring himself to articulate how it made him feel.

He shoved his hands into his pockets as Ella continued to stare. Her gaze slowly dropped to his mouth, and his body heated as he took a step forward – just as Wyatt decided to bark.

'I'm sorry!' Ella jerked away. 'I don't know what's got into me. You must be cold. Do you want to sit?' She turned and quickly charged down the hallway leading him into a sitting room.

The room was small, but there was enough space for a small green sofa and a matching chair. Alex saw a glowing fireplace in the corner and went to stand in front of it, enjoying the heat. He turned and spotted a tiny Christmas tree in front of the window – it had been covered haphazardly in decorations, suggesting Ella hadn't had much time. A pile of papers sat on a small glass coffee table next to the sofa. Beside that was a large basket filled with washing which Alex guessed belonged to Ella's step-brothers because he recognised some of the shirts. 'Ignore the mess,' she said, looking embarrassed. 'That's just ironing Lucinda asked me to do.'

'You haven't spoken to your stepbrothers, have you?' Alex blurted as he finished looking around.

Ella's shoulders sagged.

'You're good at being kind to others – why aren't you doing the same for yourself?' he asked.

Ella swallowed and then plucked a letter from the pile on the table. 'I was going to. On the day after the rehearsal.' Red skimmed up her cheeks as if she were suddenly recalling their kiss and Alex had to stop himself from reaching for her. 'I got as far as Lucinda's house. I was going to talk to her about Clyde and Dane.' She frowned. 'But before I could, she gave me this.' She sighed and waved the envelope. 'It's from the bank. It's not the first one we've had, but this is a final warning.' She handed it to Alex. 'You can read it if you like.'

He unfolded the paper and scanned the contents. 'Magic Mops is in debt.' He winced at the numbers.

'Aye.' She looked weary. 'It has been for a while. Da took out a loan before he died and since then things have just got worse.'

'Because you're the only one doing any work,' he said sourly. 'You should leave.'

She laughed, but the sound was sad. 'If I could just get my hands on some money, I'd pay off the debt and then I probably would. But—' She pulled a face. 'I can't leave them in this mess.'

'It's not *all your* mess, Ella,' Alex said, folding the letter and putting it back into the envelope.

'Da asked me to take care of the business. He begged me. I wouldn't be able to forgive myself.' A tear trickled down her pale cheek, and Alex gritted his hands into fists. This wasn't his mess to fix either.

*This is not your problem.* He told himself, even as he found himself stepping forward and taking Ella into his arms. 'You can still talk to your stepbrothers, this doesn't change that,' he said as she pressed her face into his chest, making everything inside him heat up.

'Clyde thinks they've both got tonsillitis. I don't know what to think. They could be lying – but what if they're telling the truth?' She shook her head, and Alex got a waft of eucalyptus again, found himself breathing it in and closing his eyes.

He let out a long breath. 'I saw your stepbrothers earlier.' Ella went still. 'They were throwing snowballs in the high street. One hit me. Neither of them looked sick.'

'It's snowing, lots of people are out in the snow,' she said, speaking to his chest. The warmth from her breath seeped through his clothes, making him shiver, but not with cold. 'How do you know it was them?'

'I'm not sure how many other burly men would be running around Mistletoe's high street wearing their wigs and pantomime dresses,' he muttered.

Ella pulled back, her eyes wide. 'They were wearing their costumes? Aggie and Blair will murder them.'

'Unless we do it first?' he joked and grinned at her when she laughed. 'Or we could just catch them out?'

'You mean now?' Her eyes widened.

'It's the only way anything's going to change.' He stared at her. She looked terrified. But there was a spark in her eyes too – something that looked a little like hope. 'Isn't it time you stopped being Cinderella?' he asked gently. 'I'm not saying you should walk away from Magic Mops, but your stepbrothers have to start stepping up.'

Ella blinked and Alex wondered if she was going to refuse – then she slowly nodded. 'Okay, but let's go now before I change my mind.' She offered him her hand.

Alex took it and squeezed, ignoring the rush of warm pleasure he felt. Something inside him was changing – he just didn't know if he should embrace it or run.

# 21

ELLA

'We're sick, you can't come in,' Clyde rasped as Ella pressed her fingertips into the letterbox on the door of her stepbrothers' house, trying to prise it open so she could see. She and Alex had been knocking for the last five minutes, but so far, he'd refused to let them in.

'Dane's been googling our symptoms,' Clyde shouted in between a couple of hacking coughs. 'It's worse than tonsilitis. We might have a tropical disease. It's infectious and we feel *really, really* bad. Even mam's not come to visit.'

Ella rose from where she'd been kneeling and met Alex's eyes. He was staring at her with an odd expression, one that said she couldn't possibly be falling for their lies. She shook her head to confirm she wasn't as she turned to peruse the front garden. Two snowmen had joined the single one she'd seen the week before. One of the new ones wore Clyde's bright orange pantomime wig, and Ella stomped across the envelope of glittering snow so she could grab it. It was soaked. She sighed as she shoved it into her pocket. The McBrides were going to be furious – but she wasn't going to be covering for her stepbrothers this time.

Ella turned in time to see Alex rise from where he'd been kneeling. The doormat was askew, and he was waving a door key. Ella grinned and took it from his hand, then opened the door.

'What are you doing?' Clyde gasped as Ella walked into the hallway and took in her stepbrother's hastily tied dressing gown which was bulging. Ella guessed he was wearing his snowsuit underneath, probably with the legs pulled up. But a red and white spotty petticoat poked from the hem giving him away. His cheeks were bright pink – almost the exact same shade as the last time she'd visited.

Wyatt suddenly nudged past her and pressed his nose to the carpet, taking in a couple of noisy sniffs before he padded towards the two pairs of large snow boots that were sitting by the kitchen door. Ella saw a puddle of water had spread from the soles at the same moment her stepbrother noticed and widened his eyes.

'I don't know why they're wet,' Clyde blustered. 'I think Wyatt just peed on them,' he accused, snarling at her dog in an attempt to intimidate him.

'I think you'll find Wyatt prefers doing his business on my Volvo,' Alex said dryly as he followed them in and shut the door.

'You need to leave!' Clyde complained, shooing them away petulantly with his hands. 'I feel really bad, and I want to go to bed. If you've brought food, you can just leave it in there.' He wafted a palm towards the kitchen door.

Ella regarded him as she began to unbutton her coat. 'I'm here because we need to talk and I'm not going anywhere until we do,' she said quietly. She knew she should be angry, but seeing her stepbrother exposed just made her feel foolish. It was way past time they had this conversation, and she wanted to get it over with so she could go home.

Wyatt let out a low whine and left the snow boots, heading into the sitting room.

'He's probably cold,' Ella said as Clyde watched her dog disappear.

'He needs to leave,' her stepbrother snapped. 'You all need to. I don't feel good.' He pressed the back of his hand to his brow.

'Clyde, you're not ill,' Ella said wearily.

'Oh, yes, I am!' He opened his eyes again looking surprised.

'Oh, no, you're not,' Alex said, emphasising each word, clearly making the most of the pantomime phrase which just helped to punctuate how ridiculous Ella's life had become. Alex stepped forward until they were standing side by side.

It felt good to have his support. She'd felt so alone for so many months. Not that she was going to allow herself to get used to it. Alex was leaving; he had his big important job to return to. His father to impress. There was no place in his world for her.

'Where's Dane?' she asked.

If they were going to have this conversation, it might as well be with both of them.

'In bed,' Clyde said just as there was a noise from the stairs and Ella's jaw dropped as Dane came trotting down wearing a black snowsuit with his pantomime skirt pulled over the top. He had a pair of blue earphones over his ears and was singing 'We Wish You a Merry Christmas' at the top of his voice. The words trailed off when he reached the bottom and spotted them. 'Um.' His eyes shot to Clyde's and widened. 'What are you doing here?' he croaked.

'I have some things to say,' Ella said, feeling sad. She'd suspected her stepbrothers were lying when she'd visited the other day – and her suspicions had grown at the pantomime rehearsals. Then the light Alex had shone on their behaviour in the form of his sketch had been the point she'd finally accepted the truth.

But there something truly hurtful about seeing it in all its glory – with realising she really had been taken advantage of. By her so-called *family*.

She cleared her throat. 'You've been lying to me,' she said simply. 'About being sick.'

'No, we haven't!' Dane said, hastily removing the pantomime skirt from around his waist trying to look indignant. 'Ella, we just went for a walk. We've been cooped up in this house for days. I thought some fresh air would help, but it didn't...'

Wyatt trotted back into the hallway from the sitting room carrying something between his teeth.

'What's that?' Clyde asked, trying to grab the bloodhound's collar and missing.

Wyatt wandered up to Alex and dropped the item by his feet.

'That's mine, you need to give it back!' Dane said urgently, trying to grab it but not before Alex picked it up.

It was a circular golden container and Ella watched as he turned it over and flipped open the top. 'This looks like—'

'The blusher the makeup department have been using at the pantomime,' Ella said, shaking her head at her stepbrothers. 'I *knew* you looked strange when I visited the other day. You were wearing blusher to make yourselves look sick. You've been lying to me all along.'

Dane gulped and Clyde shook his head. 'Oh, no, we—'

'Haven't?' Alex asked, his tone sarcastic. Her stepbrothers both flushed. 'You've been caught, boys, the least you can do is admit it.'

'You've been letting me do all your work for months,' Ella said as tears pricked her eyes and the truth unfolded in her mind. 'Ever since you finished university and joined the business.'

She didn't know what was worse – the fact that they'd lied, or that she'd been stupid enough to believe them. If Alex hadn't come to Mistletoe, would she have covered for them for the rest of their lives?

'We don't like cleaning.' Dane pouted.

'You think I do?' Ella snapped, getting into his face. Her stepbrother grimaced and his chin dropped. 'I did it to help out, because I thought it was my duty. Do you know how many hours I've worked this week?' She threw up her hands. 'I've been cleaning, mopping, dusting and keeping on top of all of our clients – alone! This is a family business. Only it's not, is it?'

'What do you mean?' Clyde asked, looking genuinely confused.

'I mean I have no family,' she said, her voice cracking. 'I lost all of it when Da died.'

'You have us,' Dane said. 'We're your brothers, Ella.'

She shook her head as she gazed at them. 'If you were, you'd never have left me to do all of the work.'

'We're young,' Clyde complained. 'Ask mam. We just need to grow up.'

'Now you sound like Lucinda. The thing is, boys, you're twenty-two and that is grown up. It's about time you started behaving like men.' Ella blinked as they gaped at her, and Alex took her hand giving her the strength to continue.

'You need to know Magic Mops has debts.' Dane and Clyde both frowned. 'Aye, but I'm going to do whatever I can to pay them off. After I do, the rest is going to be up to you. I'm not covering for you anymore. You come to work or the job doesn't get done.'

Her voice hardened. 'My da wouldn't want me to live like this. We either thrive and survive together – or the business dies.' Ella stared at them wondering how she'd missed all the signs. Wondering if her father really would forgive her for giving up. 'You two need to decide what happens now. Are you in or out?'

'We're in, obviously,' Dane muttered.

'Of course,' Clyde echoed.

'Aye, well, time will tell,' Ella said before she spun around and marched to the door, guiding Alex and Wyatt through it, before turning and shutting it in her brothers' pale faces.

'I think they just got the shock of their lives,' she said to Alex. 'I don't know how I feel about it, though. We might lose everything.'

'It was time to make a change. But for what it's worth, I think they might step up. They looked really upset,' he said.

'Thank you.' She turned to him. 'I don't know if I'd have done that without you.'

'You would have, Ella,' Alex said gently. 'It just might have taken you a little more time to get there.' He took her hand. 'How about I walk you home and you get some rest?'

'Aye.' She sighed.

'And I'll expect you at Pinecone Manor bright and early. You've got a picture to paint.'

'Don't worry.' Ella squeezed Alex's hand. 'I'll be there. I'm definitely due a few days off...'

## 22

### ELLA

'Can I help you paint?' Hunter begged for the fourth time as he paced the stage in the Mistletoe Village Hall. 'I'd be really good,' he implored, bouncing towards Alex who was unpacking pots and brushes, placing them next to a backdrop and a couple of fountain-shaped constructions which were going to be part of the scenery. The boy picked up one of the brushes and flicked it in the air.

'It's too late, lad,' Aggie said as she fluffed a hand over the mouse ears Hunter never seemed to take off. 'You've got school tomorrow, and we're going to be back here for another rehearsal after that.'

'Aye, boys need plenty of rest if they want to perform well,' Henry ground out as he wiped his hands over his white Rolling Stones T-shirt, smearing green all over the logo. 'Lasses too.' He raised an eyebrow at Ella.

'I've been sleeping fine.' She grinned back at him because for the first time in a year, she wasn't on her knees with tiredness.

'Aye, I've noticed the bags under your eyes have reduced,'

the older man joked. 'I also hear Clyde and Dane have been working their shifts for a change.'

'Yep,' Aggie agreed. 'They've started looking after their pantomime costumes too. I've no idea what's got into them all of a sudden, have you?' She wagged a finger at Ella.

Ella shrugged. In the four days since she'd spoken to her stepbrothers, their whole attitude had changed. Suddenly they were working hard, turning up to their cleaning shifts, and even offering to cover hers – and there was no talk of toothaches, tonsilitis or tropical diseases. In fact, they seemed to be enjoying taking on their responsibilities.

It felt like a fairy tale, but she was still waiting for them to switch back – like one of the carriages in the panto transforming into a pumpkin once the clock had struck midnight.

'I noticed Lucinda isn't talking to you,' Aggie commented. It wasn't the first time the housekeeper had mentioned it, but Ella didn't feel up to sharing.

'Are you talking about all those angry glares she's been shooting at the lass during rehearsals?' Mae asked as she appeared from the back of the stage wearing a swishy blue skirt that emphasised her figure. Henry's jaw dropped as he gazed at her, entranced.

'She's going all out playing the evil stepmother,' Aggie said.

'Aye, her acting has definitely improved,' Mae agreed. 'I've started to believe she actually hates Cinderella for real.' Her gaze turned to Ella, and she grimaced.

'She never speaks to me, but I think she hates mice too,' Hunter said glumly as he swiped the brush in the air. 'She makes a funny face whenever I'm around.'

'She's not very happy with me,' Ella admitted. But she was trying hard not to care. Her stepmother had used her for months, making her feel guilty each time she'd so much as suggested having a day off. It was only now that she was able to accept the truth. Because of Alex.

'Aye, well, it's good to have you in my studio painting rather than mopping for a change,' Henry said gruffly as he shot Mae another longing look which she ignored. Ella smiled at him. She'd made so much progress with her secret project over the past few days, felt like she was finally finding her painting feet again.

'Are you sure I can't help you with the scenery?' Hunter repeated, skipping around the stage with his brush, swiping at them. 'Mice like me don't need much sleep and we really love painting.' He yawned as he swept past Ella again.

'Lad, if you don't get enough sleep, you won't be able to work on your drawings,' Alex stepped in, his voice kind.

'I suppose.' Hunter looked thoughtful. 'I've been working on some new pictures.' He perked up as he wandered back to the pots of paint and put the brush down. 'One of a dog for my da and another for you. I'll show it to you at our next rehearsal,' he said eagerly.

'That's a deal.' Alex bumped fists with him, his cheeks flushing charmingly when he noticed everyone was watching.

'We should go,' Aggie said, taking her grandson's hand.

'So should I,' Mae sighed. 'I've got to work through some paperwork and check on ticket sales.'

Henry looked crestfallen. 'Aye, I should go too.' He turned to Alex. 'Is it okay if I leave you to work on the scenery?' He pointed to the paint on his T-shirt. 'I've been at it all evening, but I need to get back to my latest masterpiece. It's really important I get it done.' His eyes strayed to Mae and warmed.

'That's fine with me,' Alex said as Sprout came to give his shoe a swift lick.

A week ago, Ella knew Alex would have pulled a face, but instead he patted the terrier's antler headband and fed him a carrot from his pocket. As soon as he had, Wyatt's ears pricked up and he sniffed his way across the stage until Alex fed him too. 'Do you want to leave the dog? I can take care of him,' he asked Henry.

'Nae, Sprout's okay to come with me,' the older man muttered, clipping on his lead and turning towards the stairs before he stopped and twisted around to look at Ella. 'How in Jackson Pollock did you get your stepbrothers to pull their weight?'

She shook her head. 'Christmas magic.' She glanced at Alex. 'Plus I got a little help.'

'Perhaps one day you'll tell me the story,' Henry mulled. 'I need to get off,' he said abruptly, following Aggie, Hunter and Mae as they walked away.

When the door to the village hall swung shut behind them, Alex moved so he could study the canvas that Henry had laid down. The artist had already sketched the picture he wanted recreated and had begun to paint the grass.

'You know you don't have to help?' Alex said. 'I'm the protégé. This is supposed to be my job.'

'I want to.' Ella held out a hand, and he picked up a brush and gave it to her. 'I owe Henry for being so patient with me – and I owe you.'

'You said you don't do tit for tat – and neither do I.' Alex's eyebrows dipped. 'At least I don't do it here.'

'Maybe I just want to help?' she asked, holding her breath in case Alex told her he didn't want her to stay. They'd rarely been alone since he'd walked her back to her house after speaking with her stepbrothers – and she wanted to talk with him. Wanted to see that same flicker in his eyes from the night he kissed her.

He watched her face for a moment, and then nodded. 'Do you want to work from the bottom and I'll start at the top?'

'Or we could begin at each end and work our way towards each other?' Ella suggested.

Alex's mobile began to ring and he pulled it from his pocket and frowned. 'It's my father.' His voice was dull. 'I need to talk to him. But...' He sighed, stabbing at the screen. 'I think I'll do it later, when I get back to Pinecone Manor.' There was something about the deliberate rejection of the call that made Ella wonder if things between them had got even worse.

'Have you got your da a ticket to watch the pantomime?' she asked as she opened one of the pots and carefully loaded her brush.

'He won't come,' Alex said as his mobile rang again and he ignored it.

Ella studied Alex as he got to work. Could she help to fix whatever had happened between him and his father? After all he'd done for her, it only seemed fair. The pantomime was going to be brilliant, and Alex was a large part of why.

Her father had always been excited to watch her perform, sitting in the front row, enthusiastically clapping and laughing. Surely Michael Charming would do the same? They might have their differences, but a father was a father, after all. Alex clearly wasn't a man who was comfortable with singing his own praises, so perhaps he was just embarrassed to ask? Could she step in?

She could ask Henry tomorrow. He and Michael definitely knew each other, so he was bound to have his contact details. Happy with her plan, Ella began to hum and dab her brush on the canvas.

'I've never been involved with anything like this before,' Alex shared, as he watched her for a moment and then began to paint too.

'I've mucked in a couple of times,' Ella told him. 'Henry's protégés aren't always as talented as you – and he's sent a couple of them home before the panto even began.'

'You think I'm talented?' Alex sounded so surprised Ella turned to look at him.

'Don't you?' she asked, surprised. 'It's not like you'd be working with Henry if you weren't.'

'I have skills.' He shrugged. 'But that's not why I'm here. I'm an emergency replacement because someone dropped out. Henry would have struggled to get anyone else around Christmas at such short notice.'

Ella pulled a face. 'Can you imagine Henry Lockhart putting up with just anyone who could pick up a brush?'

'I can paint, but I'm not particularly gifted.' He looked unconvinced. 'My father can be very determined when he sets his mind to something – most people find it's easier to say yes. I'm sure Henry would tell you if you asked that I was a hard sell – it's why I need to work twice as hard to be even half as good as you.' The words fanned Ella's ego even though they weren't entirely true.

'But you're really talented, Alex,' she insisted. His arrogance had faded so much over the last two weeks, and she liked him so much better because of it. But surely Alex understood he deserved his place at Pinecone Manor?

His brows knitted and his paintbrush hovered a few centimetres from the canvas. 'I'm not fishing for compliments, Ella, you've already given me more than I need. I'm not a charity case who needs their ego building – it's large enough without your help.' His voice was stiff, and his body arched away from her. Then he shook his head and put the brush back on top of the pot. 'I'm sorry, that was rude. I'm just—'

'Surprised?' she guessed. 'You're amazing. That picture you did of me.'

He flushed.

'I might not have liked what it said, but it was brilliant. The details, every line, the way you brought so much to life. It must have taken hours?'

Alex looked uncomfortable. 'I believe in consistency and hard work.'

'You're embarrassed,' she gasped. 'Aren't you used to people saying nice things to you?'

Alex might not get on well with his father, but he was hormone-stirringly handsome, smart and funny – when he felt comfortable enough to share his humour. He had an incredible job and a real talent for art. He kept his kindness and warmth hidden – but Ella had seen enough hints of it now to know it wasn't just there, it was genuine. Surely other people had seen that. Told him?

'Too much approval can make people idle – and they stop trying,' Alex said as his face went crimson.

'That's not my experience,' Ella countered. 'I have to admit, I don't get that many compliments. But when I do, I feel amazing. They make me want to try harder, so I can feel that way again.'

Alex studied her. 'Aye, well, that's something my father says. I suppose I've always believed he was right.' His face clouded and he picked up his brush looking thoughtful. Ella watched. It was clear from their time together that Alex wasn't used to sharing and he certainly wasn't used to opening up. But she wanted to know more, wanted to understand him and the only way to do that would be to continue to poke at him until he broke.

Alex stroked his brush across the bottom of the canvas. 'You're doing a great job of that,' she said, trying out another compliment to gauge what reaction she'd get.

Alex's face twisted into an awkward smile. 'I'd be doing a better job if you helped,' he said gruffly. Although the fresh flood of colour across the tips of his cheeks suggested he wasn't immune to her words.

Ella grinned and picked up her brush and began to paint too, edging closer to the centre of the canvas until her elbow brushed against Alex's a couple of times.

'You smell good,' she said as her nose picked up the spicy

scent of lemongrass and cardamon, and her skin tingled and fizzed.

Alex shifted until they were facing and gave her an odd look. 'It's just my aftershave,' he said roughly. But his eyes had darkened a few shades despite the overhead lights, and she guessed he was pleased with this compliment, perhaps even stirred by it? Although she knew he'd probably never admit to that.

But she liked that she'd affected him, had managed to burrow between the layers he used to protect himself.

'I couldn't believe you knew all your lines when we were rehearsing earlier,' she said, painting the canvas without looking at him. 'You were word perfect. It took me ages to memorise mine. You work so hard; I've never met anyone with a work ethic like yours.'

'Except for yourself,' Alex said, looking at her oddly. 'What are you doing?' he asked.

'Complimenting you.'

'Why?' He eased away, his shoulders tensing.

Ella leaned onto her haunches, mirroring him. 'I don't know,' she admitted. 'It's just I've a feeling in your world people don't do it enough.'

'You're right. People don't pay me compliments in my world,' he said, his forehead pinching. 'Not unless they want something.' He turned and carefully put his brush on the top of the pot. 'So, what do you want?'

Ella's brain helpfully suggested a couple of things which she wasn't going to share. But her cheeks suddenly felt like she'd been sitting in the Mediterranean sun for the whole afternoon – and she could tell Alex noticed because his eyes skimmed her face and he swallowed nervously.

'I don't want anything, Alex,' she said. 'You helped me face what was happening with Clyde and Dane – helped me to call them out.' She brushed a hand through her hair. 'And it worked.' Her eyes rounded. 'I wouldn't have changed a thing without you. If you hadn't shown me what an eejit I've been. Without you—'

'Highlighting your faults?' he asked, his tone tight. 'Aye, I'm good at that,' he said gruffly. 'It's easier to focus on other people's than your own.'

'You have faults?' she gasped, deliberately using a teasing tone.

Alex dipped his chin and his chest bounced.

'Did you just laugh?' Ella offered Alex a wide grin.

'No.' He half laughed, half choked and thumped a hand on his jumper. 'I think I might have broken something, though.' He offered her a shy smile.

'Oh damn.' She swiped the back of her hand across her brow. 'I think I'm going to swoon. I've told you already, you'd better not do it on the night of the pantomime, the whole of the front row will probably black out, then Mae will hit you with her magic wand.'

This time, Alex laughed out loud and the sound had something inside Ella tripping over itself in its eagerness to get him to do it again.

'Aye, well, you don't need to worry about that. Could be this is just a temporary blip due to paint fumes.' He nodded at the pots. 'Normal service will resume shortly. You'd only have to speak to my team at the office to get an idea of the type of person I am.' He gazed at her for a moment before reaching out to pick up the paintbrush again, clearly shaken.

'You don't know yourself very well, do you?' Ella asked quietly. 'Because from what I can see, you're really quite something.'

Alex cleared his throat but didn't look at her. Instead, he leaned into the canvas and began to slowly paint. She could see she'd affected him because his hand wasn't steady and after a few moments he gave up and put the paintbrush down. Then he turned back to her and his gaze grew fiery, making everything inside Ella go hot...

## 23

### ELLA

'I...' Alex shook his head and gulped. 'I'm... I don't know what to say without sounding like I have a huge ego or I'm conceited. Neither appeals.'

'When we met, I thought you were both, so you've got nothing to lose.' Ella joked.

Alex chuckled, his chest vibrating, and Ella wondered if he'd ever laughed this much in one go.

'You might as well try me,' she pressed. 'I promise to listen without judgement – at least until you're done.'

He shook his head. 'I don't talk. No one wants to listen to someone whining.' He sounded frustrated.

'Is it really whining, though?' Ella asked. 'I bend Mae's ear off all the time if I'm having a bad day and if Aggie or Blair are around, I go to them. It's important to share. We all need to offload onto somebody. It's what keeps us sane.'

Ella realised the irony as she said it. How many times had she shrugged off that advice herself, preferring instead to ignore her problems?

He winced. 'I have my mate Stan, he talks to me.' He paused. 'I'm not sure if I've ever talked back, but I don't think so. He was surprised the other day when I told him I was pleased to hear from him.' He fell silent considering the revelation. 'It must be exasperating for him,' he said faintly. 'But he never said.'

'Perhaps he's just waiting until you're ready?' she suggested. 'Friends do that, good ones anyway.'

He let out a long breath. 'Maybe. He's in New Zealand at the moment – but he's coming home soon. He wants me to work with him, but I don't know what to do.' His eyebrows met and his chest heaved. 'Talking like this, sharing, feels, I dinnae know—'

'Terrifying?' Ella guessed.

He raised an eyebrow. 'Jeez. You sound like Henry. You don't hold back, do you?' He swallowed. 'I don't think I'm afraid, it's hard to explain. If I was going to try, I'd say my feelings don't matter. They're an indulgence – something to work through and ignore. All that's important is what I do and achieve. How high I climb. My success and happiness are linked to how well I paint, how much money I make, how good I look, who wants to work with me or date me – and what people say when I'm not around.' His lips pinched. 'Although scratch that, I'm not sure that matters either because I doubt anyone says anything nice behind my back.'

'I do,' Ella blurted. 'To Wyatt,' she followed up, her tone teasing. 'Tell me, who decides what matters?'

Alex took a moment to respond. 'Me?'

'You're not sure?' Ella asked, her voice hushed. 'Can we try something?' She leaped to her feet. 'It might help.'

'We're supposed to be painting.' Alex pointed to the canvas.

'We've got all night,' she sang, and Wyatt whined from where he'd gone to lie down. 'Okay I promise this won't take long.'

She ran to the edge of the stage and flicked off the lights, plunging the stage and main hall into darkness.

'Where are you going?'

'Bear with me. We need a blanket.' She ran to the back and picked up a couple from the props basket before spreading the thickest and fluffiest on the ground. 'Lie on your back and shut your eyes.'

'Is this a trick?' Alex looked at the blanket and then at her, confused. 'Are you going to paint a moustache on me and take a lot of embarrassing photos?' He sounded nervous.

'Nope.' Ella snorted. 'We're friends, remember?'

She saw the pulse beat at the edge of his jaw as he considered, watched him lick his lips as if they'd suddenly gone dry. The man clearly didn't trust anyone aside from his friend Stan. But he did as he was asked and went to lay on his back. Ella felt something inside her click as she acknowledged the gift he'd just given her.

'One more minute.' She jogged to the edge of the stage and searched for the light panel. Mae had shown her where to find the switches the first year she'd joined the panto and she flicked one down, then grinned when the ceiling filled with swirls of luminous spinning stars. 'You can look now,' she said, jogging back and stretching onto the rug beside Alex.

'So... we're doing this because?' he asked after a few moments of shocked silence.

'It's going to help you relax – and stop overthinking so we can get to the good stuff.' She looked up and linked her fingers on her stomach watching the stars spin round and round. 'Now you need to wish on one of those. It's going to help you work out what matters to you. Mae made me do it once.'

'What did you wish for?' Alex asked, and she could hear him shift on the blanket, guessed he might be looking at her because her cheek began to prickle.

'I wished for time to paint, for something in my life to change.' She'd been bone-tired, and she'd skipped Henry's lesson again because there'd been no time to make it to

Pinecone Manor. She'd been missing her father so much and the days had felt like they were all merging. She was getting older and older, and her life felt like it was filled with nothing but cleaning and a million chores, and she'd felt trapped. 'It took almost a year, but I suppose my wish came true in the end.' She looked at him. His mouth was quirked in the corner, and she wondered if he was laughing at her.

'I think that was less about star magic and more about you finally speaking to your stepbrothers,' he said dryly.

'You say that now, but you haven't experienced the magic for yourself... Go on, make a wish. What have you got to lose?'

'My dignity and self-respect,' Alex said dryly, and she heard him sigh long and hard. But he didn't move, and she took comfort from that because a week ago she doubted he'd have even considered lying down, let alone staying. 'Is this a fairy godmother thing?' Alex asked after a few moments of charged silence. 'Because you need to know Prince Charming didn't have one.'

'A flaw in the story,' Ella shot back. 'He had a father with expectations that he'd marry – who knows if the prince wanted to do something else? He could have been harbouring a secret wish to—'

'Collect shells?' Alex jumped in, his voice wistful.

'Shells?' Ella repeated.

Alex cleared his throat. 'This is ridiculous.' He made to get up, but she reached over and pressed a hand to his forearm.

'Just give it more time,' she begged, turning back to watch the stars, leaving her hand resting on Alex's arm when he didn't move. After a few more moments, Ella felt his muscles relax. He didn't shake her hand off and she took comfort from the connection and the fact that he hadn't broken it. 'You helped me with my dream,' she whispered. 'Now it's my turn. Watch the stars, aren't they hypnotising?'

'Not the word I'd use.' Alex sighed, but when Ella glanced at him, he was staring at the ceiling, frowning.

'Just say whatever you want – it can be the first thing that comes into your mind. I won't tell anyone, and Wyatt's lips will remain sealed – so long as you keep feeding him carrots.'

'I hope you're right about that,' Alex said, and Ella grinned. He was finally relaxing, giving her his trust. 'Fine,' he said eventually, then he went quiet again.

Ella stared at the glittering lights as they swirled. She could hear creaks from the floorboards under the blanket and let herself soften into them, giving Alex the silence that he needed to find the answers to her question.

'I want to be enough,' he said eventually, his voice so hushed she almost didn't hear.

'Enough?' she repeated, holding her breath and waiting for him to say more.

'This is stupid,' Alex growled, and Ella turned as he began to get up.

'Perhaps,' she said as he caught and held her gaze. 'But it's a few moments of your life, and it's not going to kill you. You keep talking about all the things you need and have to do – you never talk about what you want or what matters to you.'

She stared at his profile when he looked away, saw his jaw flex – a tiny movement in the corner where the bone connected to the bottom of his ear. 'What does *enough* mean?' she pressed, determined to make him crack wide open.

Ella wasn't sure what she expected to happen, but she knew getting Alex to confess all might be the first step to helping him. And she wanted to help him because he'd helped her. It had nothing to do with her overwhelming attraction to him. At least that's what she was telling herself.

He remained silent, but he moved onto his back again and gazed at the ceiling. She could see his jaw grinding and felt ice pool in the pit of her stomach when his frown deepened. She shuffled until their shoulders touched and a wave of need drenched her limbs.

'You know you've got this all wrong,' he said finally. 'You're Cinderella, I'm supposed to be saving you.'

'Don't deflect. You've done that already,' she said. 'Besides, the world's evolved. Cinderella can save Prince Charming now.'

His eyes darted back and forth following the stars on their never-ending race in the darkness.

'I don't know what enough is,' Alex said gruffly. 'Perhaps I never will. I only know that I'm not – but I wish I was.' His chest heaved as if releasing those words had made something inside him pop.

'Okay.' Ella sighed. 'Not enough for who?'

'I'm...' He paused, then shook his head. 'I was going to say my father, but... me, I suppose.'

She moved her hand so she could press it against the side of his jaw, then eased his face around until he was staring at her. 'That's a shame,' she whispered. 'Because from where I'm lying, you seem like plenty. I mean just how much enough does a man need to be?'

Ella hoped Alex would laugh, that the intensely sombre atmosphere might lighten. She knew they had to get back to the scenery, but she'd started this and wasn't ready to stop.

'More compliments?' Alex arched an eyebrow, but this time he looked thoughtful.

'Nae.' She smiled. 'I don't want you getting a big head.'

He stared back at her and the brown of his irises darkened as his jaw began to grind. Then he eased forward and gently pressed his mouth to hers, making her gasp and melt into him.

Then Alex broke off the kiss and rose, offering Ella his hand. He waited until she took it so he could help her get up. Then he quickly walked across the stage, back to the paint – leaving her wondering what had happened, and aching because the kiss had left her wanting so much more...

# 24

## ELLA

'Alex?' Ella gasped as soon as she opened her front door to find him hovering on the doorstep, looking embarrassed. Snowflakes were drifting from the icy, silver sky, and he'd obviously been standing there for ages, because his hair was soaked. Although that did nothing to detract from his beauty.

'What are you doing here?' She'd left him painting the scenery in the village hall half an hour earlier, after Wyatt had begun to tug at her jeans because he was hungry and tired. Ella had been hoping Alex would ask her to stay, had been wishing he'd at least repeat their gentle kiss. When he hadn't, she'd considered begging him to follow her home – but instead they'd stared at each other awkwardly, until his mobile had begun to ring and she'd decided to leave.

'You left your glass slippers behind,' Alex said gruffly, holding up the bag she'd put by the stage and forgotten. 'I thought you might need them.'

'Tonight?' Ella nodded, hoping the good deed was just an excuse to see her. 'Of course, Wyatt and I often dress up before bed,' she teased.

He looked embarrassed. 'Aye, well...'

'Sorry, I'm nervous,' she said, flushing. 'Thank you, I'm supposed to practise walking in them and losing one. Mae told me she's going to test me tomorrow.'

Alex smiled. 'Then perhaps you should put them on now?'

'I will if you come in,' she blurted, taking the bag from his hands as hope bloomed, filling her chest.

Alex stared at her for a beat, his dark eyes registering something Ella couldn't read. 'Deal,' he said softly.

'I've almost finished cooking a lasagne,' she said, trying to give Alex an extra reason to stay. 'Are you hungry?'

'Aye.' He jerked his chin and Ella stepped away, giving him room. 'Thanks.' His voice was clipped, almost as if he wasn't sure which words to use.

Ella didn't wait as Alex took off his shoes and coat; instead, she headed into the kitchen clutching the bag before opening it and slipping the glass slippers on. They were surprisingly comfortable, and the extra height made her feel more confident and sexy.

She glanced around. She'd lit some pine-scented candles while she'd been cooking, and fairy lights hung across the window giving the small kitchen a festive glow. She toyed with the idea of putting on the overhead lights, before dismissing the thought. Instead, she checked the food as the timer went off and took the bubbling dish from the oven. When Ella turned, Alex was standing in the doorway with his arms folded, frowning.

'Is everything okay?' she asked gruffly as his frown deepened. 'I mean.' Her stomach roiled. 'Did I annoy you earlier, with the stars and all those questions?'

Maybe she'd misunderstood his reasons for visiting – perhaps he was here because he was upset? He'd kissed her, sure. But what if after she'd gone, he'd had time to think – to get angry?

Alex blinked, looking shocked and took a small step forward

before thinking better of it because he immediately stepped back. 'Why would you say that?'

Ella looked at her feet. 'No reason,' she muttered. 'How hungry are you?'

She turned again and opened a cupboard, drew out two plates. Her stomach had been grumbling a few moments ago, but now Alex was here she knew she couldn't eat. She felt flustered and unsure and wished she had a script to follow.

'Not very,' Alex said, sounding as tongue-tied as Ella felt. 'I'm not upset. I wanted to talk to you...' He sighed.

'About?' she asked, turning so she could lean back against the counter, folding her arms, feeling defensive.

He pinched his lips.

'Because if I made you feel uncomfortable earlier, I'm sorry,' she said.

'You didn't.' Alex shook his head. 'I mean you shouldn't be sorry.' He winced, his jaw grinding. 'I suppose I shouldn't be surprised that's what you'd assume. I've spent the last couple of weeks criticising everything you do.'

'That's not true!' Ella gasped. 'You helped me.'

'You've done nothing wrong, Ella.' Alex waved a hand. 'I'm here because I wanted to finish our conversation on the stage.' He took a step forward, his gaze intense. 'I had some time to think when I was finishing off the painting.' He looked less tortured now, more thoughtful. 'Time to think about what you asked.'

'About what you want?' Ella checked, trying not to hold her breath. This conversation kept changing and she felt off balance because she wasn't sure what to expect. But there was hope now, hope because she could see something in his face.

He nodded. 'I don't have all the answers.' His eyes clouded. 'There's a lot of unfinished business between me and my father. A lot I need to talk with him about – when I'm ready to do it. I do know since I've been in Mistletoe...' He paused, searching for the right words. 'Since I met you...' He cleared his throat. 'There have been some days when I've felt like I'm enough. When I've been able to see beyond all the things I've been told, all the expectations I keep failing to live up to. And, I realised – while I was cleaning the brushes of all things –' He half smiled. '– and I saw the slippers you'd forgotten, that I knew there was at least one thing I wanted.'

'What's that?' Ella croaked, watching as Alex slowly tracked across the kitchen and placed his hands on the counter, effectively hemming her in. Her heartbeat pitched up, and blood began to rush in her ears.

'This,' Alex whispered as he leaned in.

The kiss when it came was exactly what Ella had been anticipating. There was no slow burn this time. Alex was clearly a man who'd decided what he wanted, and in this moment, it was her. He pressed his body into hers, taking her mouth with a confidence she hadn't experienced before. He was demanding, the kisses hard and hot from the outset, which proved he'd been thinking about her – thinking about this... And that he had no doubts.

Ella matched him in form and finesse as their kiss deepened and she found her hands wandering, eager to take things to the next level, because she'd been wanting this to happen since she'd realised that he wasn't the judgemental, arrogant man he pretended to be. She ignored Alex's jumper and instead tugged his shirt out of his jeans before skimming her fingertips across his skin and breathing in his spicy fragrance. She felt his low answering growl vibrate against her lips and grinned.

She'd been waiting for this – wishing for it. Now he was here, now Alex had decided to take this step, Ella wasn't about to hold back. She didn't care what his reasons for coming tonight were. Didn't need him to explain. Her life had been all about expectations and guilt – she'd barely had time to open herself up to anything resembling want and had let go of all her needs. So she let her hands roam, and told Alex with her kisses exactly what she wanted. Hoped he'd be able to read what was in her mind.

'You're sure?' Alex asked after a few minutes, his lips still secure against hers. He was penning her in, pressing her against the counter – his hard body moulded close. As if something he'd been holding in had broken, and by finally admitting what he wanted, a dam had burst. The rush of release sweeping him to her.

'Aye.' She gently bit his lower lip.

He groaned. 'Then you're wearing too much. You can keep the slippers on,' he added, tugging at the bottom of Ella's blouse. 'But this needs to go.'

'My clothes *your* problem,' Ella shot back as Alex spun her around and moved her until she was pressed against the kitchen cabinet, trapped again.

Her chest heaved, her skin tingling because she loved this new side of Alex. Loved him taking control. He slid his hands upwards along her sides and across her collarbone and neck, then pressed them to either side of her jaw as he took the kiss deeper, tipping her head.

Ella surged against him, her insides heating, as she savoured the evidence of his arousal, pressing herself into it. She drifted her hands lower and fiddled with the buttons on Alex's shirt. Her fingers were shaking so much she couldn't undo them, so she tugged his jumper over his head instead, throwing it onto the floor before moving back to the buttons.

They were fiddly and the tiny openings too small. 'Damn,' Ella complained, wishing she could just rip it up the front and pop the buttons off. She only didn't because she was afraid Alex would have to ask Blair or Aggie to sew them back on.

So instead, she dipped her fingers under Alex's shirt again and stroked the hard planes of his stomach, trailing her fingernails into his skin, dipping down until she was stroking under the top of his belt, edging lower still.

Alex moaned and let go of Ella's face so he could begin to work on her clothes. He shoved the bottom of her jumper up, pulling it off and tossing it over his shoulder. When it hit the floor, he made quick work of the buttons on her jeans and shoved them down her legs, moving back so she had space to step out of them without getting tangled in her shoes. When she had, he kicked the jeans aside and gazed down, his breath quickening.

Ella shuddered as the cold air cooled her limbs and he must have noticed because he frowned.

'We should find somewhere warmer.' There was need in Alex's eyes, a need that made Ella shiver again.

She jerked her chin in agreement and wound her arms around his neck before leaping into the air and wrapping her legs around him, losing one of the glass slippers in the process, despite trying to catch it with her toe.

'You can tell Mae you did your homework,' Alex teased as it clattered onto the kitchen tiles. Then he hugged her closer, and pressed his palms into her bottom, stroking his large thumbs beneath the material making her gasp, her insides liquifying. The buttons of his shirt dug into her stomach as he pressed her closer still and began to walk towards the kitchen door. 'Where?' he rasped.

'Bedroom. Upstairs,' she shot back, nibbling his ear. Smiling when he sucked in a breath and shuddered. 'Do you need to put me down?' she purred, as he stopped.

'No. I just needed a moment,' he ground out and then carried her quickly into the hallway. Wyatt growled as they passed – but instead of following, the bloodhound lumbered in the opposite direction towards the sitting room, where Ella had left his bed.

'Which way?' Alex demanded as he reached the top of the stairs.

'First on the right,' Ella said as she continued to nibble the side of his neck – breathing him in and sliding her tongue across the tiny pins of his stubble.

Alex sighed as he entered her bedroom and marched to the bed. Ella had put a lamp on earlier and it glowed, highlighting the hard planes of his face. He dropped her onto the duvet, before standing back and gazing at her.

Ella sat and then rose to her knees so she could track forward and work on the belt around Alex's waist, slipping it from the loops in his trousers and shoving them down. Then she set to work on the buttons on his shirt again.

'Do you think Prince Charming had buttons this small?' she asked, irritated as she failed to undo even one. 'Or maybe he had servants to do it for him?'

'I'll do it. Watch and you can learn.' Alex tipped Ella back onto the bed. He took off his cufflinks and placed them on her bedside cabinet, then began to work on the bottom button of his shirt. He fiddled for a moment, all fingers and thumbs before shaking his head and yanking the material until it ripped and three of the buttons pinged off. 'I told you it was easy,' he joked, bunching the blue cotton and making quick work of using the small gap he'd created to escape.

'You'd better not tell Aggie or Blair I did that,' Ella muttered as he climbed onto the bed beside her and lay until they were facing.

'You want me to put it back on?' Alex teased, taking a moment to gaze down her body. Ella was only wearing her underwear now, that and the one Cinderella shoe which she'd somehow managed to keep on. Her stomach pitched as she met Alex's eyes. They were dark and hooded, and she could almost read what he wanted to do. 'You're beautiful,' he said, his forehead pinching as he leaned in to kiss her again.

This one started slow; the glide of lips and tongues, the warmth of two bodies sliding against each other. Ella shuffled on the mattress until she could feel Alex's skin brush hers. He'd somehow removed his jeans when he'd climbed onto the bed and something must have happened to his socks because aside from a pair of skimpy black boxers, he was naked.

Ella continued to kiss Alex, reaching around with one arm so she could unfasten her bra. The slow skate of their lips hastened as she unhooked it and slid it from one shoulder before tugging it down her arm. She heard Alex's hum of approval as her nipple pressed into his chest. Then suddenly his large hand was palming her behind, and working her pants down until everything inside of her was heating, turning into a molten, fizzing mess.

Alex slowly peeled off Ella's remaining clothes without breaking their kiss, although they were both panting hard. Somehow he managed to take off his underwear because he eased her over and suddenly Ella could feel his smooth hardness pressing into her belly. She wriggled, teasing until she heard him moan.

The ache inside her core was building, and Ella stroked her hands over Alex's shoulders, pulled him against her, enjoying the weight of him as he pressed her down into the mattress. She stroked his large arms and wide shoulders before skimming her fingertips along to the rough hair on his legs. Exploring, dipping into the curves of his spine and trailing across his firm bum.

Alex broke off their kiss and began to feather his mouth along the sensitive skin on Ella's neck, drifting across her collarbone before he shifted lower. She lay back and shut her eyes as he licked and flicked his tongue over her breasts, making her body shudder and her insides climb.

Ella began to writhe and groan, almost floating off the bed when his clever mouth stopped just below her bellybutton and he began to explore the soft space underneath, before edging lower.

'Oh, oh, oh,' she moaned as he licked and sucked, and everything inside her fizzed and sparked, clenching and rising until she could bear it no longer.

'Now!' she yelled, grabbing Alex's arms and tugging him until he was on top of her. 'I want to do this with you this time,' she whispered against his mouth, and he nodded.

Then suddenly Alex was inside her and they were moving. Slowly at first, but he was as impatient as her because the thrusts quickly grew in intensity and speed.

'Are you there?' Alex rasped as their bodies rocked. Faster and hotter, wilder and rougher until they felt out of control. Ella could feel the curl of something inside of her, knew she was about to explode.

'I'm there!' she gasped as the wave crested and she shot after it, her insides exploding into a fever of pleasure. Alex rocked once more, then he let out a loud groan and shuddered.

Ella wrapped her arms around him and hung on tight, absorbing the aftershocks, until he calmed and stilled. Alex's breath was hot against her ear, and he eased himself to the side, taking her with him and hugging her tight.

Ella lay in the soft light knowing whatever happened in the future, however long Alex stayed in Mistletoe, she was glad they'd had this night.

## 25

---

### ALEX

'Are you all ready?' Mae shouted, her wide sparkly skirt swirling as she strode to the front of the stage to survey the members of the pantomime cast. Everyone began to whisper anxiously at the same time, the low hum reverberating around the village hall. 'I know you're nervous, but remember, this is our dress rehearsal. In two days, it'll be Christmas Eve and you'll be performing the real thing.' She waggled her eyebrows, dislodging a flurry of glitter onto her cheeks. 'I know we can make this perfect.'

Alex adjusted his Prince Charming costume for the hundredth time, tugging at the blue hat with the silver feather that Blair had made him wear at the last moment – because it made him look more 'princely'. He knew it suited him, but he still felt foolish.

'Do you know your lines?' Hunter, who was standing beside Alex, whispered in an extra loud voice.

'I should hope he does, lad,' Mae bellowed from the stage. 'Otherwise, I'll be turning him into a pumpkin.' She grinned as she waved her magic wand.

'And then I'll be putting him in soup,' Aggie teased.

Somewhere in the wings of the stage Alex heard Henry let out a loud groan.

'I know my lines, so you don't need to do magic on me!' Hunter shouted, hopping from foot to foot and nudging Maxwell who was standing on the other side of him.

'So do I,' Maxwell exclaimed. 'And I've been eating cheese all week because that's what mice do.' He wriggled his nose.

'Are you ready?' Ella came up behind Alex and whispered into his ear. He turned and stared at her, absorbing the punch in his belly as he took her in. He hadn't seen her since he'd left her house early this morning and something inside his stomach did a slow, happy spin. They'd been working on their paintings in the studio and spending their nights together for a week and Alex wasn't sure if he'd ever been so happy.

He knew this would be over soon – that the curtain on his new world was going to come crashing down in a few days. Then he'd have to rejoin his real life in Edinburgh. But he wasn't ready to face that yet. Didn't want to think about life without Ella. Or what was going to happen with his father, Stan or anything else. For now, it was just easy to avoid and ignore, to hope that somehow things would work out. So he leaned down and kissed Ella slowly, losing himself in her.

'Gross!' Hunter complained and Ella giggled as Alex turned to scowl at the boy.

'One day you'll learn it's not,' Alex said as he gave Ella another quick peck on the lips.

Hunter squished up his nose, then his face brightened. 'I have a present for you,' he said, reaching into the pocket of his mouse costume and pulling out a piece of paper. 'I posted my da his picture today with a Christmas card. He'll get it before he comes on Christmas Eve to watch the show.'

His eyes shone. 'I can't wait to see what he thinks. I tried really, really hard and mam said it was brilliant. I did this drawing for you at the same time – for luck.' The boy nodded at the picture, his mouse ears wobbling. 'It's a picture of you, Wyatt, Sprout and Ella,' he said proudly, his small chest puffing out.

Alex unfolded the artwork and gazed at it. 'Aye.' It was drawn carefully, and he could see the small details in the background which told him that Hunter had spent a long time on it. There was a castle with a chimney that had smoke billowing out. A dozen Christmas trees lined either side of the building and Wyatt was sitting beside a Volvo and sniffing one of its wheels. Beside him, Ella and Alex were holding hands, and Sprout was gazing at them. Above the image Hunter had written *Good Luck Prince Charming* in big swirly capitals.

'It's really good,' Alex said, a little overcome by the boy's thoughtfulness, wishing he'd thought to do something similar. 'You're talented,' he added because Ella had taught him about the power of compliments. How important it was to give them.

Hunter flushed with pleasure and then tapped a finger on one of the pockets on Alex's princely coat. 'Put it in there. It's meant to be for Ella too, so you'll have to share.'

'Thank you,' Alex said as emotion filled his throat, and a longing he couldn't explain slid through him. He wouldn't be in Mistletoe in a few days – would he take the picture with him, or leave it for her? Another, happier ending slipped into his mind: of him staying, working with Stan, and being with Ella. Then Alex shook his head, knowing he couldn't walk away from his father. He'd spent too many years earning his approval to go anywhere now – and he was so close.

'Right, I need you all to take your places. The curtains are down, and I want you behind them ready and waiting. Either on the stage or in the wings. You know where you should be,' Mae yelled. 'Don't forget your lines, break a leg and remember you're all going to be fabulous.' With that, she hopped, skipped and jumped to the back of the stage, leaving a trail of pink glitter.

'Well, everyone's going to be fabulous except for Cinderella – as usual,' Lucinda muttered as she stormed past Ella, her bright red costume swishing around her legs. She passed Dane and Clyde who were both tugging at their wigs, and grabbed their arms, marching them up the stairs to the stage.

'She's angry with me for talking to the boys and threatening them – at least those were her words,' Ella sighed as she followed. 'I've tried to talk to her a few times about what's fair, but she says I've let the family down. That my da asked me to step in and helping out was my job.'

'You know that's not true, Ella. It's past time for you to walk away and leave your family to it,' Alex said softly.

'I can't do that until I've paid off all the debts.' Ella sighed. 'Until then I'm going to have to stick it out. But while I do, Lucinda is going to do everything she can to make me feel terrible.' Her shoulders sagged and she looked miserable. 'Trouble is, it's working.'

Alex watched Ella walk away looking unhappy. He had some money saved; would she agree to take it so she could pay off the company debts? It would be a way out of this situation – a way for her to get back to her art. He'd talk to her about it later he decided as he followed her onto the stage.

Ten minutes later, Alex stood in the wings of the stage, as Ella, Hunter, Maxwell, Lucinda, Clyde and Dane waited in front of the curtains in position for the start. The backdrop, which Henry had recently finished, showed a small house and garden with a scatter of pumpkins on the ground, a candlestick and some chunks of cheese meant for the mice.

Alex could hear a hum of voices from the other side of the curtain. Mae had mentioned they might have a few locals in the audience to help the cast get used to being watched.

His heart thumped as he waited, surprised by how nervous

and excited he felt. Something had changed since he'd arrived in Mistletoe. The icy armour that had frozen around his heart had begun to melt. For the first time in years, he was starting to feel something, but he wasn't sure what to make of it. A part of him was afraid it meant he was weak, but another recognised he'd never felt so happy or alive.

'Are you ready, lad?' Henry asked, coming to stand beside him. He'd been touching up some of the scenery first thing and his Rolling Stones T-shirt was covered in blue paint. 'Did you know Michael was going to be here?' he asked curiously.

'Michael who?' Alex asked.

'Your father,' Henry said gently.

Alex blinked, as everything inside him froze. 'But he doesn't know about the pantomime,' he said, feeling stupid. 'At least he doesn't know I'm in it. I definitely didn't tell him.' Because he knew his father would be horrified.

Henry glanced back at the curtains and winced. 'Lad, he definitely knows.' He patted Alex's shoulder. 'Because he's sitting in the front row, and I don't think he's come to admire the scenery.'

Alex's heartbeat skipped and he made a tentative step onto the stage before shaking his head and retreating. 'You're mistaken.'

The great Michael Charming wouldn't take time out of his busy schedule to watch his son make an eejit of himself in a village panto. The music started to play. 'He's not here,' he promised as he watched the curtains slowly rise.

Then Alex's whole body stiffened and his blood went cold, because sitting in the front row with his arms folded, wearing a frown, was Michael Charming.


Alex's steps faltered as he stood on the stage after the final bows and the clapping died down. He should have enjoyed the performance – he'd been word perfect and everything had gone brilliantly. Clyde and Dane hadn't messed around once, and they'd even remembered their lines. But his father had watched the whole thing with a thunderous expression – curling his lip each time Alex had walked onto the stage.

When the tiny audience had roared with laughter at the funny lines, or silly scenes, Michael's face had remained expressionless, his mouth set into a forbidding line. Even now at the end, he hadn't clapped or smiled, and Alex had a very bad feeling.

'Is everything okay?' Ella asked as she took off her glass slippers and padded across the stage to join him.

'My father's here,' Alex said grimly. 'And I don't think he was impressed.'

He shut his eyes for a beat, trying to block his disappointment at being caught out. This should never have happened. All the work he'd been doing on his painting – thinking about how proud his father was going to be – it was wasted. 'I don't understand how he knew. I didn't tell him.' Had Stan?

Ella's cheeks paled. 'I'm so sorry, Alex – it was me.' She reached for his hand, and he had to stop himself from shaking it off. 'I know you said he wouldn't come, but I guessed it was because you thought he was too busy. I was sure he'd want to see you, though. You were brilliant, so I...' She looked stricken.

'Has Cinderella upset the prince?' Lucinda said nastily, as she swept past them, clearly picking up on the tension. 'Seems to be a special talent of yours, dear – letting people down.' She tipped her nose in the air and headed for the back rooms.

'I'm so sorry, Alex,' Ella repeated, her voice small. 'I thought your da would love to see you perform.'

'How did you even tell him?' Alex asked, his tone cool. It didn't really matter, but he wanted to know what had happened. Wanted to make sure there were no more surprises in store.

Ella must have picked up on his tone because she frowned. 'Henry gave me his email address. I invited him to the pantomime last week. I told him we had a dress rehearsal today, but I wasn't expecting him to come. I got him a ticket for Christmas Eve and I sent it to your offices. I found the address on Google.'

'I guess he wanted to surprise me,' Alex said. His voice barely a whisper. It was typical of his father to try to catch him out. Also, he wouldn't want to be spotted in the audience by anyone of consequence – and there was a lot less chance of that today.

'I thought you were exaggerating about him. But he didn't laugh once, or clap.' Ella wrapped her hands around her waist. 'He just glared at you.' A tear bubbled from her eye. 'I've made everything worse.'

Alex felt a prickle of annoyance. He knew Ella hadn't meant to mess things up, but why couldn't she have just left this alone? 'You can't change it now,' he said as his father rose from his chair and Alex saw Henry making his way across the hall to speak to him.

'I'd better go and face the music.' Alex sighed, ignoring the flurry of compliments from the other cast members as he went. It didn't matter how good he'd been, or what anyone said. Today was a disaster and now he had to face the full consequences of that.

'Alex,' Michael said stiffly, turning away from Henry as he approached. His father took a moment to look him up and down, his nose wrinkling. 'You really need to take off that costume, you look ridiculous,' he said coldly. 'What would your clients say? What were you thinking – and are you actually wearing glitter on your face?' The question was delivered with such an air of alarm that Alex immediately pulled the hat from his head and began to swipe his cheeks.

'I didn't expect to see you here,' he said.

Michael jerked his chin. 'That's perfectly obvious. But I got a special invite for the performance – from Cinderella of all people.' He grimaced.

His expression darkened. 'I assumed it was a mistake, but I decided to come and see for myself.' His stare was hard and unforgiving and reminded Alex of all the other times he'd been disappointed. 'Now I understand why I've not heard from you much.'

'I've been keeping up with work,' Alex shot back. 'Emailing every day.'

'I would have expected nothing less – I hope you don't think I'm going to congratulate you for doing your job.' He dismissed Alex and turned to Henry. 'I appreciate you taking my son into your studio. I can only apologise that he allowed himself to be distracted by—' His mouth bunched as if he couldn't bear to finish the sentence.

'It's been a pleasure to have him,' Henry said, surprising Alex. 'He's quite the talented artist.' He took in Alex's costume and smiled. 'In more ways than one.' He scratched his beard as Michael's frown plunged.

'It's a foolish man who puts triviality before serious work,' his father snapped, before turning back to Alex. 'Lockhart offered to show me his studio. I understand the landscape you've been working on is almost done. I'd like to see it to ensure you've not been wasting *all* of your sabbatical.'

Alex's throat tightened. 'I've still got some work to do on it.'

'I've told you. It's looking good, lad,' Henry soothed, his eyes shifting between them. 'I told your da that he might as well see the masterpiece in progress while he's in Mistletoe.'

'It think it would be better if he waited until I've finished,' Alex said.

He wasn't ready to share his painting yet. He'd wanted to impress his father and present it at the office tied up in a bow. Had already imagined Michael's reaction – which couldn't have been further from this. He was on the back foot now and needed to salvage the situation.

'Shall we go now?' Henry glanced around. 'I think Ella should come too.'

'Cinderella?' Michael glared at Alex. 'The more the merrier, I suppose. Perhaps you could change before we leave – I've brought my car, and I don't want to get glitter on the leather.'

'I've got my Volvo,' Alex said, feeling ill. This was a nightmare, but he had to get it over with. Had to see what he could do to salvage his dignity and his father's respect. 'I'll change and meet you outside.'

'Do it quickly so I can follow you,' Michael ordered. 'I'll be waiting in my car.' With that, he turned and marched towards the exit.

'I'll get Ella, but if you're ready first, go ahead,' Henry told Alex once they were alone. 'You know where I keep the key. Show Michael my studio and your painting, I'm sure that'll soften the man up. We'll join you as soon as we can.'

With that, the artist said his goodbyes and spun on his heels, leaving Alex staring after him, his insides churning as he fought the feeling of absolute dread.

ALEX

Alex's stomach was in knots as his father stood beside him in Henry's studio studying his landscape. He tried to quash the stirrings of foreboding as his father frowned.

Why had Ella thought it would be a good idea to invite him to the pantomime? Surely he'd told her enough about their relationship for her to understand it was a mistake.

He heard the sound of vehicles crunching on snow and guessed Henry and Ella were about to park. In a few moments, they'd join them, but he wanted his father's take on his painting while they were alone.

'What do you think?' he asked, his voice more eager than he'd intended, knowing any hints of emotion could prove a mistake.

His father took a step closer to the canvas, his top lip curling. Alex's body felt like it had been wrapped in rubber bands – someone was pinging each of them in turn, making everything hurt from the top of his head to his toes. He scrubbed a hand over his face and dislodged a spray of glitter which fluttered to the ground.

Michael noticed and shook his head. 'You're ridiculous.' His gaze returned to the painting and then back to Alex again. 'This isn't what I expected from you, Alexander.'

Alex felt his blood thicken and slow as shame got the better of him.

Sprout's barking and the patter of small feet indicated that he'd missed any chance of privacy. Of absorbing the impact of his father's reaction to his work without an audience. When the dog immediately made his way towards Alex, he took a step away as his father let out a muffled curse.

'Pets are a waste of energy,' his father murmured under his breath, pulling a face at the terrier who was sporting snowman headgear tonight.

'How are you getting on?' Henry asked as he wandered up the stairs and made his way towards them. Ella followed, more tentatively, her freshly scrubbed face a picture of guilt as she glanced between Alex and his father, clearly not liking what she saw.

'This is Ella McNally.' Alex garnered his manners as she approached. A part of him wanted to reach out and hug her, wanted to tell her everything was all right. But another, spikier side of him was furious. He'd been blindsided and everything he'd been working towards was ruined. All because she'd invited his father – had interfered. This is why you didn't make connections – this is why you didn't let people in. 'She's playing Cinderella in the pantomime.'

'Ah,' his father said, his tone disinterested. 'My mystery inviter.'

'This is my father,' Alex said, out of politeness because he hardly needed an introduction. Michael held out a hand and shook Ella's, dropping it almost the instant they touched. Making it clear he had no interest in getting to know her.

'Do you like the lad's work?' Henry tried again, walking to stand beside Michael so he could study the landscape too.

'I suppose,' his father said. 'I've seen a similar thing in a couple of chain hotels I frequent.'

Alex flinched as the barb hit.

'It's so much better than that, it's amazing,' Ella jumped in, sounding shocked.

Alex tried to catch her eye, tried to signal for her to stop. He knew Michael would like the picture even less if it was praised.

'Alex has done such an amazing job on the shadows and colours,' she continued, moving closer to him. 'I can almost imagine stepping into that snow.' The trees and lochan seemed to shimmer under the lights in the studio – taunting Alex with their playfulness. He'd added a tiny robin on one of the branches and felt his insides curl into themselves when his father leaned forward to study it. How had he let himself get seduced into producing such foolishness?

He thought he heard his father mutter something about frivolity under his breath.

'I love it, don't you, Mr Charming?' Ella gushed.

'Love isn't the word I'd use.' His father's voice was flat.

'Your lad is talented, there's a lot in that picture I'd be proud of if I'd painted it myself,' Henry said, his forehead crinkling in the centre as he studied Michael. 'He's good – and I've seen such a marked improvement since he arrived. You should be impressed.'

The words seemed to hang in the air as if waiting for his father's agreement, or at least an acknowledgement that they could be true – when neither came, they evaporated as if they'd been snuffed out by Mae's wand.

Michael sniffed and paced away from the picture, almost tripping over Sprout, ignoring the dog when he let out a warning howl. He moved until he was standing in front of Ella's easel. The sheet, which she'd placed over her work every evening, was back in place. Ella had told Alex she wanted the work to be a surprise, so he hadn't seen it, but watching his father eye the mystery canvas had all his senses tingling.

'That's mine,' Ella cautioned.

'So you're a painter too. Why the big secret?' Michael asked, bending and picking up the edge of the sheet and tossing it off as Ella leaped forward trying to stop him.

'No!' she shouted.

'Oh!' his father gasped, his face rearranging itself into what passed as a smile. 'Now that's good...' His eyes widened as they explored Ella's work.

Alex watched the look of absolute awe take over his face. This is what he'd wanted and he'd worked so hard over the last few weeks, hoping for this exact reaction.

'It's brilliant,' Michael said, almost lost for words. 'You're very talented for such a young lass. Far more talented, it appears, than my son.' He glanced at Alex, his face emotionless. 'Or perhaps you simply work a lot harder than him.'

'That's not true...' Ella said, her voice filled with a combination of indignation and shock. 'I've never seen anyone work as hard as him.'

Alex took in a stiff breath, working to still his disappointment, trying to defeat his feelings and find the iceman again. He knew he was in there, buried under the thin layer of hope that had grown since he'd arrived in Mistletoe. It was easy enough to tear through it. Then he paced around to the other side of Ella's canvas so he could look at it too.

What he saw made what was left of his heart crack. His eyes skidded over the drawing – it was brilliant of course, but so much more. Ella had recreated in perfect detail the picture from the Charming Capital Management logo. The three dogs sniping, yapping and vying for attention, but she'd added others too. One sitting at their feet, another that looked like Sprout was nibbling a carrot, Wyatt sat in the centre wide-eyed and magnificent, his ears flapping. It was filled with life and colour, packed with emotion and meaning – and it was utterly brilliant.

Alex felt sick.

'It's a dog-eat-dog world. You've caught that exactly. How much for it?' Michael said, turning to Ella.

'What do you mean?' she asked, glancing from Alex's father to him, her eyes skimming his face and widening when she read Alex's expression, realised he knew exactly what she'd done.

'I want to buy it.'

'It's not for sale – I was drawing this for Alex.' Her eyes were shining, and Alex could see the crocodile tears waiting to fall.

'I'll give you whatever you want,' Michael continued as an odd calmness settled over Alex – as all his remaining feelings and emotions seeped away. 'This is perfect. It's the only picture that could possibly suit the reception area of my company. Don't you think so, Alex?'

'Aye,' Alex said flatly. He should have seen this coming. Should have known if he got close to someone, they'd turn on him in the end.

It was a dog-eat-dog world, after all; his father was right. But somehow since coming to Mistletoe, since meeting Ella, he'd forgotten.

'I'm not selling,' Ella insisted, glancing back at Alex as one of the tears spilled over and trickled down her cheek. 'You need to take Alex's – it's so much better,' she pleaded, her expression almost wild. If Alex didn't know she was lying, he would have believed she was upset.

'I'm sure Ella will come up with an appropriate figure if you give her time,' he said. All emotion gone from his voice. 'She's obviously got your contact details.' He gave her a hard look. 'Why don't you give her a day or two to get back to you?'

'I'm not selling.' She gaped at him.

His father shrugged. 'I'm a businessman, so I understand

about needing time, Ms McNally, it's an excellent way of driving up the price– so I'll give you some. You have until tomorrow to send me a figure. Believe me, I'm willing to be generous.' He gazed at her picture again. 'I'm very impressed. I'm going to leave now. It's getting late and I think I've seen all I need to.'

He gave Alex a long look before picking up the coat he'd placed over one of the chairs in the studio when they arrived. 'I'll expect to see you back at work by lunchtime on Christmas Eve. We can discuss what's happened and ensure you're sufficiently prepared for our client meeting the following day.'

'But— the pantomime...' Ella trailed off as Alex gave her a dark look. Michael nodded at them both before heading towards the stairs.

'I'll see you out,' Henry said, following him.

The room remained silent as both men left. Alex could hear his father's footsteps as he got further away. The heavy thump of them pounding a death knell on his dreams.

'Well, I suppose you got your happily ever after,' he said tonelessly as he turned to face Ella.

She looked dumbfounded. 'What do you mean?' she croaked. 'I didn't mean for that to happen. I told you, I'm not going to sell.'

'You can stop now, Ella.' Alex swallowed. 'I should say bravo.' He clapped his hands and watched her face crumple. Gritted his teeth when he felt a corresponding crush in his chest.

'How did you even know what our company logo was?' he asked, scouring her face, trying to find all the things he must have missed when he'd decided to trust her. She was good – he had to admit that. Then it suddenly fell into place and he nodded. 'Of course, I asked you to hold my cufflinks when I was changing your tyre.'

'Alex...' Ella paled. 'The picture was always for you.' More tears spilled as she watched him.

'Then inviting my father to the pantomime – you must have guessed it was the best way to get him to the studio.' His forehead pinched as he tried to track back, tried to mentally find all the clues that had led them here.

'I didn't know he was coming tonight, I invited him to the performance on Christmas Eve – I thought he'd be proud of you. You were brilliant. Everyone said so,' she choked.

'Michael certainly didn't,' he shot back. 'I wonder, was that the icing on the cake?'

'Alex, I don't understand why you're saying this.' She gazed at him as tears continued to fall, staring at him blankly like she was trying to see inside his head.

Alex could feel whatever was left of the man he'd found in Mistletoe flake away. He'd be back in Edinburgh soon – and then Ella, the pantomime, and everyone else would become a dim and distant memory. He'd have to work even harder to earn his father's respect and approval, but he'd do it.

He shut his eyes as he imagined walking into the reception area of the company and seeing Ella's picture every day.

'I'm so sorry...' she repeated. 'I don't know how to put this right. I don't know how to make you believe me.' She twisted her fingers together, tangling and untangling them. 'You must know I had no reason to trick you.'

'I think we both know that's not true.' Alex paused as she looked at him blankly. Did she really think he was this stupid? 'What about the money you need to clear Magic Mops' debts?' he asked, remembering he'd almost offered to pay them off himself. The thought crushed him – he'd been totally taken in by her. 'My father will pay whatever you want for your picture. You'll be able to pay off your stepmother and leave the business like you want.'

Ella gaped. She opened her mouth to speak, but no words came out.

'You needed to get away from your family, to get back to your art and now my father's delivered that to you on a plate.' He sighed. 'Make sure you ask for plenty of money. He's good for it. But I'm sure you already know that.'

'Alex. You know that's not—'

'If they're not expecting you to knife them in the back, they won't see it coming,' he told her, his heart crumbling a little more. 'My father's been teaching me that for my entire life. This is the first time I've realised how right he is...'

The devastated look on Ella's face had Alex's insides tumbling, proving he wasn't totally over her. But he would be.

Ella seemed to wilt then – it was as if she couldn't handle the weight of his words, the guilt of all that truth. She swallowed. 'I need to go now.' Her voice was wobbly. 'We'll talk tomorrow when you've had time to sleep on what's happened. I'm going to prove that nothing you're saying is true.'

'I'll see you out,' he said as she half ran, half stumbled towards the stairs.

Alex was so angry and hurt, it made no sense that he wanted to reach for her. He knew he had to stamp these feelings out of his heart, and he would – just as soon as Ella had gone.

She was sobbing by the time she reached the porch. Alex watched dispassionately as she tugged on a pair of pink wellington boots, then turned to face him, taking in a long shuddery breath.

'Alex, I care for you,' she said, her eyes shining. 'I understand why you're upset with me, but I'd never betray you.'

'Goodbye, Ella,' Alex said as she gave him one last look before opening the door and stumbling out. He couldn't stop himself from watching as she began to run towards her van.

'What's the lass doing?' Henry gasped as he appeared from the hallway and stood beside Alex. Heavy snow was falling again, and swirls of wind gusted through the open doorway, the cold slicing its way under Alex's clothes. But he didn't flinch, didn't want to feel anything.

When Ella reached her van, she flung open the driver's door. She quickly threw herself into the seat, but as she did, one of her wellingtons caught in the snow. Alex watched her glance over her shoulder to where he was watching. Saw her sob, then shake her head and slam the door.

'What's the lass thinking, she's leaving her boot?' Henry asked, tugging on a pair of shoes before heading out into the storm.

'She's leaving.' Alex shook his head, ignoring Henry as he walked in the direction of the pink wellington which was still stuck.

Instead, he watched as the van slid jerkily from where it was parked. He couldn't tear his eyes away as it drove slowly down the bumpy driveway, before disappearing into a squall of ice and wind – taking Ella and his broken, black heart along with it.

# 27

## ELLA

'Mae!' Ella called out as she guided Wyatt through the entrance of The Art House, feeling wrecked. She swiped a tear from her cheek as her godmother appeared from the back room and immediately swept her up in a warm hug. She'd called Mae as soon as she'd got back to her house last night, unable to stop herself from sobbing as she'd explained what had happened with Michael Charming, and how Alex had reacted. How he'd believed that she'd somehow tricked him and was determined to leave both her and Mistletoe behind.

'I'm so sorry, lass,' Mae murmured into Ella's hair. 'Have you heard anything from the eejit today?'

Ella shook her head, gulping in a wave of grief. 'It's not his fault. You should have seen how cold his da was.' She could hardly believe how he'd behaved. 'I've messaged Alex and tried to call a few times, but he's ignoring me.' She shouldn't be surprised – he'd been so excited about showing off his landscape to his father and she'd ruined everything.

'Ah lass, I expect he'll come around now he's slept on things.' Mae pulled back and stroked a hand across Ella's cheek, brushing away a fresh tear. 'What about your picture?'

Ella sniffed. 'I need you to sell it for me. I'm not going to let Alex's father get anywhere near it. Alex needs to know that.' She paused, long enough to supress the sob forming in her throat. 'He needs to know he can trust me,' she said roughly as her mind recalled the devastation on Alex's face when his father had offered to buy her drawing. The way he'd looked at her, as if his entire world had crashed.

He'd been so wounded, but he'd hidden it well, tried to switch his feelings off, reject everything, especially her. Another tear tracked down her face and she brushed it away, irritated. She'd cried enough. She needed to do something positive.

'So, where's this masterpiece?' Mae looked behind her and raised an eyebrow at Wyatt. 'Did the dog eat it, or is it in your van?'

Ella had planned to pick it up this morning after she'd cleaned a client's house. But as she'd approached Pinecone Manor in the van, she'd lost her nerve. Alex hated her and she couldn't bear to see that look in his eyes again yet.

'I asked Henry to bring it here,' she said and winced when Mae's smile dropped.

'The bampot's coming to my gallery again?' she grumbled, letting out an impatient sigh as she began to fluff her hair and stroke her hands over her purple suit, smoothing it. 'Do you think he'll be long?' She glanced at the front window and pulled a lipstick from a pocket in her jacket.

'He's due any minute,' Ella said as Mae carefully applied red to her lips.

The entrance swung open and Sprout came bursting inside. He bounded up to Wyatt, his Santa hat bobbing cheerfully. The bloodhound groaned but let the terrier jump all over him as Henry walked into the gallery, carrying two canvases. 'I'm here,' he panted as he carefully put them on the ground, then he straightened again and spotted Mae.

'So you are,' she said, her tone cool. She strode across the gallery and frowned at the pictures which were wrapped in sheets of white paper. 'You brought two?' she asked Henry, clearly confounded.

'Aye – one belongs to the lass.' He pointed to the first canvas. 'The other I painted for you.'

Mae huffed. 'I don't want any more of your truth, old man,' she snapped, waving her hands as if warding him off. 'You can take that away when you leave.'

'We need to talk.' Henry scrubbed his beard, his voice so soft Ella almost didn't hear. 'Just give me five minutes.'

Mae's shoulders tensed and she stared at him with unease filling her eyes – then she seemed to give in. 'Let me look at Ella's picture first – once I've seen what the lass has done, you can have those minutes.' She tapped her watch. 'But I'll time you – then you can go.' She turned to Ella. 'Do you want me to unwrap it?'

'Aye, yes please,' Ella said. She wasn't ready to see the picture. She'd put so much emotion into the work, knew when she saw it again, it would hurt – but she steeled herself as Mae ripped off the covering and held her breath when the dogs were exposed.

'Well, that's—' Her godmother's tone was hushed. 'Absolutely incredible, Ella...' She shook her head as she took it in. 'I knew if you had time to work on your painting, you'd only improve. You're an amazing artist, lass.' She squeezed Ella's shoulder before nodding at Henry. 'Perhaps even more talented than you.'

'Aye,' the artist said. 'You've done everything I asked, lass. I can see the truth in this, and I can see flaws too.' His agreement should have pleased Ella, but she couldn't bring herself to care.

'Do you think you can sell it for me?' she asked, turning away. All she could think about was Alex's expression the last time she'd seen him, the accusation burning in his eyes.

'I've got a few regular buyers I can call. I'll take some photos and put it in the window of the gallery now. You really are a talent, lass.' Mae sighed as she scoured the work, her expression filled with wonder.

'Just don't sell to Michael Charming,' Ella insisted. 'You can give it away – I don't care – but not to him. The painting was for Alex.' She gazed at the picture.

'Does it have a story?' Mae asked.

Ella nodded. 'I based it on the logo of Charming Capital Management because it was important to Alex. But I added a little of Mistletoe in there too.' Ella sighed. If you looked closely, the German Shepherd, Great Dane and husky were smiling at each other and wagging their tails. There was no rivalry here, no contest or need for approval – it was all about friendship, community and love.

'Is that Sprout and Wyatt?' Mae asked, pointing to the terrier and bloodhound.

'Aye,' Ella said. Alex had changed so much since he'd arrived, and it had started with the dogs. She'd hoped that including them would help him remember his time here, and her too...

'I promise I won't sell your picture to Alex's father,' Mae said firmly.

'Thank you,' Ella murmured.

Mae's eyes drifted back to Henry who was watching them, and her dreamy expression suddenly disappeared. 'You'd better take your five minutes now, old man. I've got a painting to sell.' She tapped her watch.

Sprout let out a yap and abandoned Wyatt. He bounded across the room to Henry, perhaps intending to give him support.

Henry gulped and nodded, scratching his beard. He looked nervous. 'You told me once you didn't like my truth,' he said gruffly.

Mae flinched. 'You made me look like an old hag. If that's

your truth, I don't want it. This was never about my vanity.' She stopped and took in a long breath, visibly upset. 'It was always about how you saw me.' She blinked. 'The picture in your head when I wasn't around.'

Henry stared at her for a beat, his heart in his eyes. Ella wondered if her godmother had any clue as to how much this gnarly, grumpy and talented man cared. Then he took in a deep breath and knelt, ripping the white paper from the canvas before holding it up so Mae could see.

'It's me,' Mae whispered after a few beats of heavy silence.

'Aye.' Henry swallowed. 'And do you like this "you", lass?' His tone was muted and he waited for her reaction, scrutinising every reaction that flittered across her face.

'I—' Mae stopped, clearly lost for words.

Ella took a step back, almost tripping over Wyatt who was watching the couple too. It was as if no one else was in the room and she felt a fresh tear leak down her cheek – only this one was happy.

In the painting Mae wore a long, red shimmering dress – it bunched in at the waist and then flowed like water down her long legs. She looked curvy and her figure mirrored Mae's exactly: voluptuous and full-on sexy. Even the neat blonde bob looked familiar, only in the picture it had been clipped away from her face, exposing the globes of her cheeks and clear, smooth skin. There were wrinkles, but they gave her face character, with a hint of wisdom, and somehow made her even more gorgeous.

She looked exactly as she did in this moment – but there was a brightness to her in the painting, a glow Ella recognised. One her godmother emitted when she was happy.

After a long silence, Mae shook herself. 'That isn't the truth.' She turned to Henry, narrowing her eyes as she wrapped her arms around her middle. 'I thought that's all you dealt in?'

Henry scratched his beard. 'That is the truth.' He paused. 'I just needed to look again.'

'I don't understand,' Mae said. But there was something in her expression now. A sharpness. Curiosity. Maybe hope?

'Perhaps the truth comes in more forms than I once believed,' Henry muttered, his cheeks flushing. 'I know for me, it changes from one day to the next. The last picture I painted wasn't supposed to hurt you.'

'It did,' Mae said soberly, glancing again at the canvas Henry was still clutching, the bow of her mouth drifting up and then falling again as if she couldn't decide how she felt.

'I know.' Henry gulped. 'I want you to know I think you're beautiful from any angle, in every light. I loved every inch of you in the last picture I painted because I adore everything you are. And I love you just as much in this one. You're the same to me however my brushes, pencils or paints recreate you. That is my truth. I know I can be clumsy and thoughtless and I'm sorry I got things so wrong. But I love you, Mae.' He shrugged. 'That's all my truth. I can only hope it's enough.' He cleared his throat, looking a little mortified by his declaration. It was so out of character, but so completely honest – Ella could almost see the truth seeping from his pores.

Mae brought her hands to her mouth as her eyes filled with tears.

'I'm sorry,' Henry cursed. 'Lass, have I upset you again?'

'Nae, you old fool – I just think I'm going to cry,' Mae gulped.

'Cry?' He looked terrified.

'In a good way, you eejit,' Mae choked.

The artist gazed at her for a long moment, then he visibly relaxed. He balanced the edge of the portrait against one of the walls of the gallery, then slowly walked towards Mae.

She watched as he approached, as if fascinated by every

movement, measuring and judging – her face alight. When Henry reached her, he took her into his arms.

Ella took a second step back, watching as they kissed. Her eyes burned with tears, but her heart was full. She might not have the ending with Alex she wanted, but at least Mae and Henry had theirs.

When the couple finally pulled apart, Henry noticed Ella standing in the corner. His cheeks burned a brighter shade of red and then Mae turned and saw her too.

'Oh, I'm sorry, lass,' she said, looking flustered. 'We were talking about your picture.' She cleared her throat noisily. 'Perhaps we could pick this up later?' she asked Henry.

'Aye.' The older man grinned. 'You could come to Pinecone Manor – I'll ask Aggie to cook.'

'Soup?' Mae asked, roaring with laughter when Henry's jaw dropped. 'Will Alex be there?' she added, sobering when her attention flicked back to Ella. 'I might have a thing or two to say.'

'He's not left yet.' Henry pulled a face. 'But he told his da he's leaving today.'

'I thought he might change his mind,' Ella whispered.

'What about the pantomime?' Mae gasped.

Henry winced.

'Then who'll play Prince Charming?' her godmother turned to stare at Ella, distressed. 'There's no one to step in.' Ella opened her mouth, but there was nothing to say.

'I can do it,' Henry offered. 'I know I'm a little long in the tooth, but—'

Mae put a finger to his mouth. 'My truth is you're the most handsome man I've ever met.' She pressed her lips to his again. 'If the lad's determined to go...' She glanced at Ella, sympathy in her eyes.

'Seems he is,' Henry said gruffly.

Mae nodded. 'Then I'll call an emergency rehearsal this evening – everyone will need to know.'

Ella nodded, ignoring the ball of pain that had lodged in her throat as she watched Henry kiss her godmother again. Alex was really leaving. Even after he'd told his father that he'd return to Edinburgh, she'd secretly hoped he'd change his mind and give her a chance to explain. Then again, what could she say now that she hadn't already said last night?

Ella glanced back at the picture. It might be her only hope – once Alex heard she hadn't sold it to his father, perhaps he'd finally listen and forgive her for what she'd done.

## 28

ALEX

Alex rubbed his eyes. They felt grainy and he was bone-tired from a sleepless night. He'd tossed and turned for hours thinking about Ella and his father – trying to tamp down the feelings of rejection and hurt. He'd made a mistake – but he'd learn from it and move on.

Shaking his head, he ran up the stairs and into Henry's studio, expecting to find his mentor working, despite the lack of Rolling Stones music blaring from the speakers. But the room was empty. Instead, Christmas decorations fluttered gaily on the ceiling, taunting him.

Memories from last night assaulted Alex as he slowly crossed the room heading towards his easel and spotting a tiny patch of glitter on the ground. *'You're ridiculous,'* his father had told him as the makeup had fallen – and in this moment, Alex couldn't have agreed more.

He moved to his easel and stared at his painting. The work, which had given him such a sense of pride when he'd been crafting it over the last few weeks, mocked him. *I'm not good enough,* it seemed to shout. *And neither are you. You never will be.*

Alex shook his head vigorously, batting away the voice. The painting was almost done – there were just a few splashes of light to add, and he could finish it if he put in a couple more hours. His father didn't want his work, and Alex had no clue what he'd do with it, but he'd finish what he'd started and then take it – and himself – back to Edinburgh.

He began to mix his paints but couldn't stop his attention from straying to Ella's easel. Someone had moved it closer to the window and he couldn't see her work from here. Just the edge of the canvas, and the sheet which had been thrown over her betrayal. No wonder she hadn't wanted anyone to see it.

He took in a deep breath and tracked across the room, unable to stop himself. He'd been so shocked and hurt last night that he'd barely had a chance to study her work. So he'd look again, burn the image of treachery into his brain – the picture that proved that no one could be trusted. That his father had always been right.

Alex suspected he'd have weak days in the future, moments when he might wonder if Ella had really meant what she'd said about the painting being for him. He might find himself wondering while staring at the ceiling in the dark hours of a lonely night, if perhaps she hadn't tricked him. If she'd been telling the truth. But the picture would prove once and for all that she had been lying. Alex would know in his gut when he saw it again if it had been for him. He reached for the edge of the material, let his hand hover for a moment, not quite ready to face the pain as his stomach churned. In the end, he had to force himself to rip it off in one quick sweep, like he was removing a plaster. It might hurt more, but the pain wouldn't last as long.

Then Alex started feeling sick. Any hope he had that Ella had been telling the truth disappeared like a snowball in sunshine and he shuddered. Because the painting was gone – and in its place someone had left a blank canvas. Her work was probably already on its way to Edinburgh and his father, the deal obviously done. He swallowed and nodded, acknowledging the irritating prickle of tears as they flooded the edges of his eyes and forcing them away, along with any lingering feelings.

Ella had betrayed him and the sooner he finished his picture and left Pinecone Manor, the faster he'd be able to get on with his life.

Two hours later, Alex heaved the damp painting and his suitcase down the stairs as Aggie let herself in through the front door.

'Surely you aren't leaving, lad?' she gasped, frowning as she perused his luggage and the canvas.

'I'm sorry, I have to,' Alex said gruffly.

Aggie nodded as understanding dawned. 'Mae's called an emergency pantomime rehearsal for later today. I wondered what might have happened.' She took a step forward, her face filled with sympathy. 'Is everything okay?'

'It's fine,' Alex said. 'I've just...' He didn't want to lie to the older woman – but he didn't want to tell her the truth either. It was still too painful, and he felt stupid just acknowledging what had happened. 'I need to get back to my father.'

'A family emergency.' She grimaced. 'Aye, I understand. When will you be back?'

'I won't,' Alex said, cringing as Aggie's face fell.

'Ah, okay. I might be an old gossip, but I'm not going to ask you why, lad. I can see this is difficult for you.' She frowned as she nodded towards the door. 'Are you going to see Ella before you go? The lass left a wellington boot in the porch. I've no idea how she got home with only one. Do you?' She turned back to him, her face a picture of confusion and worry. She might not be asking Alex what had gone on, but it was clear she was trying to puzzle it out.

Alex shook his head. 'I won't have a chance to see her, sorry.'

'Well, can you take the time to say goodbye to Hunter at least?' Aggie pleaded. 'The lad's very fond of you. He'd be devastated if you left without saying goodbye.'

'Aye.' Alex sighed. 'But—'

'He's in Blair's tea room now. You could just pop in?' she implored.

Alex took in a long breath. 'Okay,' he promised. He didn't want to stop in Mistletoe Village, but he knew whatever happened, he couldn't let the boy down. Alex wasn't like his father – at least not yet...

'Alex! Mr Charming,' Hunter shouted from the booth in the corner of The Snug Tea Room as soon as Alex opened the door.

'Hunter.' Alex glanced around, ensuring Ella wasn't here as he made his way towards the small boy. 'Shouldn't you be in school?' He slid into the seat opposite, taking in the sketch pad and colouring pens piled on the table.

'Don't be silly.' The boy giggled. 'It's the Christmas holidays now.' His smile dimmed. 'Da isn't going to make it back until tomorrow. But Mam told me he's definitely coming to the pantomime this time.'

'That's good,' Alex said, thinking of all the Christmas events his father had missed due to his important work. How each absence had chipped away at his confidence. But ironically, when his father had finally attended his show, it was the last thing in the world he'd wanted. 'Did he get your picture yet?' he asked.

Hunter shook his head. 'It's going to arrive today.' He bounced on his seat. 'I can't wait until he gets it. Nana promised she'd let me know as soon as he rings.' He glanced up as Blair made her way across the tea room carrying a tray.

'It's good to see you, lad. Mae's called an emergency rehearsal for later today, any idea why?'

'Um.' Alex swallowed as Blair put a mug of coffee in front of him. He wasn't ready to tell Hunter he was leaving yet, to pop his happy bubble. He just wanted to chat, to take a moment before he upset him.

Luckily, a crowd of people bustled into the café at that moment, distracting Blair. 'I'll bring over some cake in a moment,' she said, eyeing them. 'Don't bother the man too much, lad.'

'It's okay. We're friends,' Alex said quietly.

'We are friends,' Hunter said, beaming at him. 'I drew you another picture.' He flicked through the pad and carefully tore out a page. 'It's of you and Ella this time.' Hunter slid the paper towards him and Alex felt as if something inside of him had just been punctured. She was wearing the Cinderella ballgown and he was dressed up as Prince Charming. Beside them were two mice. 'I'm in it and so is Maxwell,' the boy said shyly. 'I thought you could take it with you when you go back to your work. It'll remind you of me.'

'It will.' Alex nodded, a little overcome. Hunter's kindness and determination to befriend him was humbling. All that innocence. Had he been like this once, what had happened? 'It's really brilliant, lad,' he croaked suddenly wishing he could talk to Stan. His friend might be able to help him make sense of the feelings he'd always been able to control. The ones that were now threatening to consume him.

'Hunter, your da's on the phone,' Blair said, appearing again at the table. She placed a mince pie in front of Alex. 'I thought you'd like to take it in the office, it's quieter there.'

Hunter gave Alex a quick smile and then bounded after his aunt. Alex sat staring out of the window of the tea room, his mind swirling. He took his mobile from his pocket and quickly calculated the time in New Zealand. It would be late evening, not too late to call his friend.

He tugged his coat back on and left the mince pie, quickly swigged a gulp of his coffee before indicating to Blair that he'd be back. When he was outside, he dialled Stan's number, pacing back and forth on the snowy pavement as it continued to ring. When the message clicked on, he frowned.

'Stan. I don't know where you are, but can you call me when you can? I've got some things to say.' He frowned. 'Probably things I should have said a long time ago. Like I value your friendship.'

He swallowed.

'I don't think I ever really realised how rare it is to be able to trust someone so completely. I know you always tell me that I don't say how I feel, and I'm not going to suddenly start doing it now.' He shut his eyes. 'But I will say you're the best person I know. I got your email about the business and...' Alex honestly didn't know what to say next.

He hung up and shoved his mobile back into his pocket and walked into the tea room again. He could see Hunter was sitting back in the booth – but something was different. The boy was drawing again, hunched over his pad, his body rigid.

Alex caught Blair's eye and saw her lips were drawn. She motioned him over.

'What happened?' he asked, glancing back towards the booth.

She sucked in a breath. 'The lad's da told him his picture isn't any good. Said he needed to try harder.'

Alex frowned. 'But the picture was brilliant.'

'Ach, well. The eejit never thinks anything his son does is good enough'. She sighed. 'He's always been the same. He believes in harsh words and the power of criticism. He's never realised how easy it is to break a spirit. To make a wee lad feel like he's not enough. Doesn't seem to matter what any of us say.'

She looked at Alex, her expression hopeful. 'I know it's a lot to ask, but could you talk to him? I think he might listen to you.'

Alex felt a knot form in the centre of his chest. 'I can try,' he muttered. 'But I need to get something first.' Before Blair could say anything, he headed out of the tea room. He knew exactly what he needed to do.

Alex returned a few moments later, carrying his canvas. He slid back into his seat in the booth opposite Hunter and rested his picture beside him on the bench. He hadn't bothered to wrap it so put it facing the seat so the boy didn't see it yet, but Hunter didn't look up from his drawing. He watched the boy work. He was concentrating hard, but his mouth was tense and unhappy – a sharp contrast to the way he'd looked when Alex had arrived. 'What happened with your da?' he asked gently.

'He said my drawing was really bad,' the boy said. 'It's not real enough, and the colours are all wrong. He said it was ridiculous.'

The familiar word had something vicious spiking inside Alex's heart. 'What do you think?' he asked gruffly.

'About what?' Hunter looked up, as if he were surprised that mattered.

Alex mulled what to say. He knew every word counted; mere syllables had the power to snap a spirit or build it. His father had always had the same choice – why had he chosen to break it every time?

He leaned forward and held Hunter's eyes. The boys were red from tears. He understood those too – not that he'd shed any recently. Not until last night. He cleared his throat. 'I showed my da my painting yesterday,' he said and saw the boy's forehead twitch as he finally noticed the canvas beside Alex.

'What did he say?' Hunter leaned forward as Alex turned the picture around, distracted momentarily from his misery.

'He told me it wasn't good enough,' Alex said, shaking his head. 'What do you think?' Hunter looked equally dazzled and bewildered, and Alex wondered why he'd always given his father's opinion so much weight. Why had he spent a lifetime allowing him to control how he felt – hadn't Stan said as much? Why hadn't he listened?

'But your picture is fantastic.' Hunter frowned, his young face twisting as he tried to come up with an explanation. 'You paint brilliantly. Even Mr Lockhart thinks so and he doesn't think anyone can draw.' The boy sat back, a tumble of emotions flickering across his face as he studied the work. 'I don't understand.'

Alex shrugged. He wasn't sure how to articulate something he was only just beginning to comprehend himself. He turned to look at his painting again, allowed himself to see it properly. It *was* good and he was just as talented as everyone said. 'I wonder if some people only know how to look for the bad in the world.' Perhaps they were born with a mind intent to criticise. Maybe it made them feel better about themselves?

He didn't know how to put that into words and wasn't sure he should. He wasn't here to knock Hunter's father down, to make him look small in the eyes of his son. All he could do was provide a few hints so that one day the boy might work it out for himself. Hopefully, it wouldn't take *him* thirty years.

'But why?' Hunter looked bemused.

Alex shrugged. 'I can only tell you I think my father does it because he thinks it's going to help. He wants to make me into the best version of myself. Only.' He paused. 'I'm not sure his best version is the same as mine.'

Alex breathed out as the words sunk in, looking for a space where they could live, and form a new truth. He'd spent his life living up to the belief that if he just tried harder, did more, he'd be enough – but in this moment, he wondered if he ever would.

Was it time for him to start living for himself and not Michael Charming? The realisation floored him, and it took him a moment to notice Hunter was nodding.

'I think I know what you mean,' the boy said. 'In school we learned not everyone likes the same things.' He glanced at Alex's mug. 'I hate coffee, but I love hot chocolate. As long as it's not too hot and has extra sugar in it. Maxwell likes haggis, but I think it's—' He pulled a face and Alex laughed, then the little boy began to laugh too.

'Aye, which means we all need to decide what we think is good. To believe in ourselves,' Alex agreed. 'Do what we think is right, like what we want to like, be proud of what we accomplish.' He pulled a face – he didn't want to overstep. 'That doesn't mean I'm saying your da is wrong...' he added carefully. 'I just don't agree with him, so I say draw what you love, lad. Don't let anyone tell you it's not good enough. Also...' Alex turned to his picture as a thought occurred. 'I wondered if you'd like to keep this picture?' he asked.

'You want to give me your painting?' Hunter marvelled, his voice hushed.

'Aye,' Alex said, handing the canvas across the table. The boy took it, his eyes rounding with delight. 'I owe you a picture or two, and I can't think of anyone I'd rather give this to...' Alex paused, taking his time so he got the words right. 'I hope it'll help to remind you not to listen to everyone's opinion.' Hunter blinked. 'Sometimes, the only one that matters is your own.'

'Aye.' Hunter stared at the canvas before carefully placing it beside him in the booth – then he nodded before giving Alex a thoughtful smile.

He picked up his mug and sipped, swiping foam from his lip before he tore out a blank piece of paper from his sketch pad and offered it. 'You can use my pens,' he said before starting to colour again. This time, when he began to work, Hunter was smiling.

Alex stared at the blank piece of paper. Was it time for him to make a new start too?

## 29

## ELLA

Mistletoe Village Hall was subdued when Ella arrived. She headed towards Mae as her godmother swiped a hand across her brow, looking stressed. Henry was hovering beside her, and kept darting adoring looks in her godmother's direction.

The artist was dressed in full princely regalia and looked dashing and far younger than his years. Blair and Aggie had outdone themselves, creating a lavish outfit in one afternoon.

'Thanks for coming to this emergency meeting everyone,' Mae shouted, waving her hands, as she encouraged everyone to gather closer. 'I called it because I've got an announcement to make, and I was hoping we could do a quick run-through of the show while we're all here. That's why I asked you to come in full costumes and makeup.'

'What's going on?' someone shouted. 'I heard something's happened to Prince Charming?'

Mae's lips pinched. 'Aye, that's right. I'm sorry to have to tell you that Alex can't play the prince in the pantomime. He's had to return to Edinburgh, unexpectedly.'

There was a hushed gasp from the crowd. 'Why?' Lucinda chirped, shoving her way to the front, elbowing Ella out of the

way as she passed, before turning and staring – her expression
venomous. 'I don't understand,' Lucinda continued. 'Did something happen or did someone –' Her glare intensified. '– upset
him?'

'I'm afraid the lad didn't give me any information that he
wanted shared,' Mae said, her expression stern as she took in
Lucinda's combative stance.

'He told me he was going to see his da when he was in the
tea room today,' Hunter said sadly as he pushed his way to the
front. 'He said he's not coming back. But we're going to talk a lot
on the phone. About our art.' The boy's mouse ears seemed to
sag. 'I'm going to miss him. He's my friend.'

Ella felt her insides shrivel. She missed Alex too. He hadn't
answered any of her calls. But it seemed he'd managed to speak
to some people before he'd left Mistletoe. It was clear from his
lack of contact that he wasn't going to forgive her or give her a
chance to explain. He must know by now that Ella had refused
to sell her painting to his father, but the news obviously hadn't
changed anything. He was never going to forgive her. His feelings had clearly been far less strong than hers. She felt sick.

'So, who's going to play Prince Charming?' Clyde asked
from the back of the horde and some of the cast members began
to speculate.

Mae clapped her hands encouraging everyone to quiet
down. 'Luckily, Henry has offered to stand in, which means the
show can go on,' she said, giving him a soppy smile.

'Bravo,' someone said loudly and began to clap, while a few
others joined in.

'Thank you,' Henry said grandly.

'He's a little old, isn't he?' Lucinda piped up.

'I'm no spring chicken, lass, but I still scrub up okay,' Henry
said gruffly.

'Henry will make a wonderful Prince Charming,' Mae
snapped, her eyebrows drawing together as she frowned at

Lucinda. 'I'm grateful that thanks to him the show can still go on. We've all worked hard, and we need to make the best of this situation.' She shook her head. 'We're in this together – the show's almost sold out and we need to put on the performance tomorrow night. Mistletoe is relying on us.'

'Fine,' Lucinda said angrily, folding her arms.

'Then let's get on.' Mae looked weary. 'Can everyone take their places please and we'll try to do the run-through as quickly as we can. I know it's almost Christmas and we all have lots we need to get done.'

'Some, more than others,' Lucinda muttered as she shot Ella another bitter look and headed for the stage.

Ella sighed as she hung back. She was used to being taken advantage of, but being hated was more difficult to deal with. And it wasn't just Lucinda now, it was Alex too.

Mae sped up until she was beside Ella, close enough to tug her arm, stopping her in her tracks. 'Henry, why don't you go ahead?' she suggested as he came up to join them. 'I just want to have a quick talk with the lass.'

'Blather away,' Henry said affectionately, leaning down to give her godmother a swift kiss before heading for the stage.

'Everyone's really unhappy,' Ella said, taking in a deep breath. The room didn't smell right anymore. The hot light-bulbs had an odd burnt fragrance, the McBride sisters hadn't had time to bake, so there were no delicious scents wafting from the kitchen. Even the Christmas decorations looked lacklustre and nothing seemed to sparkle now.

'Aye.' Mae's shoulders drooped as she looked around. 'But there's nothing we can do except get on with things,' she said gently. 'I do have some good news I wanted to share. The kind of news that makes me feel like a fairy godmother for real.' She grinned, then glanced towards where Lucinda had cornered – and was admonishing – her sons. 'News I'm hoping will make life better for you.'

'What?' Ella asked. Unless Mae was about to magic up Alex's forgiveness, she wasn't sure how things could get better.

'I emailed all my favourite collectors this morning about your painting,' she said, then waved her magic wand over Ella's head. 'And ta da – I had two offers for it within an hour.'

'What, sorry?' Ella stuttered.

'I've sold your picture, lass.' Mae smiled. 'I've probably sold your next one too because the client who lost out asked if he could have first refusal on your next. It might not make up for everything, but at least now you can focus on your art. It's time to get back to it, time to stop giving all your time to people who don't deserve it.'

Wide-eyed, Ella turned to where Clyde, Dane and Lucinda were still arguing and frowned.

'Your da wouldn't expect you to still be helping them,' Mae said gently, reading her mind. 'I happen to know your mam wouldn't either. You've put your life on hold for the last year. You've scrubbed, cleaned, and done chore after chore. You've been taken advantage of for little to no thanks. Now it's your turn. Go back to college, do what you love.'

'I don't know...' Ella said, wishing Alex was here so she could talk it through with him. She already knew she couldn't leave her stepfamily in the lurch, no matter how much she wanted to. She had to pay off the company debts before she could consider leaving.

'Perhaps it would help if I told you how much my client paid?' Mae asked. When Ella turned, her godmother named a figure that had her insides popping like a firecracker had just gone off.

'How much?' she checked, widening her eyes.

Mae told her again. 'It's a new start for you, lass,' her godmother said, hooking her arm through hers. 'I've already sent the money to your bank, and I'll be expecting a new painting as soon as you've got the time. This is a chance for a new life.'

One without Alex. But as Ella walked beside her godmother, she knew this was a chance she had to take.

Ella found Lucinda at the interval. The crew had just told them to take ten minutes because they were making a few last-minute adjustments to the lighting. Her stepmother was standing at the edge of the stage watching Ella's stepbrothers who were fighting again.

'So you finally decided to face me, did you?' she snapped. Ella's stomach twisted and her first impulse was to turn and spin on her heels. But she thought about what Alex and Mae had said and steeled herself to stay.

'I'm sorry, I should have spoken to you earlier.' She stepped closer instead.

'When you forced Clyde and Dane to work when they were sick?' Lucinda snapped. 'Your father would be horrified at the way you've treated us—'

Ella held up a palm. 'I think Da would have been more upset about my long hours and how hard I've been expected to work,' she said quietly. 'And that I've had to do most of it by myself.'

Lucinda paled. 'He asked *you* to take care of the business,' she said coldly.

'He asked me to help out.' Ella swallowed. 'I don't think he expected me to do it on my own. And I don't think he wanted me to stay in Mistletoe forever.'

Lucinda sniffed. 'I'm sure he thought you'd at least stay on until you'd helped to sort out the mess we're in.'

Ella nodded. 'He might, or he might not,' she said. Realising that was true. 'Whatever, I now know things need to change.'

'What made you decide that?' Lucinda demanded.

Mae had been telling Ella off for a long time about all the things she'd forced herself to give up. Aggie, Henry and Blair had all agreed. It was only Alex who'd made her take a second look at the life she was leading.

If it wasn't for him... She swallowed and shook her head. This wasn't about Alex Forbes-Charming. It was about reclaiming her life. 'That doesn't matter. What does, is Mae's sold one of my paintings,' she said. 'And I'm going to use the money to pay off the company debts and then I'm going to leave.' She'd even have a little left over to live on until she sold another.

Lucinda looked shocked.

'I'm giving my notice now, so you've got time to find a replacement. I've barely taken any holiday, so I could leave today – but I'll give you a month to get things sorted.'

'That's not enough time,' her stepmother blustered as underneath her makeup, her cheeks paled. 'Surely you can't expect—'

'For you, Clyde and Dane to step in and work?' Ella asked. 'I think it's time for you to take on the responsibilities of running the business and managing your lives. I think Da would be happy if you did.'

'What are *you* going to do?' Lucinda's eyes fired and Ella had to draw in another gulp of air, to stop herself from backing out.

'I'm going to paint,' she said. 'With Henry – and then I'm going to enrol back in college next year.'

'You can't!' Lucinda said as Ella turned away, feeling something inside of her shift.

She might have lost Alex, it might take her years to get over him, but for the first time since her father had died, she was going to put herself first...

## 30

---

### ALEX

Alex took in a long, steadying breath as he parked in the marked bay reserved for him in the company car park. He switched off the engine and wondered why this familiar space suddenly felt so wrong.

He'd arrived at his home in Edinburgh late last night, after taking his time driving from Mistletoe. He hadn't rushed his journey. His need to impress his father had faded since his sabbatical and their confrontation at Pinecone Manor.

He'd spent the night in his cold quiet home – wishing Sprout or Wyatt were there. Craving something to distract him from staring at the ceiling. He'd slept badly, waking fitfully as he'd imagined he could see Ella's face frowning from the shadows, could hear the patter of paws on the bare floorboards.

He checked his mobile again. He hadn't heard from Stan and after a barrage of texts and messages yesterday, Ella had stopped trying to contact him. He'd never felt so alone.

His insides twisted painfully as he tried – and failed – to push all thoughts of her away. Then he took another deep breath and opened the car door.

Alex paused as he walked through the imposing glass doors

of Charming Capital Management, preparing himself to see
Ella's painting in the reception area – a reminder of her
betrayal. Then he frowned as he took in the freshly painted wall
which glowed stark white. Someone had hung a set of new
silver hooks, but the space was empty. Where was Ella's painting? Why wasn't it here?

Frowning, he nodded to the security guard, taking in the
scant Christmas decorations and lack of smiles or laughter
coming from the staff. Had it always been so grim and unhappy
in the office, and why hadn't he noticed that before? Alex
waited, readying himself to say hello when he was buzzed
through the security gates, but the guard didn't even look up
from his computer.

'Merry Christmas,' Alex said as he passed, earning himself a
double take.

'And to you, sir,' the guard eventually said, his brows
dipping as, looking confused, he studied Alex.

Alex straightened his spine as he marched into one of the
elevators and pressed the button for the top floor. Then he
stared at his reflection in the floor-to-ceiling mirror – taking in
the shadows under his eyes and the way his mouth wilted as the
lift travelled upwards.

By the time it arrived, Alex had found his iceman again. He
took his time walking along the chrome, glass and grey corridor,
passing his office – which was bare of tinsel or anything jolly –
as dread seemed to drill tiny holes in the pit of his stomach. He
stopped momentarily in the doorway of Stan's office, noticing
the new furniture, frames filled with pictures of strangers and
shiny Apple computer that all signalled someone new had
already moved in.

'Alex,' Michael Charming barked as he opened his father's
office door. 'You're late.' He took in his son. 'At least you made it
in time for our meeting. I want to talk about tomorrow... Take a
seat, I've not got much time.'

His father began to tap on his computer, accessing which-ever file he wanted them to discuss. After a few moments he looked up, his lips bunching in annoyance. 'Why are you still standing?'

'Where's the painting Ella McNally sold you?' Alex asked, glancing around the room. He shouldn't care, but he had a feeling something odd was happening and he needed to shake it off.

Michael sat back in his leather chair and folded his arms. 'Is this jealousy because I wanted to buy her picture instead of yours?' His mouth set into an unrepentant line as Alex stared at him without responding. 'It's a dog-eat-dog world, remember?'

'Aye. I remember,' Alex said softly. 'I'm just not sure I agree with you anymore.'

His father lifted an eyebrow. 'You sound like your mother.' He sighed.

'Perhaps.' Alex nodded. 'Maybe I'm more like her than I realised. Perhaps that's not such a bad thing.' He went to take a seat so he was the same height as his father and could look into his eyes. 'I did want you to like my painting,' he said. 'In fact, all I've thought about for the last few weeks is what you were going to think.'

Michael nodded as if that wasn't a surprise.

'But I've realised I have to stop looking for your approval.' The moment he said the words, Alex's body loosened, as if a bunch of suffocating knots had been untied. 'Because for the first time, I understand you're never going to give it to me.'

His father's expression cooled. 'Seems you've spent a little too long out of the office, Alex. I think we should get started – we haven't got all day.' He waved a hand as if dismissing their conversation but for the first time in his life, Alex wasn't going to fall into line. Wasn't going to do what was expected.

'Tell me about Ella's painting,' he pushed. He wasn't sure

what he expected to hear, but he had to know why it wasn't up in the reception yet.

The canvas hadn't been in Henry's studio yesterday morning. A courier wouldn't have taken long to bring it here – and Alex knew his father would want it hung the instant it arrived. Michael Charming wasn't a man known for his patience. He glanced around the office again, wondering if he'd somehow missed it, if it was propped against a desk or wall.

His father sighed. 'Ms McNally wouldn't sell it to me. She told me I should hang yours because it was better.' He rolled his eyes. 'It's obvious she's not a businesswoman. I had the space repainted; I'm assuming you brought your picture with you from Edinburgh?' His tone was offhand, and Alex didn't bother telling him that he'd given it away. 'It'll serve as a temporary solution until you paint something better. If you can.'

'Ella wouldn't sell her painting to you?' Alex checked. He swallowed as a wave of guilt threatened to overwhelm him. Had she been telling the truth? Had her painting always been for him? Hope made him stand up again.

'That's what I said.' His father looked him up and down. 'You look ill, lad. Pull yourself together. You've been out of the office for long enough. We've got a lot to get done this evening.'

'It's Christmas Eve.' Alex glanced at his watch and winced. 'What time does a pantomime usually begin?' He couldn't remember what time Mae had told them to arrive.

Michael snorted. 'How should I know? Can you focus now, lad?' His tone hardened.

Alex sighed and gave his father a long look – then he spun towards the door.

'Where are you going?'

'Back to Mistletoe. I'm sorry, but I've got something I have to do – a lot of important people I don't want to let down.'

'What's got into you, Alexander?' His father rose. 'Stop talking nonsense. You need to get on with our meeting.'

'I can't,' Alex said as he reached the door and opened it.

'If you leave this office now, you won't be welcome back,' his father said, his voice like ice.

Alex turned and stared at him as a thousand memories assaulted him – every moment between them that he could remember over the years, each conversation, argument or idle exchange. None of them were good. 'Aye. I'll email my resignation as soon as the pantomime is done.'

'Alexander?' His father gaped. 'Is this about the painting?'

'Nae.' Alex shook his head. 'It's about me finally realising I'm never going to be enough for you. I can't please you. It's time I stopped trying and started thinking about what I want instead.'

'Alexander!' His father yelled again as Alex walked out of his office and into the hall feeling light. He checked his watch again and broke into a trot. The pantomime would surely be starting soon.

If he left now, he might be able to make the second half. Would hopefully get there in time to play his part – if traffic and fate were on his side. He'd just needed to pop into Pinecone Manor on the way. He'd call Henry from the car; perhaps his mentor could make sure his costume was ready when he arrived? His stomach pitched as he broke into a sprint, suddenly feeling excited and nervous all at once.

His life was changing, but he was in control. He'd left his job; now it was time to talk to Ella, to beg her for forgiveness. For the first time in years, Alex knew exactly where he was going and what he wanted, and it had nothing to do with his father – and everything to do with him.

# 31

## ELLA

'We've got five minutes until the curtain goes up!' Mae called out, as the pantomime cast assembled onto the stage in full costume. A hush fell over them as they began to take their places.

'Are you okay, lass?' she asked Ella – her mouth crinkling as she studied her.

'He's not going to come,' Ella murmured, patting a palm on her stomach to still her nerves and calm the ache that had seeped into every cell of her body. 'I've been hoping.' She pressed her lips together – there was no point in going over it again. Alex had ignored all her calls; it was Christmas Eve and the pantomime was about to start – and he still wasn't here.

Instead, Henry was dressed as the prince and waiting in the wings ready to stand in.

'Ah, Ella,' Mae soothed, squeezing her arm as Hunter came running out of a side door carrying one of the pumpkin props.

'Can you do some magic for me, please?' he pleaded with Mae, putting the vegetable on the ground and tugging her glittery pink skirt.

'What magic, lad?' she asked, leaning down to look into the

boy's powdery white face. He was dressed in his mouse costume and fully made up. He should have been excited, but behind the glitter and makeup, Ella could see he was as unhappy as her. What a stark contrast to the rehearsal just a few days before when everyone had been buzzing with excitement.

'Can you try turning it into Alex?' Hunter asked seriously, pointing to Mae's magic wand and then to the pumpkin. 'It works with me and Maxwell – and the carriages,' he added.

'Oh, lad. You know it's pretend. Just a bit of Christmas magic for the audience,' Mae said sadly, her eyes skimming the boy's face.

'It's still worth trying, though, isn't it?' Hunter begged. 'My da's on his way, but Mam said he's going to be late and he might miss everything. Alex is only in Edinburgh, so he could get here before the end. That's what Nana told me.'

He blinked, the long lashes the makeup department had added to his eyes made him even cuter and almost impossible to resist.

Mae regarded the child for a moment and then she shrugged. 'Aye. You're right.' She waved her sparkly wand in an arc spraying glitter, then then tapped it dramatically onto the pumpkin.

Ella waited with bated breath. She couldn't help it. She didn't believe in magic, but she did understand the power of wishes – and was still hoping Alex was going to appear dressed in his costume, ready to forgive her. She looked left then right, and her heart sank as any lingering hope disappeared.

'It didn't work.' Hunter sighed.

'Perhaps we can try again later, lad?' Mae suggested kindly.

'Aye,' the boy said, his small shoulders slumping.

'We need to take our places, now,' Mae told them as Aggie came racing across the stage looking flustered.

'There's a man in the audience – Stanley Bailey or something,' she whispered. 'He's asking after Alex. He's very keen to speak to him, but I don't know what to say.' The older woman patted a hand nervously on the top of her bun. 'Should I tell him he's not here, he might want his ticket refunded?'

'I think he could be Alex's best friend. He's supposed to be in New Zealand, but perhaps he's come to see the performance,' Ella guessed. 'I expect he just wants him to know he's here,' she said gruffly.

If only Stan had been the one to come to the rehearsal a few days ago instead of Michael Charming, things might have been different. 'I can talk to him if you want?' She'd like to meet the man Alex trusted. He might have some advice on how she could apologise to his friend and make him listen to her.

'Nae, lass. It'll have to wait until the end,' Mae said, waving her wand at Aggie and Hunter, encouraging them to go back-stage as music began to play in the main hall, signalling they were about to begin.

Her godmother paused for long enough to wink at Ella. 'Break a leg, lass, and try to believe,' she whispered enigmati-cally, before trotting away in a haze of sparkles.

Ella sighed and turned to face the curtain as it began to rise, forcing a smile on her face, even though every inch of her body wanted to curl into a ball. She could do this, go through the motions – isn't that what she'd been doing for the last year?

And perhaps when the pantomime was over, she'd talk to Stan, then pick up Wyatt and drive to Edinburgh to find Alex and try to explain.


'Are you ready for the first ballroom scene?' Blair asked Ella forty minutes later. Mae, Hunter and Maxwell had just deliv-ered her to the ball and now the scenery was being changed into a sumptuous glittering ballroom in the king's palace. Music was playing and some of the cast members were performing a dance, distracting the audience from the props team as they rearranged the set.

'Where's Aggie?' Ella asked, searching behind Blair because usually either Mae or the housekeeper helped to calm the actors before they appeared on stage.

'Ach, she had an emergency to deal with. A costume to find.' Blair flushed. 'Nothing for you to worry about, lass.' She glanced over her shoulder and grimaced. 'I expect she'll be here soon.'

'Is everything okay?' They didn't need any more problems. Ella wriggled, trying to get comfortable in the flowing blue ball-gown she'd changed into after Mae had magicked up a dazzling makeover with her wand.

'It's fine, lass. The play's going well.' Blair winced.

'You know that's not true. It's lost all its sparkle.' Ella sighed. Everyone had gone through the motions so far and nothing had gone wrong, but there was a dullness around the cast, a flatness they couldn't seem to lift. It was turning into a disaster.

'Aye, but the show must go on.' Blair nodded. 'Hopefully, the ballroom scene will wow the audience. Come on, lass, you're on soon.'

Blair took Ella's arm and gently guided her to the edge of the stage. Ella closed her eyes momentarily, waiting for the line that would signal she needed to go on. She knew the first thing she'd do is lock eyes with the prince.

Only instead of Alex, she was going to come face to face with Henry. She gulped in a breath of air, and when the line was delivered, she forced herself to take a step, plastering a fake grin on her face as she swept onto the stage. Then Ella stopped in her tracks as everything around her seemed to freeze.

Because standing in the middle of the sparkly palace set, dressed in a billowing Prince Charming suit and wearing almost an entire pot of glitter, was Alex.

Ella couldn't speak – instead, she missed her line as she

continued to gape, tracing every chiselled angle of Alex's gorgeous face. It had been less than two days since she'd seen him, but it had felt like so much longer. Everything inside her began to hum, as her fractured heart seemed to fix itself.

Alex must have realised Ella had lost the power of speech, because he quickly stepped forward and took her arm, spinning her around in a circle and pulling her close so he could whisper. 'You look stunning.'

'I...' Ella pulled away and pinched herself, checking she wasn't dreaming. 'You're here,' she said stupidly. 'Mae's pumpkin magic actually worked.'

'Magic?' Alex looked confused. 'Aye I'm here. Sorry I'm late, but—' He shrugged and then spun Ella around again before dipping her in time to the music, making everyone in the audience gasp and then begin to clap.

'It took me a while to realise what an eejit I've been,' he whispered, spinning Ella and dipping her once more. 'I've got some things to say, but—' He righted them both and tipped his chin towards the audience, flashing her a smile. 'It might have to wait.'

'I can wait,' Ella said, her voice hushed, before she leaned in and kissed him on the mouth. It might be off script, but she couldn't help herself. 'But not for long.'

Alex grinned and nodded, then they both turned to the audience and picked up the scene.


'We've not got long before you and the prince are back on stage!' Aggie said urgently as she guided Ella into the wings, after touching up her makeup in the small changing room downstairs.

'Where's Alex?' Ella whispered, desperately searching the corridor for some sign of him. They still hadn't had a chance to speak alone, but he'd held her hand and sneaked in a couple of secret kisses when they'd been out of the audience's eyeline. They should have a few minutes now before they were performing again, and he was asking her to try on the slipper – but the man had disappeared. Where was he? Had he changed his mind?

'Oh, yes, I am,' Clyde yelled from the front of the stage as he and Dane acted out one of the comedy sketches – giving the props team time to refresh the decor ready for the penultimate scene.

'Oh, no, you're not,' Dane shot back as someone suddenly looped an arm around Ella's waist before spinning her around.

'I'm here,' Alex whispered, pulling her closer. 'I'm sorry, I had to get something.'

'Finally!' Ella wrapped her arms around his neck. 'I'm so sorry.' She burrowed her face into his collarbone, wondering how she was ever going to let go. 'You need to know the picture was always for you. Your father can't have it.'

'He told me,' Alex said, gently moving away, still holding onto her. 'I should never have said all those awful things, Ella. Or believed them. I hope one day you'll be able to forgive me.' His eyes burned into hers and she saw the truth in them. Felt everything inside her finally relax.

'Of course I forgive you,' she said, hugging him again. 'And I understand. I should never have invited your father to the pantomime. I thought he'd be proud of you. How could he not be?' She let out a sigh. 'How could he not understand how talented you are, how brilliant. You helped me see the truth about my stepbrothers so I could get my life back. Everyone loves you, Stan, Wyatt, Sprout, Henry, m—'

He pressed a fingertip to her lips. 'More compliments?' he teased, looking delighted when she kissed it. 'I don't need them anymore, Ella. I know who I am and who I want to be, that's what matters. That and being with you...'

'I just wanted to say—'

'It'll have to wait. You need to get on stage, lass,' Aggie barked, pulling Ella out of Alex's arms and gently twisting her around. 'Your scene is about to begin. You need to find the glass slipper, lad – you're going to need it.'

With that, she propelled Ella onto the stage, so Hunter and Maxwell could lead her to the small bench, ready for Prince Charming to get her to try on the slipper.

Ella sat carefully and fluffed her orange dress around herself as the mice skittered around her on the ground, keeping her company. She knew the moment Alex walked on to join them, because Hunter made a sudden squeaking noise and when she looked up, he was pacing towards her.

'What?' Her jaw dropped when she saw what Alex was carrying.

Some of the audience began to chuckle, and Ella had to stop herself from laughing too.

'May I?' Alex asked, grinning as he knelt and waved her bright pink wellington boot.

Ella snorted. 'What are you doing?' she whispered.

'I picked this up from Pinecone Manor,' he said under his breath. Then he turned to the audience. 'I know this is a little untoward, but before we try on the glass slipper, I want to see if this fits first. It's important you see. Part of a love story that's a lot like this one, with two people who are meant to be together, only it takes one of them a while to figure it out.' A few people cheered as Alex turned back to Ella and stared into her eyes.

'I've been searching for you for my entire life. I just didn't know it,' he began. 'Instead, I followed the wrong path.' His mouth pinched. 'Tried to please the wrong person. I didn't appreciate who I was, didn't value anything about myself because he didn't, and I realised now – since coming to Mistletoe – that he never would.'

A male voice in the audience cheered and Ella wondered if it was Stanley.

Alex must have heard, but he didn't take his eyes off her. 'I didn't see the truth – the warts, lines, wrinkles, any of it.' He took a moment to nod at Henry who was hiding behind a piece of the scenery with Mae.

'Until I met you. You taught me I should be proud of who I am. You gave me the confidence to express myself without feeling weak, or stupid.' He grimaced. 'Mostly.'

There was a small smattering of laughter from the audience again.

'May I?' Alex asked, nodding to Ella's foot.

'Um, yes?' she croaked, watching with her heart in her throat as Alex carefully lifted her foot and slid the wellington on.

'It fits perfectly – just like you fit me,' he said, and Ella hurled herself off the bench and into Alex's arms before she kissed him.

The audience began to clap and stamp their feet and above the din, Ella could hear Aggie, Blair, Mae and Henry cheering enthusiastically. While Hunter and Maxwell ran rings around the stage, squeaking and laughing as they joined in with the celebration.

Then Alex pulled back and pressed his lips against Ella's cheeks. 'I almost forgot my most important line. I love you,' he said quietly, then he leaned in and kissed her again. In that moment, Ella caught Mae's eye, and she wondered if perhaps her godmother might be magic, after all. Because right here, in front of her, was the most perfect prince she could ever have imagined. And if she got the ending she was hoping for, they were going to live happily ever after from this moment on.

# A LETTER FROM DONNA

I want to say a big thank you for choosing to read *A Christmas Romance in the Scottish Highlands*. If you enjoyed it and want to keep up to date with all my latest releases, just sign up at the following link. Your email address will never be shared and you can unsubscribe at any time. Also, you'll receive a copy of my free short story, *The Christmas Mix Up*!

*www.bookouture.com/donna-ashcroft*

*A Christmas Romance in the Scottish Highlands* is a modern-day twist on the Cinderella story. A tale of a glittering pantomime and magical romance set against the reality of a day-to-day life filled with crushing expectations and guilt. It's a story of two people who need to see the truth in all its glory – warts, lines, wrinkles and all – in order to change their futures and get the happily ever after they deserve.

I hope you enjoyed meeting Ella McNally and Alex Forbes-Charming and the quirky and sparkly community of Mistletoe Village; from Henry Lockhart and Mae Douglas to Hunter, Aggie and Blair McBride. Did you both love and hate Ella's evil stepmother Lucinda, and her unreliable stepbrothers, Dane and Clyde? They provided plenty of life lessons along with humour – and were the hurdle Ella had to overcome in order to reclaim her life. Did you feel sympathy for Alex who strived to make his father proud? And did you celebrate when he finally realised it was a goal he could never achieve, so chose to move on?

If you loved this Christmas story with its sparkle, glitter, and pantomime antics, then it would be wonderful if you could please leave a short review. Not only do I want to know what you thought, it might encourage a new reader to pick up my book for the first time.

I really love hearing from my readers – you can get in touch with me on social media or via my beautiful website.

Thanks,

Donna Ashcroft

www.donna-writes.co.uk

 facebook.com/DonnaAshcroftAuthor

 x.com/Donnashc

 instagram.com/donnaashcroftauthor

# ACKNOWLEDGEMENTS

People often ask me if writing gets easier with each book that I write. Logic says, after fourteen novels, that it should. But the reality is, every story is different, each tale brings new characters, arcs and plots – many of them tricky, all with their own particular snag, push or pull on the story.

One thing that never seems to change is my terror that this time the end won't come, and what I've created on paper simply won't measure up. (I admit, I am a catastrophiser.)

So, this book is dedicated to the person who tells me day after day that it will. The one who pushes me forward when fear holds me back. Thank you, Jules. I know I'm an absolute pain!

Thanks also to my wonderful writing community. There are many of you, but I wanted to name a few: Anita Chapman, Liz Finn, Sarah Bennett, Bella Osborne, Rachel Lake, Erin Green, Suzanne Snow, Ian Wilfred, Pernille Hughes, Ruby Basu, Liney Hogg, Nancy Peach, Lauren Forsythe, Caroline Roberts, Olivia Beirne, Kerry Kennedy and Susan Buchanan.

Thank you to Jackie Campbell, Julie Anderson, Soo Cieszynska, Andy Ayres, Alison Phillips, Caroline Kelly, Giulia Pitney Coope, Sue Ward, Tess Thorpe, Amanda Baker, Mel and Rob Harrison, Claire Hornbuckle, Danel Munday, Linzi Stainton, Caroline Smail, Emma York, Meena Kumari, Grace Power, Fiona Jenkins, Cindy Wilson, Cindy L Spear, Sarah Rothman, Helen Neaves-Wilde, Anne Winckworth. Dad, Mum and John, Lynda and Louis, Peter, Christelle, Lucie,

Mathis, Joseph, Tanya, James, Ava, Rosie, Philip, Sonia, Muriel and Stephanie. Not to mention, Chris, Erren and Charlie Cardoza.

As always, thanks to the fabulous team at Bookouture, including Natasha Harding, Ruth Jones, Lizzie O'Brien, Lauren Morrissette, Melanie Price, Noelle Holten, Kim Nash, Jess Readett, Ria Clare, Hannah Snetsinger, Natasha Hodgson, Catherine Lenderi, Peta Nightingale, and the wonderful Richard King and Saidah Graham.

Thanks to the incredible and generous blogging community who are so supportive to me and other authors. Being a writer would be a much lonelier and more difficult experience without you all.

Finally, to the readers who have been there with me throughout my journey – thank you. Xxx

# PUBLISHING TEAM

Turning a manuscript into a book requires the
efforts of many people. The publishing team at
Bookouture would like to acknowledge everyone
who contributed to this publication.

## Commercial
Lauren Morrissette
Hannah Richmond
Imogen Allport

## Cover design
Debbie Clement

## Data and analysis
Mark Alder
Mohamed Bussuri

## Editorial
Ruth Jones
Sinead O'Connor

## Copyeditor
Natasha Hodgson

## Proofreader
Catherine Lenderi

Printed in Great Britain
by Amazon

49031849R00158